During the 1920s and 1930s, around the time of the Harlem Renaissance, more than a quarter of a million African-Americans settled in Harlem, creating what was described at the time as "a cosmopolitan Negro capital which exert[ed] an influence over Negroes everywhere."

Nowhere was this more evident than on West 138th and 139th Streets between what are now Adam Clayton Powell, Jr., and Frederick Douglass Boulevards, two blocks that came to be known as Strivers Row. These blocks attracted many of Harlem's African-American doctors, lawyers, and entertainers, among them Eubie Blake, Noble Sissle, and W. C. Handy, who were themselves striving to achieve America's middle-class dream.

With its mission of publishing quality African-American literature, Strivers Row emulates those "strivers," capturing that same spirit of hope, creativity, and promise.

COLLEN DIXON is the author of *Simon Says* and *Behind Closed Doors . . . In My Father's House*. She has worked in corporate America as a consultant and in management and sales. She enjoys a wide variety of hobbies, including online auctions and collecting art. She resides in Mitchellville, Maryland.

BY COLLEN DIXON

Simon Says

Behind Closed Doors . . . In My Father's House

EVERY

SHUT

EYE

EVERY
SHUT
EYE

COLLEN
DIXON

STRIVERS ROW/ONE WORLD
BALLANTINE BOOKS
NEW YORK

Strivers Row
An Imprint of One World
Published by The Random House Publishing Group

www.striversrowbooks.com

Library of Congress Cataloging-in-Publication Data

Dixon, Collen.
    Every shut eye / by Collen Dixon.—1st trade pbk. ed.
      p. cm.
    ISBN 0-8129-6882-4
    1. African American men—Fiction. 2. Washington (D.C.)—Fiction. 3. Missing persons—Fiction. 4. Drug traffic—Fiction. 5 Mayors—Fiction. I. Title.
    PS3604.I94E94 2004
    813'.6—dc22   2004045446

Manufactured in the United States of America

2   4   6   8   9   7   5   3   1

First Trade Paperback Edition: November 2004

This book is dedicated to my dear friend, Brian Wesley Garland, and to my beloved grandmother, Susie M. Dickens.

God sent you special angels here to always give me a kind word, a warm smile, and to say to me, "I love you." Even during my darkest moments, you have been His emissaries on this earth, bringing care and brightness into my life. I know in my heart that your love is real, and for that I can never thank you enough.

You are truly two of the most beautiful beings God has ever created. For all who have been in your presence, your warmth and compassion have been a comfort and a blessing.

I love you both dearly.

Collen

Acknowledgments

Thanks and all praises to God . . . for what He has done, what He does do, and for all that He has planned for me . . .

To my family: my father, Leonard; mother, Frances; sisters, Linda and Lynette; nieces and nephews, Brandon, Mickey, Morgan, and Portia. Thanks for who you are and what you are to me.

A special thanks to my sister Lynette . . . I appreciate your friendship and your sisterliness.

To Twanda, for being my friend and family.

To my extended family: Cousin Mary, Cousin Yolande, Butch and Phyllis Fisher, the Browns, the McIvers, Lori and Phil Gilliam, the Lakins, the Palmers, the Woods, the Cambells, the Savages, the Applewhites, Vivian Gaunt, Ida Hutchinson, the Garlands . . . Thanks for all of your support.

To my friends who are like my family . . .

To Tomika . . . Thanks for being an excellent teacher of some very difficult lessons. I'll forever be grateful.

A special thanks to Mena . . . For always being there, no matter what time or what trouble. You're very special to me, and I'm glad that you are my friend . . .

The Kels in my life . . . Kellie "Minor" Muse and Kelli "Major" Wynn. Thanks for not only being my sorors, but my friends. We're bonded not only by the colors but by the creed. Thanks for being a part of my world.

To Rodney Akers, Brenda Brown, Dujuan Brown, Emile Brown, Darnell and Cynthia Carpenter, Wanujiru Chege, Pamela

Cranford, Barbara Coles, Maurice Davis, Tina Dowhite, Yolanda Ezzel, Mike Graham, Robb Jackson, Lisa Jeffress, Gene Lowe, Toney Monroe, Darrell Morgan, Vonda Munden, Ros Murphy, Reggie Oliver, Greg Parrish, Val Robertson, Mario Scribner, Pat Sugick, Louis Thomas, Doc Walker, and Mike Walker. Thanks for keeping a sister up!

To my other mothers, Mrs. Pat Buck and Dr. Sandra Newsome. Thanks for adopting me!

A special thanks to Shirley and Melony . . . thanks for taking such great care of my grandmother.

To the book clubs, stores, and organizations that really support me and help to get the word out . . .

Nubian Knowledge (MD); VLP—Village Learning Place (BMore), Shirley Johnson and The Enoch Pratt Library System (BMore); PG County Schools—Nathan Burns (Central Senior High) and Denise Buck (Fairmont Heights Senior High); Just Friends, Woodmore South Chapter One Book Club (MD); Novels and Nutriment Book Club (MD); Sistas in Voice (MD); Divas are Reading (DC); Club Mimosa (PA); APOOO (www); RAWSISTAZ (www); Circle of Friends (TN and NC); Indigo Book Club (NJ); Girlfriends Reading Circle (MD); Almost Gold (MD); Sisters Rising (MD); Journey's End Literary Book Club (NC); AmiGals (NJ); Star Bookclub (NJ); Mahogany Literary Circle (MD); Deep in Thought Book Club (NJ); Boston Blacks Online (MA); PSSST Book Club (VA); Barnes and Noble Book Club (VA); Booking Matters (GA); S.T.A.R. Book Club (PA); Dr. Richard Cooper of WURD (Philadelphia, PA) and Widener University KARAMU; Alpha Kappa Alpha Sorority, Inc., and the Iota Lambda Omega Chapter (MD); Dr. Sandra Newsome of Bowie State University (MD); Dr. Gwendolyn Parker Ames and the AmiGals Literary Retreat; Dr. Delores Scott at Virginia Union University; Donna Blackwell of Baltimore Reads (MD); Gary Johnson of www.blackmenin america.com (www); Anne Beers Elementary School (DC);

Howard University Bookstore; Karibu Books; Sibange Bookstore; Reprint Books; and The Alzheimer's Association (US).

My editor, Melody Guy of Random House . . . Thanks for going the extra, extra mile! I can't thank you enough!

My agent, Sara Camilli . . . Thanks for believing in me and my work . . .

To my sisterfriend, Zane . . . Thanks for being my friend, inspiration, and mentor. You made things happen for me and for many like me, and all I can say is thank you for being you!

To my special friend, Dywane Birch . . . Congrats on the new book and for always having my back.

To my brothers and sisters in the ink: Terrance Dean, Chris Chambers, Laurinda Brown, Brenda Thomas, T. J. Butler, Eric Pete, Alicia Singleton, Nikki Turner, and anyone else I might have missed. We are united in promoting the cause of literacy. Keep the faith and stay inspired!

My industry friends and mentors: Tonya Howard, Marc Gerard, Earl Cox, Manie Baron, Anita Peterson of "The Literary Cafe," Lashunda Hoffman.

> *Reflective changes can occur at anytime . . . We don't know the day*
>   *or the hour . . .*
> *Time is of the essence. Let that essence be defined by what is really*
>   *important to you . . .*
> *Your loved ones, your friends, your family, your causes.*
> *Every moment is a priceless, precious commodity, so spend them*
>   *carefully, and cherish them accordingly.*

Remember . . . Always support a cause. You never know when you might have cause for support!

Peace and Blessings,

Collen

EVERY
SHUT
EYE

H E MOLDED YO' ass into what he needed most, a good cover," Fortune said to Alex. "And you played the role perfectly, 'cause you really was a good kid, you know, to the bone. A good little yassa boy. Like a damned puppet. He had your head so far up his ass, he had to tell you when it was daylight. Watchin' you was just like watchin' that game Simon Says. Simon says do this, and you did it. Simon says do that, and you jumped to it. Damn, you was a sucka. And it worked fo' him and fo' you, too. Till you had the bright idea to start thinkin' fo' yourself. . . ."

CHAPTER 1

ALEX CRACKED his sore knuckles and stared blankly at the bathroom door. His wife, Tiffany, was on the other side, taking one last moment to check her appearance before they finally left the secure ward near the intensive care unit of Sibley Hospital.

Only a few days had passed since the night his once secure world had flipped upside down. The night of his deadly showdown with his father-in-law, Mayor Simon Blake, on the murky waters of the Potomac River.

Since that night, Alex had stayed with Tiffany, refusing to leave her side while she recovered. Curled up in a chair beside her bed, he barely slept. He was too focused on Tiffany's breathing and movements to relax. And it showed. Alex looked like a prisoner of war. Tall, fit, and handsome, his normally bright, flashing eyes were now bloodshot, with dark circles under them. One of his muscular arms was bandaged and wrapped. He was achy and bruised but determined to put his best foot and face forward for Tiffany's sake.

Dressed in wrinkled khakis and a periwinkle blue polo shirt, Alex gathered his shirttail and tucked it into his waistband. He tapped his fingers on the steel railing of Tiffany's hospital bed and tried not to seem impatient. "Are you all right in there, Tiff?" he asked. It seemed as if a lifetime passed before she replied.

"I'm okay, baby," she said slowly. "It's just taking me a minute to get myself together."

Tiffany Renee Blake Baxter was an extremely beautiful woman, and Alex knew there was no way she was going to be seen in public appearing less than her normally gorgeous self. The swelling in her face had gone down significantly, and her bruises were fading slightly, but Tiffany had still summoned her personal consultant from MAC cosmetics to ensure that the bruises on her face were covered.

Their life was out of control, and Alex really didn't know to whom or where to turn. He thanked God that he'd had the where-withal to contact Lisa Adams, one of his closest friends, who also happened to be the head of the investigation department of her family's insurance company. An experienced, semiprofessional private eye, Lisa was a wunderkind and a true ally. She had arrived from Atlanta on the day Tiffany had been admitted to the hospital, and she had single-handedly commandeered every facet of his and Tiffany's shredded lives. Alex had even entrusted Lisa with his knife until he could think more clearly. It had been his brother's knife, the same one that had surfaced during the most critical times of Alex's life. He'd used it to defend Tiffany's honor when they were college students at Hilliard Institute, when her boyfriend Sid tried to rape her. And it had saved Alex's life in his deadly battle with Simon.

In the smoking remains of what was left of his former life,

there were few people Alex could trust. Lisa was one, and Fortune Reed was the other.

Fortune was an old childhood friend of Alex's older brother, Ivan. For years Alex had hated Fortune because he'd blamed him for Ivan's murder, an event that had influenced everything Alex thought and did from age thirteen to eighteen. Determined not to let the streets claim him, too, Alex had buried himself in his books and become isolated from those around him. That was until Mayor Simon Blake took him under his wing and miraculously exorcised the past demons from Alex's life, introducing him to a world of wealth and privilege.

Under Simon's tutelage, Alex had blossomed, and even fallen in love with Simon's daughter, Tiffany. Alex lived a lavish life beyond his wildest dreams. He became an attorney and was given a cushy position in Simon's administration, where he was clearly being groomed for bigger things. For years, Alex had lived in ignorant bliss, until Fortune reentered his life and shattered all of those lofty dreams. Through Fortune, Alex found out that Simon had an alter ego named Moses and was a two-faced, double-dealing, low-down criminal and murderer. Moses was the top drug dealer in Washington, D.C., but more important, Moses was the person who had really been responsible for murdering Ivan. Initially, these revelations had been difficult for Alex to believe, but Fortune managed to rip the shroud of obliviousness Alex had thrived under and forced him finally to accept that Mayor Simon Blake was nothing more than a heinous thug who had systematically crafted, manipulated, and then tried to destroy Alex's life.

"How do I look, darling?" Tiffany emerged from the bathroom wearing a long-sleeved pale yellow linen jumpsuit with a colorful silk scarf tied loosely around her neck and a pair of two-carat diamond studs glittering in her ears.

Jarred from his thoughts, Alex looked at his wife, taking in her honey brown skin and shapely figure. "You look wonderful, Tiff. Absolutely lovely." He opened his arms and walked over to her. He kissed her gently on the forehead. "I love you, Mrs. Baxter."

"I love you, too, Mr. Baxter," she said, and hugged him gently around his solid abdomen. "I just want to get out of this place and see my babies. And my *fa*"—she paused mid-word—"*ther*."

Tiffany fell silent, and Alex caressed the back of her head. As he held his wife, tears stung his eyes. But he forced them back in and held Tiffany close. He placed his chin on the top of her head and saw their reflection in the mirror.

Alex felt dishonest, because he couldn't disclose the full truth about what had happened between him and her father on that fateful night. Tiffany's doctors had warned him that she needed calm and peace in order to fully recuperate, and he wanted to ensure that she did get better. It bothered him to have secrets from her, but in the tight crevice where he now resided, which was between a jagged rock and a hard place, Alex's options were few. How could he tell Tiffany that everything she knew about her beloved father was a lie? And that her own husband was responsible for her father's death? A father who had plotted against and even tried to poison her, his only child?

Tiffany had seen the newspaper headlines and was aware that there had been an accident on her father's boat, but was sketchy about the details. She vaguely remembered being at Simon's fundraiser, and not much after that. Howard Norman, Simon's public relations man, had concocted a story to protect Simon's reputation. His version was that the mayor's yacht, *The Masquerade,* had experienced some major engine problems, and that Alex and Tiffany narrowly escaped while Simon gallantly tried to save the vessel. Both he and the boat went under, and after countless hours of search-and-rescue attempts, the mayor's body had not been found.

For the unsuspecting public, their beloved mayor had died a highly revered, unblemished hero. To them, Simon Blake was a visionary whose mission had been to bring statehood and a new football stadium to D.C. He left behind a legacy of being the "people's mayor," which now would be preserved in history. As much as Alex hated this deception, he had to admit that Simon had accomplished a lot for the city.

Nonetheless, Simon Blake was as dirty as they came, and if the truth was ever divulged, Alex's close association with him would make Alex appear just as soiled. Alex had worked hard to get where he was, and he wasn't about to throw it all away so easily. Ironically, that was one of the many lessons he'd learned from Simon. Nothing worth having comes easy, and never give anything away unless it gets you more in return.

Alex was determined to extricate himself from his involvement in Simon's disappearance, even if it meant having to momentarily get in bed with Howard, a man Alex completely distrusted and despised. Although they both served Simon in different capacities, there was almost a sibling rivalry between Alex and Howard. Howard always vied for Simon's attention in an imperious manner that made Alex's skin crawl. But Simon seemed to trust Howard implicitly, and evidently Howard would still go to any length to protect Simon. And for right now, that protection was covering Alex and his family, so he decided to let Howard's lies stand. When the police interviewed him, Alex claimed that he couldn't remember anything except the boat malfunctioning.

"Things are going to be okay, Tiffany. I promise you," Alex said, hoping that he sounded assured and confident.

"I-I just don't understand," Tiffany said, pulling away, her face clouded with confusion. "How could this have happened? My father's gone?" She rubbed her temples and sighed. "I can't remember anything from that evening. Nothing." She sighed again and then groaned. "I think I'm getting another headache, baby."

Alex patted his pants pocket. "I have all of your prescriptions ready to be filled. As soon as we . . ." Now his voice trailed off. He was about to say "get home," but then he remembered they weren't going home. If it was possible, he never ever wanted to step foot again in the place that he and Tiffany had called home for the past five years. Especially after finding out that Simon had had it bugged the entire time they lived there. Lisa's security folks were doing a thorough sterilization of the house, but Alex still didn't feel comfortable.

"Um, Tiff. We need to talk." He grabbed her hands and led her back to the bed, where she sat on the edge. "I thought it might be best for us not to go back home right now. I'm sure that the media is camped out there, and you know, the house might have too many memories for us."

"But that's why we should go back. Because that's where all of our memories are."

Alex caressed his wife's hands. "The doctors aren't too sure if that's a good thing for you right now. They actually think that we should get away for a while, and try to get some R and R. I was thinking about maybe going to Europe or the Mediterranean."

Tiffany shook her head. "I don't think so, Alex. We can't go that far away. What if my father didn't die that night? What if he comes home and I'm not here for him? I need to be here."

"Tiffany, it's not that I don't understand—" Alex began, but she cut him off.

"No, you don't understand. What if my father really is dead? He's the mayor of this city, and he deserves to be remembered as such. He's done a lot for this city, and the least we could do is give him a memorial service. I'm not even going to consider leaving until we do that. And wherever we go, I want you to make sure that if my father is found, I'm notified immediately."

Alex reached for her shoulders and tried to keep his tone level. "Okay, baby. You're right. We shouldn't leave until we have at least a memorial service for Simon. And I'll be sure to make the appropriate folks aware of how to reach us when we leave. But I'm asking you to trust me on this. There are enough people still searching for Simon so that if he has survived, they'll let us know. Immediately." Alex breathed slowly to keep his true feelings in check. "I realize that you can't give up hope, and anything's possible, but you can't let what happened deter you, uh, I mean us, from going on with our lives. Right now, you've got to get better, and get stronger. You know that's what Simon would want you to do."

Alex's words felt hollow and artificial, and they burned in his throat as he uttered them. He could barely stand to say Simon's name, let alone defend him. Now he had to support a memorial service that he didn't even want to attend, much less help plan. But he had to, at least for Tiffany's sake. The last thing Alex wanted to do was stand up and say kind words about Simon.

"I don't know, Alex. Going away now just seems so selfish." She paused. "This is all so much. So sudden. I can't believe that my father's gone." Tears sprang to her eyes. "Oh, I just can't bear to think about all of this right now."

Alex grabbed a tissue and placed it in his wife's hands. "I know, it is hard to believe. But, unfortunately, we have to accept the information we have right now. Your father *is* gone, and now we have a number of challenges to face. And getting away for a short while shouldn't be viewed as a bad idea."

Tiffany carefully wiped her eyes, and kept her makeup intact. "I guess we do have a lot to consider, Alex. But how can we just up and leave? We have jobs. What about the house? Who's going to manage that?"

JUST THEN, Lisa, wearing an olive-colored trench coat and shades, burst through the door. She was followed closely by a hospital orderly pushing a wheelchair.

"Hey, you two. Let's get this show on the road. The car's waiting down by the service entrance, and my men will make sure that you two get out of here unnoticed," Lisa said, peeking over her shades.

Tiffany shot Alex a look of death, and her eyes spoke volumes. She and Lisa had barely spoken during the many years Alex and Tiffany had been together, and now Tiffany was obviously bothered by Lisa's presence.

"Alex? What's going on here? Lisa? What are you doing here?"

Alex cringed, thinking now was not the time for an argument. Lisa and Tiffany politely tolerated each other, and he had asked Lisa to be careful around Tiffany, and she had reluctantly agreed. But Alex knew Lisa could be vicious when she felt she was being attacked.

Lisa smiled and motioned for the orderly to help Tiffany with her belongings. "I'm here as a friend, and to provide a service for you. Alex asked me to help him take care of some security matters, and I was more than happy to oblige. Right, Alex?"

Alex nodded, relieved and grateful for Lisa's calm response. "Yes, Tiffany. Lisa's here to help us out for a while."

"Why didn't you just call Daddy?" Tiffany cut her statement short and rubbed her temples. "I'm sorry. I know. You couldn't." She smiled weakly. "It's going to take me a minute to get used to this, you two." Tiffany stood up and reached for the wheelchair. "Thank you, Lisa. And I'm sorry. I'm just all over the place right now. I know we need the help, and we really do appreciate it."

Lisa winked at Alex and mouthed the words "You owe me big-time," to him. She turned to Tiffany. "No problem, Tiffany. That's what friends *and* handsomely paid consultants are for."

CHAPTER 2

TIFFANY WANTED the family to stay with her aunt Giselle, but Alex told her he didn't want them to be a burden to her aunt and that the media would certainly be camped out at Aunt Giselle's residence, too. But in truth, Alex felt that Simon might also have bugged Giselle's house, and that they'd be safer in a hotel. Tiffany seemed upset at first, and the ride from the hospital was tense but eased up a little when she realized that they were going to stay in the penthouse at the Four Seasons.

Tiffany couldn't wait to see their children, who were being tended to by Alex's father, Gerald, and his lady friend, Mrs. Owens. Lisa was extremely thorough with every detail and made sure that they checked in under assumed names, and that her security people and the hotel management worked fervently to ensure their family was well taken care of. Tiffany, Alex, and Lisa entered the hotel through the service entrance, and then took a private elevator up to the penthouse.

"Hello, Tiffany. How are you feeling, dear?" Mrs. Owens asked. She enveloped Tiffany in a hug, holding her close to her full-figured bosom.

"I'm doing okay, Mrs. Owens. I'm doing okay."

"Uh, hello, Tiffany. It's good to see you," Gerald said tentatively. He and Alex had been estranged until recently, so he still felt awkward around his daughter-in-law, but he wanted to make an earnest effort to reach out to her. Gerald had a commanding voice, but a very reserved disposition and shaky social skills. He was doing his best to connect with his beleaguered daughter-in-law.

"Thanks, Mr. Baxter."

"Please, um, call me Gerald."

"Okay, Gerald." Tiffany smiled tiredly; then she glanced around the room. "Where are my babies?"

"I just laid them down, but I'm sure they're not asleep yet," Mrs. Owens said. "I know they want to see their mommy." She took Tiffany by the hand and led her back into one of the bedrooms.

Lisa removed her trench coat and took a seat on the arm of the sofa where Gerald was sitting, and they both stared at Alex.

"Eh, son. She's not doing too well, is she?" Gerald said, and Alex shook his head no.

"You took the words right out of my mouth, Mr. B.," Lisa said.

"She's still a little shaky about most things. But not about something I wished she'd be more uncertain about. She wants to have a memorial service for Simon," Alex said. "Can you believe that?"

"Yes, I can; he was her father, after all. And you've got to go forward with it, Alex. If only for appearance' sake," Lisa said.

"I know. But, I can't be a part of planning that travesty. You've got to get Aunt Giselle here, as soon as possible, okay? I think that would help Tiffany immensely, and having her aunt around will get me off the hook. Hell, I'm sick at the thought of it."

"Okay, Alex. I'll give her a call and have one of my guys pick her up this afternoon. But listen to me. You've got to be strong for Tiffany and your children now. This isn't the time for you to just let your wife wallow in all of this muck and mire. Let her do the service—it'll keep her busy—and until you figure out what's really going on, you need to take the lead and get her and the kids out of here."

Gerald nodded his head, and Alex started to pace.

"I know, Lisa. But I don't know if I can take a lecture right now. My mind's running in a thousand directions," Alex said. "I'm just trying to get myself together."

From the rear of the lavish suite, Tiffany could be heard talking and playing with the children, and Alex quietly walked down the hallway to observe them. Alex II and Anya were almost three months old. He loved watching Tiffany with the kids, and as he looked at his family now, he knew they were the only things that were real and constant in his life. The only things that really mattered. Watching his family momentarily calmed him.

After a few moments, Alex rejoined his father and Lisa in the living room. He ran his hand down the back of the floral sofa as he walked to the balcony doors and slid them open. The thick summer air nearly choked him, but he inhaled deeply. From the penthouse, he could see a panoramic view of the city. The city that he once loved so much. Now it seemed as evil as the man who once ruled it.

Alex clenched his fist and thought of the hard-earned lessons Simon had taught him. *Dissect. Prioritize. Strategize. Always think ahead.* "Okay. I know everything's kind of out of control, but I've got to focus. First things first. I need to know if you found out what happened to Foody," he said to Lisa.

Rudolph "Foody" Johnson was Alex's former college roommate and best friend. An electronics whiz, Foody bounced around from one job to another, but he was always there for Alex. And when Alex had needed him to hack into Simon's computer network, Foody jumped at the chance to help. During a covert operation at Simon/Moses' drug lab, Moses' henchman, Blinky, had blown up the building in an attempt to destroy any evidence linking Simon to the lab. Alex had gotten out first, with some of Simon's files and one of his hard drives in hand; then Fortune managed to escape; but Foody never came out. According to Fortune, Foody had insisted on staying, even after he realized that the building was going up in flames. He refused to leave until he had gotten the computer files Alex needed to implicate Simon. Now, with Foody missing, Alex didn't know where those files had been transmitted.

Lisa strolled over to the full-service bar and poured a glass of orange juice. "I've been checking ever since you first called. We tried every hospital, looking for *Rudolph, Rudy,* or even *John Doe,* and no one matching his description was brought in the evening of the explosion." Lisa sipped her juice, and shook her head. "The only bright spot is that based on the information I've gotten thus far from the medical examiner's office, none of the bodies identified has fit Foody's description. I've given the authorities information on Foody, and they'll try to match his dental records from when he was in the service. But, beyond that, some of the bodies that were found intact were burned beyond recognition."

Alex shuddered. The thought of Foody having been either blown apart or burned to a crisp because of him added to his inner turmoil. "Damn, damn, damn," he said, his voice faltering.

"Son, you can't go blaming yourself for everything now. You've got to get a grip. Get your mind right." Gerald flicked a thumb in the direction of the bedrooms. "For your wife and kids back there," his father said, his voice cracking.

"I know, Dad," Alex said. "But it still doesn't change things. Because of me, everyone's lives have been impacted. And now, I have to do something about it."

Lisa poured two more glasses of juice, and handed one to Alex and one to his father. "Here, drink this. You both need some rest. Alex, this situation is nerve-racking enough, and we're only here to help you. Now, my suggestion is for you to take your family away from here. As soon as possible."

"And me and Mrs. Owens will go with you so you'll have someone to watch after the little ones. That'll give you and your wife some time to get things together," Gerald said.

Alex stepped onto the spacious balcony, and Lisa followed. He placed his glass on a wrought-iron table, and grabbed the ledge. "Lisa, you're probably right, but you've got to understand where my head is at right now. I'm having a hard time accepting that my life has been a damned lie."

"Look, Alex, I have a difficult time believing everything you've told me, especially the part about Simon leading a double life as one of the biggest drug dealers in this city. But right now, you have no choice but to deal with this. Now, you asked me to help you, and I'm trying. You've been rattling on about what happened, and I still have a lot of questions. But you can answer my questions from anywhere. I just think that it's going to be a lot safer for you elsewhere."

The loud, humming sound of planes flying into National Airport could be heard in the distance, and there was the sound of metal clanking above their heads. Both Alex and Lisa glanced up at a scaffold descending near their balcony with a lone window-washer on the metal platform.

"I know, Lisa. There's a whole lot of stuff we have to discuss. I still don't know what to tell Tiffany or if I should even tell her anything. And if I do decide to tell her, where's my proof? Where's the knife I gave you? What happened to the rental car? I left the overcoat that I was using to carry Simon's hard drives in it. And the files? Did you get them?" Alex's sentences ran together like one long, breath. "And are we really safe? How do I know some of Simon's cronies aren't going to come after us?

"I'm not looking for easy answers. I'm looking for the truth. And, how will I ever know the truth? Hell, I don't even know if Simon's really dead. I just don't know if—" Alex stopped mid-sentence. He thought about something Simon had always cautioned him about. *Don't be weak. Never show fear or trepidation to your friends or your enemies.* Alex took a breath to calm himself.

"How long before Simon can be declared dead?" Lisa asked.

"If no body is found, the law provides that a judge can declare someone dead if presented with an affidavit that describes the circumstances of the death or other similar testimony in a hearing. A judge could also declare someone dead if he or she's been missing for three years," Alex said. "But there's no way I'm going to hang in limbo for that long, Lisa."

"I understand," Lisa said. "You want to make sure that he's dead."

"No, I want to see his lifeless, bloated body," Alex said. "Half-devoured by some animal. Or maybe I could see him in a casket with a stake driven through his black core of a heart. Then I'll believe it."

Lisa gently grabbed Alex's broad shoulders. "Chill out, boy. Believe it or not, I'm pretty damned good at what I do, and I'm addressing all of your concerns. Not only from a professional capacity, but as your friend, too. Right now, you need to take the doctor's advice and not tell Tiffany anything. She doesn't need to be upset. And, the knife's in a safe place. I'm working on getting your proof about Simon, but it's going to take a little while. From what you've told me, there's a whole lot to consider. We can only assume that Simon is dead, but we can't take any chances. I'll make sure to keep checking on that.

"Now, until Simon is found or at least for the next month," Lisa continued, "the deputy mayor, Phillip Smalls, will take over as mayor. Since Simon was near midterm, a special election is going to be required. But no one's really pushing that because no one wants to appear insensitive to what has happened to the mayor. It could spell political suicide if someone's deemed too overzealous."

"Is there a special investigation into Simon's death?" Alex asked. "You don't think that they're going to want to question Tiffany and me, do you?"

"They'll probably go by the statement you made to the police. The Feds are only involved because Simon was a government official," Lisa said. "That's standard protocol, but I'm keeping on top of it.

"But, on a more personal tip, if Simon really is gone, well, then we need to make sure you can't be implicated in any of his shit. That's the most critical need. And if he happens to reappear, then we'll cross that bridge when we get to it." Lisa shifted her stance and met Alex's gaze.

She relaxed her grip on Alex's shoulders. "Everything else, I've got covered. All of your belongings were removed from the rental car you used that night, and it was thoroughly cleaned. If anyone inquires, they'll never be able to trace it back to you. We've got the files. And one of my best programmers is analyzing the hard drive as we speak," Lisa said, glancing up toward the scaffold. "And, regarding your safety, that's my primary concern. I'll make sure that you all are covered until we're sure that you're safe. Okay?" Her voice drifted, and her eyes were again fixated on the scaffold.

"What are you staring at, Lisa? Look at me when you're talking, will you?" Alex felt needy, and he didn't like it.

"I'm paying attention, Alex. I really am. In my line of work, you have to be observant of everything."

"Yeah, but you also need to make sure the person you're talking to thinks that you're paying attention *to them*." Alex's voice raised, and he felt his face getting flushed.

"Look, I've got you. You're okay for now. We'll keep checking for Foody. You wanted me to put a tail on Simon's PR guy, Howard. I've made arrangements for you and your family to go to an undisclosed location for a while. At least a month. We're sweeping your house, and I'll make sure that your new house is completely sanitized, and we'll set it up with the proper security features. I'll go through your mail, and anything that's remotely connected to you. So, do you feel better yet? Or did I miss something?"

"Yeah, you did. Where's Fortune?"

At the exact moment Alex ended his sentence, the window-washer and the scaffold swung into the side of Alex's balcony.

"Get down!" Lisa shouted, and shoved Alex to the balcony floor. She bent down and pulled a .45 from her ankle holster, released the safety, and then pointed it at the window-washer.

"Yo, what's up with the heat, lady?" Fortune asked, holding onto the ropes and levers. With a wide squeegee hanging from his tool belt, Fortune was outfitted in white coveralls, sunshades, painter's cap, and a wide grin. He eyed Lisa like a hungry man eyed a juicy steak with all the trimmings. "That's just about as sexy as hell. A big ol' girl with a big ol' gun. Move over, Pam Grier. There's a new sheriff in town, and I can dig it. Go on with yo' bad self."

"Lisa, meet Fortune Reed," Alex said, as he rested on his elbows, and shook his head.

"Pleased to meet you, Pam, I mean, Lisa," Fortune said, with a sly grin.

"Fortune?" She asked, gun still pointed at him. "What the hell?" She turned toward Alex. "Does he always make such outrageous entrances?"

"You haven't seen anything yet, Lisa," Alex said, as he dusted off his pants and struggled to his feet. "But you can put the gun away for now, okay?"

Fortune tussled with the levers, and the scaffold dropped a few feet until it was nearly level with the balcony. "I'm still tryin' to figure out how to work these controls, you dig? It might take me a couple of minutes, but I'll get it."

Lisa rolled her eyes at him and sucked her teeth. "This is incredible. Do you know that you're eighteen stories up? I don't think that now is the time to be learning how to use one of these things. Plus, what the hell are you doing here, anyway? Why didn't you just call or something common like that? Use the damned elevator like everyone else."

"What do you mean, what am I doin' here? What the hell you think? I'm here to help my boy out." Fortune winked, and when Lisa turned her head, he twisted his neck, mocking Lisa's surly attitude.

"From what I've heard, you've already helped him out tremendously," Lisa said, and planted her hands on her hips.

"He has, Lisa," Alex said. "He really has. If it wasn't for Fortune, I'd still be Simon's flunky."

"Word is bond," Fortune said.

"That might be true, but all of this started because of him, too, didn't it?" Lisa asked.

Alex couldn't deny that. Because Fortune had crossed Simon years ago, Simon had ordered a contract on him. And when the contract went down, Alex's brother, Ivan, was mistakenly killed. But Fortune had always watched Alex's back from the shadows, and finally came forward when Alex needed him most.

"What the hell's going on out there?" Gerald said, as he charged toward the balcony door. "I was over there trying to drink my juice, and I look up and see you out here with a gun drawn, Lisa. What are you aiming at?" Gerald glanced over and saw Fortune, and grimaced. "Oh, good Lord. I see what the problem is now. Here comes trouble. With a capital *T*. I see why you got a gun now, girl. Go on and shoot him. That'll be a public service if I've ever heard of one," Gerald said.

Fortune blew Gerald a kiss and said, "It's nice to see you again, Mr. Baxter."

Alex finally stood and Lisa put the safety back on the gun as Fortune leaned over on the railing. "And trust me on this one, too, Sweet Lips. I couldn't call or somethin' *common* like that because you've got this place locked up like it's Fort Knox. Plus, *common* just ain't my style, beautiful."

"Style? Hmph. Style is the last thing that comes to my mind when I see you," Lisa said, and shoved the weapon back in the holster.

Gerald chuckled and leaned on the doorjamb. "That's right, Lisa. You tell him a thing or two," Gerald said, and folded his arms. "Let him have it."

"Yeah, I think I'd like some of what she's givin'," Fortune said, with a leer.

"Enough already," Alex said. "You two haven't been in each other's company for five minutes, and you're at it already. I need both of you to work together, especially if I'm going to be out of town."

"Work together?" Lisa and Fortune asked in tenor and alto unison, and they both turned to face Alex with distinctly different expressions plastered on their faces. Lisa's was one of disgust, and Fortune's was ecstatic.

"Yes, work together. Lisa, if there's one person on this earth, outside of you, Foody, and my father that I can trust, it's Fortune."

"Jesus," Lisa said, and folded her arms across her ample chest.

"That's a sad commentary, son. You've gone from sugar to shit dealing with this hoodlum," Gerald said, shaking his head.

CHAPTER 3

THE FOUR were so caught up in their conversation that no one had noticed that Tiffany had reappeared from the bedroom, and had her arms folded across her chest. Afraid that she had overheard their conversation, Alex quickly asked, "What's up, Tiffany?"

"What are you all doing out here?" Tiffany asked, with a very perplexed and annoyed expression creasing her face.

"Oh, nothing," Alex said, and then moved toward her, with his arms outstretched. He grabbed her elbow, and guided her back inside. "We were just fascinated with the window-washer's work, and talking to him about the perils of high-rise window cleaning. It was really interesting."

Tiffany pursed her lips and said, "How charming."

Alex breathed a sigh of relief. Now was definitely not the time or the place to introduce Tiffany to Fortune. He just wasn't ready, and neither was she. It might push her over the brink if he tried to explain who this unsavory relic from his past was.

When Tiffany had been hospitalized, she had awakened once and had briefly encountered Fortune. It was right after Fortune had confronted Howard, and hastened his departure, and Fortune and Alex were discussing the nightmarish events leading up to Simon's disappearance. Fortune had been dressed as an orderly, and had slipped out as soon as Tiffany opened her eyes. Alex hadn't seen or talked to him since then, but it came as no surprise to him that Fortune would just reappear the way he did, shimmying down the side of the hotel. Nevertheless, Alex was relieved that Tiffany hadn't recognized Fortune.

Though she had already agreed to go, it took more than that to convince a steel-resolved Tiffany to actually take a brief sabbatical, but Alex wore her down after a few tense, medicated, and emotionally charged days. She and her aunt Giselle just had to arrange and hold Simon's service before they left.

Aunt Giselle was a retired educator and school-board administrator who lived in the exclusive section of Burleith, which was near Georgetown. A bright, well-read woman, Aunt Giselle was also very quiet and reserved. In the whole time Alex had known her, they had had very few conversations. She was a good and faithful servant in her church, played bridge, attended teas, and was an active member of many of the area's charitable organizations. She was part of the historic well-heeled black society, but she never looked down on Alex. She seemed to like him and was always warm and polite to him.

Tiffany's aunt Giselle was her mother's only sibling and had practically raised Tiffany after her mother's death. Since Tiffany's grandparents had also passed, Aunt Giselle was her most immediate family. Aunt Giselle had never married and was childless, and she had always treated Tiffany as her own. Outside of a few sorority sisters and her second cousin Lily, Aunt Giselle was the one person Tiffany talked to, and probably the one who knew her best. Their relationship was comforting to Alex, and he knew that Tiffany really needed her aunt at this time.

LISA HAD TAKEN UP residence on the floor below them and went about the business of strategizing with Alex. She made preparations for the Baxter family to travel to Carmel, California, for a month's stay at a spa. Fortune had disappeared again, but not before getting word to Alex that he'd keep some "eyes on Simon's house."

Even though their suite was huge, after several days its high ceilings and tall walls were already beginning to close in on Alex. He missed his freedom. But, then again, Alex had never really been free. Simon had made certain of that. But at least now he willingly relinquished his privacy and freedom. For his safety, Lisa was screening all of his mail and other forms of communication, and he felt a bit like a captive. Restlessly changing the channels on the television, he happened upon a news conference. The D.C. chief of police was live, giving a statement about the fire at Simon's warehouse in Southeast.

"The Metropolitan Police Department has been conducting an investigation into the activities of the city's drug dealers. As part of this ongoing investigation, we have determined that the warehouse that exploded in Southeast last week was the drug laboratory of a leading drug dealer in the city." A picture of Blinky appeared in the upper corner of the wide-screen television.

"Edward Blanks, also known as 'Moses' or 'Blinky,' was a lifelong D.C. resident, and had been under investigation by both the D.C. police department and the Drug Enforcement Agency. His body was found, with a number of others, in this warehouse. Initial reports from the medical examiner indicate that Mr. Blanks died from smoke inhalation. Director Robert Robeson, of the Drug Enforcement Agency, will now elaborate further on this matter."

Robeson approached the microphone. "Mr. Blanks, also known

as the notorious Moses, was responsible for over sixty percent of the area's illegal drug business. We feel that with his death and the destruction of his laboratory, Washington, D.C., is a much safer area.

"We are certain that there are still a number of smaller factions capitalizing on the area's drug market, and we are putting them on notice. We will continue to eradicate all illicit activity. You have our word on it."

Alex's jaw dropped, nearly to his chest, as he reeled away from the television. He grabbed the phone, and dialed Lisa's room.

"I saw it," she said, before Alex could utter a word.

"Do you believe it? What kind of shit is that?" Alex asked. "You know, it pisses me off that they're letting Simon off the hook like this, but I swear, part of me is kind of glad that the story's getting out like this. At least I don't have to explain anything to Tiffany, just yet. But I still can't believe that this is as twisted as it is. It's all bullshit."

"It sounds like your boy has been doing some serious damage control."

"Who, Simon? You're probably right. I know he's behind this some kind of way. I just know it."

"No, Alex. Chill out. I'm talking about Howard," Lisa said.

"I never thought that Simon told Howard about his alter ego. But now I guess he did. That's probably why Howard was always so snide."

"Well, I'm just wondering why he did it. Or, who put him up to it."

"We know who put him up to it. I'm telling you, it's Simon, Lisa. Who else could it be?"

"That's a good question. But remember, it's Howard's M.O. to protect Simon and his reputation. From what I'm being told, Howard's been keeping a very low profile. He lives and works out of his house in Dupont Circle, but there hasn't been a lot of activity there. No odd comings and goings by anyone."

"He's the ultimate spin doctor, Lisa," Alex said. "I'm telling you. And if Simon was really dead, why would Howard continue to cover for him? That's why I feel Simon's still alive. He's keeping Howard on his payroll. Did you put a tap on Howard's phone?"

"No. I didn't think that was necessary. We're just watching him."

"I need for you to put a tap on his phone. Today," Alex said.

"Okay, okay. But, you want an awful lot of things, Alex. And I love you like a brother, but unfortunately, this mission is beginning to add up. Surveillance, wiretaps, and other resources can be very expensive," Lisa said. "And I can't have my folks getting on me about this."

It dawned on Alex that although he was still employed by the D.C. government, he hadn't worked since the accident. He had annual and administrative leave he could take, but that wouldn't last indefinitely. And Tiffany was only working part-time at a non-profit agency while trying to get her fledgling event-planning business off the ground. They had pretty substantial savings, but he hadn't thought about having to use those funds for something like this. It was pretty ironic. Simon, the man responsible for Alex's financial windfall, would now be responsible for his financial downfall.

"I know, Lisa. But, you'll get paid, I promise. I'll make sure of that."

"I'm sure. But, that leads me to my next issue. Simon's estate."

"I don't want to have anything to do with his blood money, Lisa. You ought to know me better than that."

"Don't speak too soon. You don't know what's what yet. Or what you may be entitled to going forward. You've got a lot to consider, and I know you're speaking from a state of shock, so you don't need to make any concrete decisions right now. None."

They were still debating when someone knocked on Lisa's door. "Hold on a minute. That's probably room service. I'm sure you haven't eaten yet, have you? You better. You need to keep your strength up." She set the receiver down, and went to answer the door.

Alex overheard Lisa's voice rising, to the point that she was almost yelling. Then he heard the sound of the door slamming. She picked up the receiver, obviously irritated.

"What's the matter with you, girl?" Alex asked. "You need for me to come down there?"

"You better before I kill somebody. Guess what? Your buddy just showed up again. Transporting my food."

"My buddy?"

Lisa switched to the speakerphone. "Fortune."

"What's up, little bro?" Fortune's voice echoed in Alex's receiver.

"Fortune? What the hell are you doing down there?"

"I figured that I couldn't get back up to you, so I thought that I'd try to get in here with Foxy Brown. I mean, Miss Lisa. Hee-hee."

"A hee-hee, hell. Alex? You know what? Of course, homeboy had to get dressed up like a waiter," Lisa said. "You didn't touch my food, did you?" she asked, and Alex heard the sound of metal plate covers clanging. "If you did, I'm going to order some more, damn it. Some without your special seasoning."

Fortune muttered some smart remark, and then spoke back into the mic. His voice was ten decibels too loud.

"What's goin' on, Alex?" Fortune nearly shouted.

Alex jerked his head away from the receiver. "Fortune, you don't have to speak so loudly. I can hear you. We were just talking about what we need to do next. Did you hear that the cops and the DEA are trying to make it seem like Blinky was actually Moses? I bet Howard had something to do with it."

"Who?" Fortune asked. "That dude that was up in the hospital room makin' noise the other day? Simon's old mouthpiece that's always talkin' loud, but sayin' nothin'?"

"Yeah," Alex said.

"I heard something about that through the grapevine," Fortune said. "And, it sounds like some old made-up shit that jive-ass Howard probably came up with. I'm sure it was Simon's plan to have that dude put all the blame on Blinky, in case anything ever happened to him."

"That's what I was thinking," Alex said. "Because Simon's still alive. And now he can come back and not worry about being linked to his drug activities."

"Now, now, hold up. You made a coupla good points, but think about it. If you haven't been schooled about anything, Alex, you oughta know that everything ain't always the way it seems. Every shut eye ain't sleep. And every good-bye ain't gone."

"What?" Alex asked, and Fortune repeated his statement, and then continued.

"Things might look one way, an' really be a whole 'nother way. Whatever the case is, somebody wants they tracks covered. I can tell you one thing—it could be that Simon's really dead, an' it's that fancy-pants Howard behind all this. Trust me, he ain't that clean himself. Seems like Howard's been doing a little double-dippin'. Two-faced muh-fucker. Word is, he was workin' for Simon's main competitors. Them high-post Cavanaughs."

Alex was familiar with the Cavanaughs. They were a well-known, very affluent and influential D.C. family. "Competitors? You don't mean that—"

"That's exactly what I mean. They into a whole lotta criminal activity, 'cept they was smooth with their shit. They are really into sellin'. Big-time. But, they got bad blood between them and Simon from way back." Fortune paused. "Hey, ain't you gonna offer me somethin' to eat?" Fortune said to Lisa. "That's mighty damn rude of you."

"What?" Alex asked.

"No, I'm not offering you jack," Lisa said. "Alex, what is he talking about? This sounds like a damned soap opera to me. The freakin' black Carringtons versus the Colbys. Damn. I personally don't care what these folks do. We need to stick to the facts as they relate to Alex, Fortune. Like, what's going on with Simon's estate."

"Which one? The real one, or the one he wanted you to find out about?" Fortune asked, his voice infused with sarcasm.

"Wait a minute," Alex said. "I want to hear more about the bad blood between the Cavanaughs and Simon. I mean, it could have something to do with what happened, and what's going on now. If Howard was working for both Simon and the Cavanaughs, he's more involved than I ever thought and he could have the answers to some important questions."

The door to Alex's suite opened, and all of the ladies in his life strolled in. Their mood was upbeat, and their hands were filled with shopping and garment bags.

Alex lowered his voice. "We'll have to discuss this when I see you," he said, whispering into the phone. He raised his voice, and continued. "Yeah, uh, I think I'll go do a few laps in the pool now. Work off some of this nervous energy I've got."

"I got it," Lisa said. "I'll see you in a little while."

Alex hung up the phone, and stood to greet his family and give his wife a warm hug. There was still a little swelling in Tiffany's face, but her makeup was impeccable. She looked great and seemed a little calmer than she'd been when she left. Shopping must've done her a world of good.

"Who was that, baby?" Tiffany asked.

"Um, just Morgan," Alex said. Morgan was one of Alex's fraternity brothers, and his former college roommate after Foody left school. Alex made a mental note to make sure he contacted Morgan before the day was over. "I was just telling him about Simon's memorial service."

"That's nice. Everything's pretty much been planned. We're going to have it at the Rankin Memorial at Howard University this Saturday. I'm sure we have everything covered, but I really need to speak to Howard," Tiffany said, and laid her Neiman Marcus bags on the coffee table. "I want to show you this lovely suit I picked up for you, but I better go check on my babies first," she said.

"I'll do it," both Aunt Giselle and Mrs. Owens offered, both making beelines for the bedroom. Neither one of them could resist the twins.

"You can show me the suit later, baby. I'm going to go for a quick swim, and then go to the sauna. But, um, why do you need to speak to Howard?" Alex asked. His left eyebrow involuntarily raised, and twitched.

"Why not? Mainly, because he knows the proper protocol and who to invite. I want to keep the memorial small, but my father knew a lot of people. I want to make sure that I have the people there he would've wanted to be there. And who would know better than Howard?"

Alex exhaled heavily. He figured that there was no getting around this one. "Okay, but just do me a favor. Just don't tell him where we are."

"Why not?"

Alex's mind raced. "I know that he means well, but Howard's in PR and he can be a little bit over the top sometimes. I'd prefer if we had access to him, instead of him having access to us. It's probably better if he didn't know where we were. He might worry us to death."

Tiffany reached over and pecked Alex on the lips. "All right, baby. If that's how you want it, then I won't mention it." She smiled, and it warmed Alex's heart. "You don't know how glad I am that you're in my life. I know you're only trying to watch out for me, and I love you for it."

"I love you, too, Tiff. I really do. And I'd do anything for you."

CHAPTER 4

ALEX DONNED a T-shirt, a colorful pair of Nautica swim trunks, and a thick white terry cloth hotel bathrobe with a gold Four Seasons insignia on it, and sneaked down to Lisa's suite. On entering her room, Alex was surprised and amused to see Fortune, still outfitted in his waiter's uniform, sitting on a love seat on the far side of the room. His feet were propped up on a glass coffee table, while Lisa sat on a chaise lounge, still eating, but with a burning scowl on her face.

This was the first time Alex had been in Lisa's two-room suite, and he found it was stockpiled with equipment. She had several laptop computers, printers, and fax machines. There were short-wave radios, police scanners, several mobile phones and pagers. Other miscellaneous devices were neatly lined up on one of the desks. Alex took a desk chair, swung it around, and sat astride it backward.

"You've certainly got some kind of outfit down here, don't

you?" Alex was finding it difficult to believe that his world had suddenly turned into a clandestine operation. "This place is like something straight out of a James Bond flick."

"This is no joke, Alex. I need this stuff to stay abreast of what's going on," Lisa said. "I told you that I was good at what I do."

Fortune laughed, and reached for a lone strawberry on Lisa's tray. "I keep tryin' to tell her that what she needs is some good old-fashioned feet on the street. All this surveillance shit is cute, but she needs somebody that knows this area an' can get down to the nitty-gritty."

Lisa smacked his hand before Fortune could touch her fruit. "I wish you'd get that nitty-gritty out from under your fingernails, Fortune. Yuck." She rolled her eyes. "I know what I'm doing."

"An' I know what I'm doin', too," Fortune said.

"Okay, children. Both of you know what you're doing—in your own little special way. But the goal is to figure out how you both can do what you do, in a manner that's going to help me and my family," Alex said, and gave each one a reprimanding look. "So, let's get down to business. Fortune, you just mentioned something about Howard, Simon, and the Cavanaughs. What was that about?"

"Oh, yeah. Simon hates them Cavanaughs. Remember I told you about Simon's wife, an' how she was havin' an affair? She was havin' it with one of them. The uncle. I think his name was Edgar or somethin' like that."

"Interesting," Alex said. "And that may be relevant later, but right now I need to address issues that are important now. Lisa, has anything come in the mail that I need to be concerned about?" She shook her head no. "What about our travel plans? Have you made them yet?"

"Yes, I have. But I'm not going to give you a whole lot of details about it. I think the less you know, the better off you'll be. So, the minute the memorial service is over, all of you, including your father, Mrs. Owens, and Aunt Giselle, will be heading to Carmel with one of my bodyguards. I've reserved bungalows for a month at the Valley Resort and Spa. It's tucked away, but it is one of the finest in the country. And of course, you'll be checking in under assumed names."

"Isn't it like a hundred and ten degrees out there?" Alex asked.

"It's in northern California. It gets a little warm during the day, but it's nice in the evening. Don't worry, you'll be fine," Lisa said. Anticipating Alex's next string of questions, Lisa continued without a pause. "And I've made arrangements for you to be driven to another city to catch a chartered plane to a major city. From that major city, you'll fly into California. I'll make sure you have the details once you're under way."

"And, once we're gone?"

"Once you're gone, I'm going to move into your house. That way, I can save you some money, watch your property, and keep things moving in the right direction."

"What about the new house? You know Tiffany and I can't move back into our old one," Alex said. "And I want to get rid of our cars. Both of them. I'll give you a power of attorney to sell them. Donate them to charity. Whatever. Just ditch them, please. I'll worry about replacing them later."

"Got it. I'll make sure that they're gone by the time you get back. Now, I'm working with a realtor as we speak. And yes, I've checked her out, and she doesn't have any connections to Simon. None at all. She's concentrating on the areas you mentioned, like Georgetown, Spring Valley, and Chevy Chase, and I'll fax you copies of properties for you and Tiffany to take a look at. I'll even have the realtor make videotapes of the properties, to give you a better idea of what's what. But you'll have to select one while you're gone, so when you return, you can go to close relatively quickly and move into your new house."

"There's also a place out in P.G. County called Woodmore. It's a gated community, and it might be worth checking into," Alex said. He was concerned that the plan to relocate wouldn't go over well with Tiffany, and wanted to have as many viable options as he could to present to her. While they were talking, Fortune rummaged underneath the gold tablecloth that was draped over the service cart.

"What are you doing?" Lisa asked, in an annoyed tone.

"I had something for Alex," Fortune said, and he whisked a clear dry cleaner's bag from under the cloth. Inside was Ivan's letterman's jacket. "I thought you might want this with you."

Alex grabbed the jacket and rubbed his fingers across Ivan's embroidered name.

"What's that?" Lisa asked. "I know that's not yours, Alex."

"It's Ivan's jacket," Alex said. "Fortune had kept it since my brother died, and brought it to me at the hospital. I put it away because I didn't want Tiffany to see it, and I forgot about it."

"Yeah, I know. But, that's why I'm around. I got yo' back. You left it in the hospital room, but I got it for you," Fortune said.

Alex hugged the jacket, but remained silent. With all that had happened, how could he have misplaced something as important as this jacket? It was the one thing that Alex had of Ivan's, besides the knife that he had used to kill Simon.

"Lisa?"

"I know, Alex. I'll put it in a safe place."

"SO, ABOUT Simon's estate," Alex said. "We need to find his will. I've got a strange feeling that something's just not right about it."

Fortune snorted, and shook his head. "What? You think he listed his drug lab an' its contents as assets? Get real. I know you don't think that."

"That's not what I meant, smart-ass. Knowing Simon, there have to be a few surprises in there. Hell, Blinky was sacrificed, so I'm quite sure he wasn't going to spare me. I know I was disposable, or the designated fall guy."

"You might be right," Lisa said. "But we're going to confirm that. I'm looking for Simon's legal documents now, but at this moment, we're working with the D.C. police department in keeping his house secured. But since it belongs to the city, we have to be very careful about how we access it. They know that I'm working on behalf of the mayor's family, so I'm not raising any undue suspicion."

"But you have to move on it. The deputy mayor has already taken over Simon's duties. And whoever wins the election in the spring is going to want to move into the mayor's residence," Alex said. "So I'm sure that they're going to want to have Simon's things cleared out soon."

"Probably; so what do you want to do?"

"I want you to go through it with a microscope and tweezers if you have to. And then, have his personal belongings packed up and put in storage. As far as his office is concerned, I'm quite sure he had nothing there of any interest. But check it, and stow his personal belongings from there, too," Alex said.

"Okay," Lisa said. "Now, other than that, we're investigating his finances. We're checking his bank accounts and those offshore accounts you mentioned you saw in his office. And the ones that were listed on his computer."

"Lisa, I don't want to press you, but you've got to get on it. Seriously. He's got those accounts set up in my children's names. God only knows what else he might've done to get me and my family caught up in his game. I need to know that my family's going to be okay, and that whatever he's done, we can fix it. Before it's too late," Alex said.

"I'm with you, Alex. And trust me, we're on it. It's just going to take a little time. Remember, whatever Simon put in place, he didn't do it in a day. It took him a while to get you this caught up in his game, and it's going to take more than a minute to figure out to what degree you are involved. But from what my folks have told me thus far, things just aren't quite adding up. They aren't making a whole lot of sense."

Fortune smirked. "There you go with that 'trying to make sense' shit again. Y'all book-smart folks just don't get it, do you? Do you really think Simon woulda had his papers someplace in a neat little desk drawer, or in some damned file cabinet or where you could just go on a computer and find it? Get real. Y'all been watchin' too much television or somethin'."

"I saw those files with my own eyes, Fortune, and I've got his hard drive from the computer. So what are you talking about?"

"What I'm sayin' is that you might find some shit, maybe some of the more legitimate stuff, but you ain't gonna find the lowdown on where he stashed his real dough. He didn't keep no map that's gonna lead you to the buried treasure. No way." Fortune pointed to his head. "He probably kept all that up here. So whatever information that mighta got blown up in the warehouse an' on his boat probably wasn't nothin', either. Trust me, Moses had his stuff spread out, you dig?

"He probably had stashes throughout the city. That's how they do. Spread it around. Put some paper here, put some bread there, so there's always a little somethin' somethin' to fall back on, in case you gets in a pinch. I'm sure he's got safes an' strongboxes 'round here in half of these little corner stores, probably up in some old lady's house, out there on Marshall Hall, and in some of these boarded-up buildings. Hell, he might've even stashed somethin' in yo' crib."

Fortune's words rang in Alex's ears. Having worked with Simon for so long, Alex knew that Fortune was telling the truth. If Simon was devious enough to have kept Alex in the dark, there was no telling to what lengths he would have gone to protect his interests. "I believe you, Fortune," Alex said. "But I'm not about to let him get the best of me again. I'll do whatever I have to do to find out what I need to know. I'll think like him, act like him, whatever it takes."

"Agreed, Alex. And thanks for the testosterone charge. But, Fortune. Your point is—what?" Lisa asked, as she cut her eyes at Fortune, and gnawed on a pear.

"My point is that you needs me, sweet thing. You need me on this one. I've got to be the one to dig up these spots, otherwise you and your ten-foot goons is gonna get run up outta this city," Fortune said with a wink. "Or, end up like Simon's ass. And I wouldn't want to see that happen to your fine ass."

Lisa nearly dropped her fruit. "Naw-uh. There's no way you could ever work either for me or with me. Not like you are now. No way."

"What you tryin' to say?" Fortune asked, with a slick grin.

"I'm not trying to say anything. I'm saying that you've got to clean up your act if you want me to even consider having you be around me. Got it?"

"Well, then help a brother out, won't you?" Fortune licked his crusty lips, and Lisa sucked her teeth.

"Excuse me, you two. But can you work out those particulars later? You both have to forgive me, and you might think that I'm being paranoid, but I have my doubts. I just don't believe that Simon's dead," Alex said, and stood up from his seat.

Lisa and Fortune shot each other looks, their faces etched with concern. "It's still early yet, Alex. Let *us* worry about Simon," Lisa said.

"I'll try, Lisa. And it's not that I don't trust you two. It's just that I have issues trusting anyone. Or anything. Even believing what I hear and what I see. And it's not just about me, but about my family. So I need for you to promise me two things: That you'll stick with me no matter what. And I know I'm asking a lot. And, secondly, whatever goes down, I want you to find out what happened with Foody, okay? Please don't forget. It's really killing me not knowing where or how he is."

SIMON'S MEMORIAL SERVICE at Howard University's Rankin Memorial was a blur to Alex. It comforted him that Lisa's men provided additional security, while Lisa and Fortune stayed on the periphery. He felt that they would be safe, and Tiffany and Aunt Giselle had planned the memorial down to the finest detail. The service was seamless. Alex claimed to be too grief stricken to speak, so Tiffany and Howard filled the program with Simon's political allies, businessmen friends, and fraternity brothers.

All Alex wanted to do was hurry through the service, so that he could get his family out of town. Through all of the condolences and sympathetic gestures, Alex couldn't help thinking that Simon was probably sitting somewhere in the audience, taking notes on who said what. Or that he was going to come bursting through the doors at any moment, like something straight out of a soap opera.

Thankfully, none of that occurred. Alex spent the afternoon consoling Tiffany, who, despite her best efforts, was an emotional wreck. At the reception following the ceremony, Tiffany found the comfort and support of her sorority sisters, while Alex stole a few moments away from the madness. He had hoped to sync up with Lisa, but Councilwoman Winnie Sutton caught him.

Winnie was perhaps Simon's most vocal political adversary. He had claimed that Winnie's position was always contrary to anything he proposed, and he made it no secret that there was no love lost between them. Alex had come in close contact with her when he was scouting out locations, on Simon's behalf, for the new stadium in her ward. And Winnie had let the world know that she was not interested in having a gigantic stadium built in her jurisdiction at the expense of her constituents.

"Well, hello, Alex," she said, and gave him a hug. Winnie's

conservative gray suit was topped off with a bright, multicolored scarf. "I was surprised to see that you didn't speak on the program."

Winnie looked at Alex as if she were a teacher and she had just caught him cutting class. She was asking for his hall pass, and he had none. "I, um, I was too overwhelmed to really speak, Winnie. I figured that some of Simon's other supporters would do a better job."

Winnie half smiled, and then clasped his hand. "Um-hum. I see. He certainly has a number of those here today, doesn't he?"

Alex wanted to say that he and she weren't included in that number, but he thought better of it, and just nodded.

"Curious thing that happened to your father-in-law, isn't it? Shame. I understand that now that the search has been called off, he's been categorized as missing and presumed dead."

"That's my understanding, Winnie."

"It's hard to believe he's gone, isn't it? But I guess, in a sense, he'll live on. After all, he has a number of propositions he was pushing through, like statehood, and—"

"The stadium," Alex said.

"Yes, the stadium." Winnie smiled and adjusted her scarf. "I guess we'll have to see what happens with that now. I'm sure that if Simon ever thought he'd never get his precious stadium, he'd return from the dead." Winnie rubbed Alex's shoulders. "Oh, well, I guess I shouldn't have said that. I guess I must be more grief stricken than I thought."

Alex watched as Winnie turned and walked away. Again, Simon's words echoed in his head. "Winnie Sutton's like a pit bull. Once she gets those ill-fitting dentures into something, you almost have to shoot her to make her drop it." Evidently, the depth of Winnie's dislike of Simon was deeper than Alex had thought. It made him feel a little better to know that he wasn't alone.

CHAPTER 5

HE EMERGED from the murky waters of the rancid river. Exhausted and deeply wounded, he took a few wobbly steps on the embankment and collapsed. He awoke to the rumbling sound of airplanes taking off and landing at National Airport. It was nearly dawn. He warily checked his surroundings and attempted to gauge his whereabouts. He had to be somewhere down the Virginia shoreline, he thought. After his fierce battle in the choppy waters, he had lain on his back and floated downstream, far away from the point of his near fatality, to where no one would ever think to look for him.

He found a spot near the brush and rested briefly, alternating between hawking up phlegm and applying pressure to his wounds. "So, this is what has become of me," he said aloud. He glanced around and hoped that no early morning fishermen would happen upon him. "Well, if they think they've seen the last of me, they all have another thought coming," he said, suppressing the pain from the injuries that would've surely killed a lesser man.

ALEX BOLTED UPRIGHT in his sleep and nearly yelled into the darkness. His heart was palpitating, a cold, sticky sweat lined his forehead and bare chest, and the waistband of his pajama bottoms was damp. That dream was a recurring nightmare he just couldn't shake. It took him a moment, but Alex got his bearings. It was just a dream, he thought. Tiffany's shallow snores comforted him, and he breathed a sigh of relief. They were safely away at the spa in Carmel, and no one knew where they were.

Creeping out of bed, Alex felt his toes sink into the plush carpeting, and he maneuvered his way across the darkened room to the bathroom, where he quietly closed the door. The bright light burned his bloodshot eyes, and he ran some tap water into a small glass. He drank a little, then took some of the water and splashed his face with it.

So much had happened over the past week. It had been all Alex could do to make it through the memorial service, feigning total and complete grief. The dishonesty was gnawing at him, and when he glanced in the mirror, he wasn't happy with the reflection that he saw. Torn and angry, Alex still felt as if he were controlled by Simon, that he had to uphold an illusion of Simon as the honorable gentleman. To shake hands with Simon's colleagues and constituents was a struggle when Alex really wanted to blurt out what a sham and a fraud Simon was. But with Tiffany barely able to contain her sorrow, he had to mute the voices that screamed out in his head. Behind his politically correct façade, Alex felt like a fraud and a sham, too. It grated on him that Simon was still getting his way. Even from beyond the grave. Or wherever he was.

Alex closed his eyes and held on to the side of the marble vanity. He wanted to scream, shout, or break something. But with his wife and family so close, he had to be strong, so he tried to let the moment pass. He held on, gripping the vanity until his knuckles drained of their color. Fragments of those terrorizing events floated in his head like fake snow in a snow globe someone had vigorously shaken. He started praying for relief and was so consumed with his silent pleas that he didn't feel the tender touch of his wife.

"What's the matter, baby?" Tiffany asked, as she grasped him from behind and leaned to place her chin on his shoulder. Her warm, curvy body melted onto his back, her softness meeting his hardness in near perfect harmony.

Alex opened his eyes and stared into the mirror. The reflection he now saw made him smile, despite the hell he was in. Even in the middle of the night, with her hair pulled back and little sleep crumbs in the corners of her eyes, his wife was simply beautiful.

"I'm okay," he said, and tilted his head until it touched hers.

She turned him around slowly, and held his face. "I know this is hard for you, too, Alex. I haven't been getting a whole lot of restful sleep, and I can tell you haven't been sleeping too well lately, either. Are you having nightmares?"

"Sometimes. Are you?"

Tiffany nodded. "Sometimes. And the sad part about it is that even though we had the memorial service, I still can't accept that my father's gone."

"Me either, Tiff."

"I guess we both need closure. I thought that it would help to have the service, but, honestly, it hasn't. I can't seem to move past it," she said. "I really haven't."

Alex was at a loss for words. He wanted to support his wife, to make her feel better, but every supportive word he could muster about Simon made him feel like a spineless hypocrite. "I understand how you feel," he said.

"I know it's going to take a little time. For both of us. It's only been a few weeks." She paused and kissed his face. "Things'll get better, baby."

The warmth of Tiffany's kiss and her sultry natural scent stoked something in Alex. They hadn't made love for a while, the thought never entering their minds. But tonight, the thought was invading. And comforting.

He held her close and kissed her forehead. She sank her head into his chest, and spoke, her voice muffled. "It's been too long since you held me like this," she said. "Why have you waited so long?"

"I wasn't sure if you felt up to it, baby." Alex said. "I wasn't sure if it was a right time for—"

"Shhh," Tiffany said. She lifted her head and placed a delicate hand over his mouth. "Don't talk. Just make love to me," she said, and then kissed him deeply.

He swung her onto the vanity, pushing their toiletries to the side of the countertop. He slowly planted soft, wet kisses on her warm face. After a few moments, she clutched his head, and forced it backward.

"Forget what I said, Alex," she said, her chest heaving.

"What?"

"I don't want you to make love to me. I want you to fuck me." Tiffany knocked toiletries over, filling the room with an intoxicating mixture of scents. Tiffany pulled down the top of her baby-doll nightgown and exposed her breasts. "Take me someplace I haven't been in a long time. Come on, Alex. I need you to."

He took her breast in his mouth, and sucked on it passionately. He tore her gown away and gripped her other breast. Tiffany moaned, and he sucked and bit and licked her stomach, trailing along her sensuous body, while she massaged her tongue in and out of his ear.

She leaned forward, and dug her nails into his back with one hand and snatched his bottoms off with the other. When he forced her backward and began sucking her breasts like a starving infant, she grabbed his manhood and stroked him. The harder she stroked, the harder she dug her nails. No longer able to contain himself, he jammed himself deeply inside of her.

She wrapped her legs around his waist, and for every thrust, she met him with matched power and lust. Amidst deep groans and moans, they ravished each other with pent-up passion, pain, agony, and ecstasy. The harder he delved inside of her, the harder she gripped him with those vice-grip thighs and forced him further into her, savagely taking all that he gave, while begging for more.

"Work me harder, baby. Harder," she moaned, and scratched his back until he bled. "I'm coming, I'm coming," she groaned, her voice deep and throaty.

Alex pumped her until her body shook with an intensity he hadn't ever felt before. She grabbed his ears and jerked them while she rode wave after wave of orgasms. Alex exploded inside of her, but stayed with her, until she sank her teeth into his shoulder, and her entire body collapsed back onto the vanity. A wall of tears ran down her face, and Alex clung to her as if she were a slippery life raft in the middle of a raging ocean.

OVER THE NEXT FEW DAYS, Tiffany's mood darkened. Alex tried to let Lisa handle things in D.C., so that he could focus on his wife and family, but Tiffany seemed to be drifting away from him, falling into a deep depression. Neither Alex, Aunt Giselle, nor the children were able to reach her. When the realtor's tapes arrived, she was uninterested in viewing the properties. Alex wasn't sure how to proceed, but knew they had to have a new home. He decided to go with the Spring Valley property, which was set back on a half-acre wooded lot.

Though her days were filled with deep-tissue massages, spa treatments, and long strolls around the property's tranquil lakes, Tiffany seemed to grow increasingly despondent. Eventually, Alex sought the advice of one of the staff doctors, who recommended that Alex and his wife go to joint grief counseling.

The counseling sessions opened up a dialogue that led to the counselor's recommendation that Tiffany seek more intensive therapy from a psychotherapist in nearby San Francisco who specialized in intense grief counseling.

Alex conferred with Aunt Giselle, who was very aware of Tiffany's fragile state of being. She offered her home in Burleith to Alex and his family until they were settled in their new place, and Alex agreed after he figured that he'd get Lisa to check it for bugs. Aunt Giselle even volunteered to go with Tiffany to San Francisco while she received counseling. The therapist also advised Alex to make Tiffany's transition back home as unstressful as possible, and said that he probably needed some counseling of his own. But that would have to wait. Alex couldn't fathom the thought of discussing his issues with a professional until he was certain that Tiffany was going to be okay. Instead, he found himself talking to one person he'd rarely, up till now, talked to during his life: his father.

Alex called him, and they agreed to meet down at the juice bar near the serenity water-wall in an hour.

As the water danced down the copper wall, Alex watched and sipped his pineapple smoothie and waited for his father. Gerald finally arrived, beet red and sweating.

"What's the matter, Dad?"

Gerald plopped down in a rocking chair, and puffed. "I fell asleep in the steam room. Like to cooked myself to pieces."

Alex chuckled, and motioned for the waiter, then asked his father what he'd like to drink.

"A big glass of water. Nothing fancy. Just water. And lots of it. I need some to pour over my head," Gerald said, and mopped his brow with a paper napkin.

Alex slid his glass across the table toward his father. "Why don't you drink this while you're waiting?"

Gerald picked up the drink and practically downed it all in one gulp. "Thanks."

"Dad." Alex paused. "Tiffany's not doing very well, and she needs to stay here for some more intensive therapy." Gerald nodded, and kept drinking.

"But I've, I mean we've, got to get back. Lisa's been taking care of things, but I need to be there, too. I have to make sure everything's okay, and I can't do that sitting here."

"I understand, son. But, are you sure you want to leave your wife?"

Alex explained that the doctors thought that it was best and then told his father what he and Aunt Giselle had planned.

"That sounds okay, son. And I'm sure that it's going to work out. I know you want to make sure things are right at home, but you need to think about your wife and family. There's nothing more important than them." Gerald sighed. "Especially your wife. You don't want to put yourself in the position of losing her. Trust me. You don't want to see anything happen to the woman you love."

The waiter returned with Gerald's water, and another smoothie for Alex. It was a welcome diversion, because Alex was dumbfounded. His father had never discussed his mother with him. Never. And now it seemed as if he was actually trying to.

"Look, son. I know I haven't been the best father in the world. It's not easy being—well, but that's no excuse. I'm just trying to tell you not to make the same mistakes I made. If your wife needs or wants something, do all that you can to make sure she gets it. Because you never know when your last days together are going to be."

As if Alex needed to be reminded of that. "Is that how you feel? Like you didn't do enough for Mom?"

Gerald sighed and sipped his water. "Most times I do. Your mother was a good woman, but I didn't quite understand her. And when she wanted to get out and become active in the Civil Rights movement, I didn't support her. She went anyway, but not without listening to me gripe. And, unfortunately, that's what she heard before she left on that last trip. And I regret that, Alex. I really do. But I can't change what happened.

"All I'm saying is to honor your wife. Let her know how you feel. Put your feelings aside and do what you have to do to get her through this."

Alex already knew that he'd forgo his needs for the sake of his wife's. That was what the mettle of a marriage was all about. Suddenly, the wedding vows made a lot of sense. *For better or worse.*

CHAPTER 6

THE SOLES of the spit-shined British-tan Stacey Adams shoes left tracks on the dusty floor of the barn. On his small frame, his crisp off-white gabardine slacks fell gracefully down his legs, and with his mesh-leather driving-gloved hand, he bunched them up in the crotch so that his expensive trousers would not touch the filth as he made his way across the voluminous barn, with its graying wood plank walls, full of varying degrees of cracks. The evening sun crept through the roof of the barn, slightly illuminating its dreadfulness.

It was stifling in there, and the sounds of roosters, horses, and other farm animals drummed in his ears. Howard was facing his personal hell, and he dreaded breathing in the noxious air. His face was scrunched up, and he held a stark white handkerchief to his nose, hoping to filter the rank smell of horses, manure, and hay.

"How much further?" Howard sniffed, clutching his nose and

his crotch. "I don't think that I can take much more of this stench."

"He's right over there." The old farmer chuckled, and then mumbled something about "city folk." His voice was heavy and slow, with a thick Southern drawl. Slovenly, heavyset, and sway-backed, the farmer, who reeked of tobacco and body odor, held a lantern and continued to lead Howard through the barn; then he pointed to a few bales of hay. Behind them, Howard spotted a pallet of some sort sticking out.

He did a quick study of the farmer. A keen, insightful master of interpreting body language and detecting people's characteristics and character flaws, Howard found that the farmer was proving to be a difficult read. Ever cautious, Howard waited for the farmer to enter the sectioned-off area. Under the noise of the animals, Howard heard the moans of a man. An injured man. He quickly followed the farmer inside, and nearly gagged when he saw the bundled-up heap on the filthy mattress.

"Oh, my God," Howard said, his eyes fixed on the injured man wrapped in a stained, tattered green horse blanket and curled up in the fetal position. He was gurgling lowly, as if the air was shredding his esophagus, and flies buzzed around his body.

Temporarily abandoning his fashion consciousness and concern for his garments, Howard knelt down, and shooed the insects away. He reached for the man's pulse. It was faint and slow.

"And how long has he been like this?" Howard asked. He removed the glove from his left hand as he reached to feel the man's forehead. It was cold and clammy. Howard quickly replaced his glove and pulled the blanket back, and nearly gagged. The man's body was speckled with flies, and maggots were squirming around the wounds on his bare chest. Shirtless and shoeless, the man was wearing what appeared to be only his soiled trousers. The same ones he had been wearing on the last night Howard had seen him. On the boat.

With the help of the dim, flickering lantern light, Howard could see how bad Simon's condition really was. Howard had spent some time as a medic in the army years ago, and Simon's appearance reminded him of that of some of the fallen soldiers he had encountered. Simon's complexion was ashen; his eyes were dry and thick with crust. Howard reached to open Simon's lids; his pupils were alternating between being fixed and dilated, and flickering backward. He tilted his head back, and opened Simon's mouth. It was pale, and his tongue was covered with a thick white film.

Simon's wounds were swollen, discolored, and oozing pus, and his stomach felt hard and hot to the touch. He was clearly running a raging temperature, full of infections, dehydrated, and probably in some form of shock. Not to mention suffering the aftereffects of hypothermia from being in the chilly water. Howard thought, *Damn, I'm glad I'm wearing gloves.* It was a lot for Howard to digest, especially as the farmer droned on with his story.

"He's been like that ever since he washed up on the shore, down the road a piece," the farmer said as he flipped a stocky thumb over his shoulder, then shoved his hand into the flap of his overalls. He pulled out a pinch of tobacco, and placed it in the back of his rotting teeth. "But don't mind them maggots none. They're actually eatin' away some of that dead flesh."

The farmer continued. "Near 'bouts a week or such ago, I went off to the crick down there off Riverside Road to do a little fishin', and there he was. First I thought it was the biggest black bass I ever seen."

The mechanisms in Howard's mind clicked. If Simon had been here almost a week, it meant that he had floated for at least a day before he had landed down there in Charles County, Maryland. A scant fifty miles from the nation's capital.

Earlier that day, Howard and his assistant, Royce, had been returning from Simon's memorial service when Howard's mobile phone rang. The caller was taking so long to speak that Howard thought it was just a wrong number and hung up. The phone rang again, and the farmer started talking. "Hey, uh, some boy, I mean some man down here wanted me to contact you," the farmer said. After getting a few details, Howard hastily dropped Royce off and immediately left to meet the farmer way down Indian Head Highway, through a couple of counties, and off several beaten paths.

"Did he say anything else?" Howard asked, ignoring the redneck's tasteless comment.

"Nope. Not really, I reckon. Nothin' that I could understand, anyways. He's been in and out mostly," he said. "Just mumblin' a whole lot. He did call on Jesus and Moses a coupla times. Then, out the blue, he starts repeatin' these numbers, and I called you soon as he said to dial 'em. He never did call your name, though." The farmer paused. "Jeez, you must be a pretty busy fella. It took me a coupla tries to finally reach you. I tried yesterday and today."

The farmer didn't have a telephone and had to journey into the local town to use the pay phone in front of Crescent's Mini-Mart to call Howard. That's where Howard had met the farmer, and then trailed him back to his farm. Howard sniffed, and finally stood and faced the farmer.

"Mister, uh—" Howard asked, fanning his small hands and making a feeble attempt to recall the old codger's name. "Did you give him anything for his wounds? Any medicine or anything?"

"Folks call me Wallace or Wally for short," he said, and extended one of his hands, which were caked with dirt, his nails embedded with crud.

Howard could only imagine how horrified Simon would be if he were aware of his present surroundings—and of the cretin who had been administering to him. Howard ignored the old man's hand.

The farmer continued. "Well, I had a few capsules of some old penicillin that I tried to give 'im, but I couldn't get 'im to take it. Opened up his jaws and everything, but, nothin'. Just set there right on his tongue. So, I mixed up some cobwebs and a little salve to try to stop the bleedin' on some of those gashes. They worked right nice." The farmer shrugged his shoulders. "Yep, that's about it."

Howard slowly closed his eyelids, and let his pupils roll to the back of his head. He cringed, opened his eyes again, and then raised a neatly trimmed eyebrow. "I see. I'm so glad that your down-home remedy stopped the bleeding. I often wondered if things like that really worked." Howard, a product of the Deep South, knew full well that those old backwoods remedies worked, but he'd never let this hick know that.

Howard folded his arms and cast a long, sardonic look around the barn. "I'm quite curious. Did you come up with this cure yourself, or did you consult with anyone? A doctor perhaps? Or whatever you call the medicine men in these parts." Howard dusted off his gloved hands and peered at the farmer. "Does anyone else know that he's here?"

Wally shook his head, "Nope. I just figured it might help 'im out. Doctors are few an' far between, an' it's not like I could afford one. Not at all. But anyways, it's just me here, and I run things with little or no help from no one. I don't grow as much as I used to; I just ain't able. But I goes to town once a week, so I don't run into folks too often. Yessir. But anyways, I heard on the radio that one of them political types up there in D.C. had gone missing in the river, sos I figured that this might be the boy, I mean, uh, the man. I wasn't too sure, and then, since he was still livin', I figured that someone might be lookin' for 'im or somethin'. Be glad to hear that he's alive, you know what I mean?" The farmer chuckled and rubbed his fingertips together, and the dim lantern light gave him the appearance of a television character. The fat, old, greasy Otis, from *The Andy Griffith Show*.

Howard sneered and reached for his breast pocket. "Well, I can only say that at this time, we really appreciate your discretion. It is actually a matter of security, if you understand my meaning. I hope that you'll keep this issue under your, uh, hat," Howard said, and pulled out his shiny, eel-skin wallet. With his manicured fingers, he gingerly counted out ten one-hundred-dollar bills. "I hope that you'll take this as our token of appreciation. And for your consideration."

Wally's eyes lit up, and he licked his lips. "Sure thing, mister, uh—"

"*Mister*'s sufficient for now. The less you know, the better," Howard said. "Now, if you have a piece of relatively clean plastic or something with which I can line my car seat, I'd sincerely appreciate it. And if you'd be so kind as to help me get this fine gentleman out to my car, I'd be ever grateful and indebted to you."

AFTER CAREFULLY HOISTING Simon into a rickety wheelbarrow, Howard held the lantern, and alternately grabbed his crotch and nose, while old farmer Wally struggled to push Simon's dead weight out to Howard's tiny Aston Martin.

Assisted by the dim light of the lantern and the glowing moon, Howard carefully lined his passenger seat with a piece of thin blue tarp Wally had rustled up, and then watched as Wally struggled to get the ailing Simon into the auto. Tuning out Wally's trite chatter, Howard focused in on the objective at hand. Getting Simon back on his feet.

"So," Wally said, scratching his thinning gray hair with those crusted, gnarled fingers. "It was a real pleasure meeting you, mister."

"Likewise," Howard said, and walked toward the driver's side door. Wally cut his path off with his wide body.

"Yessir, I feel like I've put in a solid day's work 'round here already. That's more than I can say for me most of the time. As you can see, it sure is tough tryin' to make it as a farmer these days. Don't get too much help from those fat-pocketed folks up there in the gov'ment." Wally shrugged, and chewed on his tobacco. "Oh, well, I'm not going to bore you with my sorrows. I'm sure you got bigger fish to fry."

Howard stared at Wally, who was standing dangerously close,

in Howard's personal space. Howard sniffed, and tried not to inhale Wally's pungent odor.

Wally spit out a long line of tobacco, and it landed quietly in the darkness. "Say, those folks up in D.C. are goin' to be tickled pink that their guy's been found. Yessiree. Hell, I'm sure the folks around here would just love to know that our little town was part of finding that old boy."

Howard sniffed again, and slowly put away his handkerchief. "I certainly do have bigger fish to fry, Wally. I'm sure you understand that. But, rest assured, I can truly sympathize with your plight as a farmer. I truly can." Howard reached in his breast pocket, removed his wallet, and peeled off five more C-notes. "Perhaps this extra token will lighten your load a little more."

Wally grabbed the bills, and extracted another wad of snuff. "Sure nuff. And I do appreciate it. This ought to tide me over, at least for a month. Do you think you might be able to show me a little more appreciation? Specially since I'm an old man, and my memory slips sometimes, and I'd hate to not be able to afford my memory medicine, you know."

"Oh, yes. I know," Howard said, and opened his car door. He reached under his seat and pulled out a small case.

"Do you think you might have a little somethin' extra for my toll calls and such. It was mighty expensive callin' you like I did."

"No problem," Howard said, and opened his case. He withdrew a small, antique, silver snub-nosed single-shot derringer, and systematically blasted Wally in the center of his forehead. A clean circle burnt through his skull, and Wally stumbled backward, his eyes stuck open, and his mouth dribbling with tobacco juice. With a dull thud, Wally's thick body fell backward onto the grass, and the five hundred dollars scattered on top of the ground. Howard swiftly picked up the bills, then rifled through Wally's seedy overalls and retrieved the grand. He tossed two dimes onto Wally's lifeless body. "You can keep the change, Farmer Wally."

CHAPTER 7

WITH THE ASSISTANCE of his Dominican gardener, Hector, who barely spoke English, Howard safely transported Simon up to his attic. To avoid having anyone identify him, Howard had wrapped Simon's head and face with thick, white gauze, and had driven the Aston Martin into his attached garage, which led into his house.

Relying on his resourcefulness and copious connections, Howard was able to transform the attic into a nearly sterile environment for the ailing mayor overnight. Simon's recovery was a bit precarious, but after a week, and a round of intensive examinations and meds from one of Howard's underground doctor friends, Simon's condition stabilized. His wounds had been infected, and he was diagnosed as suffering from severe septic shock.

The attic looked like a mini intensive care unit. Simon was attached to oxygen to treat his respiratory distress; intravenous fluids were being administered to rehydrate him and restore his blood volume; and the infections were being treated with steroids and potent antibiotics.

Because his staph-infected wounds were susceptible to dirt and airborne viruses, Simon's bed was sealed within a plastic tent, and Howard took every precaution to ensure that he himself was completely covered every time he entered the room. He had to do this until he was able to get some additional help.

But, he'd had to be still more careful. Howard kept his assistant, Royce, in the dark about his ailing houseguest and busied him with minor tasks that kept him out of Howard's home office. Ever shrewd, Howard hired two full-time nurses to provide round-the-clock care for Simon. He only required that they dress as maids when they entered the house, so that none would be the wiser. It was costing him a princely sum, but it was no matter. Whenever Simon completely recovered, Howard knew that his reward would be enormous. And if Simon didn't survive, Howard could benefit from that also. Either way, he couldn't lose. Either way, he knew he wouldn't lose.

WHILE SIMON'S LIFE WAS HANGING in the balance, Howard managed to keep up appearances, making his rounds at the gym and keeping his other clients relatively content. He was walking a fine line, playing a dangerous game—still working for the Cavanaughs without disclosing the fact that he was harboring the ailing Simon. But he had rationalized that, too. If Simon didn't survive, then his other employers would never have to know. And if Simon did survive, then Howard would have access to Simon's fortune. And if Howard played his cards right, he would be a very wealthy and protected man.

WHEN SIMON FINALLY REGAINED consciousness, the nurse on duty immediately summoned Howard, who, after dressing in his sterile suit, dismissed the nurse from the room.

A groggy Simon struggled to speak, his voice barely above a whisper, and Howard strained to hear him over the beeps and clicking noises emanating from the medical equipment. He leaned over Simon's bed railing.

Simon struggled to breathe. "Howard?" Simon asked, and Howard could see Simon's bloodshot eyes squinting through the cutouts in the gauze. Wafting through his white-crusted lips, Simon's halitosis nearly knocked Howard off of his feet.

"Yes, Simon. It's me."

"What the hell's going on?" Simon asked, his voice a gravelly whisper and his words slightly slurred.

Howard held a plastic-gloved finger to his lips. "Shhhh. Try to stay calm, Your Honor."

"Where am I?" Simon paused, and his fingers strained outward. "What happened? What happened to me?" Simon asked. He reached for his face, and cringed, still obviously in a lot of pain. He touched the dressing. "What's all of this? Howard? What's this on my face?"

Howard checked the monitors, and adjusted the dosage of Simon's painkillers. "It's some covering for your face, Mayor. I had to take a few precautions to protect you. You need to understand that I've been here to protect you."

"Protect me? Protect me from what, for Christ's sake? Get this shit off of my face," Simon said, the volume of his raspy voice raised. "The last thing I remember is being on my boat, at a—at my fund-raiser. After that, everything's pretty much a blank."

Howard took a seat on a stool beside Simon's bed. He eyed the fluctuating levels of Simon's blood pressure, and tried not to register concern. The beeps on the heart-monitoring machine rapidly increased. He removed a pair of sterile surgical scissors from Simon's nightstand, and held them in his hand. Howard sighed. "Well, first and foremost, you need to try to stay calm. You're suffering from major trauma right now, and extensive injuries. But, we won't focus on that at this moment. We have to focus on you getting better."

"Damn that," Simon said, and ripped the dressing off his face. "You don't have to protect me from anyone. I fear no one." Simon's skin was ashen, and a stubborn gray beard was sprouting on his face.

Simon clutched his chest and sucked in air, and fought back an immense yawn. "You must've forgotten who you're talking to. I'm Simon Louis Blake, damn it. Don't ever forget that." His red-eyed glare was steely and full of resolve and aggravation, but it was evident that he was getting drowsy.

Howard increased Simon's medication to ensure that he fell back to sleep. Howard was not eagerly anticipating Simon's heightened state of consciousness, at least, not so soon, and certainly, not at this moment. But he quickly remembered the resolute individual that lay injured, but defiant, in the stark hospital bed.

Simon's voice was raspy and low. His whisper sounded like an edgy growl from a wounded lion. "Now, stop this song and dance. I want to know why I'm here. And more importantly, who's responsible for me being here," Simon said, and blinked slowly, struggling to keep his eyes open, but the pain medicine quickly took hold of him.

Simon fell back into a deep sleep, and snored soundly and deeply for the rest of the day. During that time, Howard finetuned the details of his story for Simon. Simon, whose mind was like a steel bear trap, eventually awakened, and immediately began methodically questioning Howard again.

It was a carefully crafted story Howard spoon-fed to Simon. There had been engine trouble aboard *The Masquerade,* and Simon, Alex, and Tiffany had been endangered. In a heroic feat, Simon had gotten his daughter and son-in-law safely off the boat, and then he tried to save the vessel, but the boat had caught fire, and it had been assumed that Simon had perished.

According to Howard, less than ten days after the accident, a helpful stranger had found and sheltered Simon until he regained enough consciousness to ask for Howard. Howard, always cautious, had decided to keep the fact that Simon was still alive under wraps until he was well enough to recall what had actually happened.

Simon motioned for some water, and Howard carefully placed a curved ice chip in his mouth.

"I'm not quite sure what to say, Howard," Simon finally said, his words carefully spoken. His glare drilled holes through Howard, who met his gaze with not so much as a flinch. "How was my memorial service?"

"Touching and well attended," Howard said, and ignored Simon's sarcasm. "I understand your concern, Simon. And the fact that your memory hasn't fully restored itself is going to make your ability to comprehend what I've told you a little difficult. But you will eventually get it back. It'll probably be fragmented at first, but you should regain complete recall in a matter of days or weeks. Worst case, maybe months."

Simon sucked on the ice chip and continued staring. "I understand that. So that explains how I got here. Who's running my office? Oh, that's right. The deputy mayor."

"Correct," Howard said. "But they've voted to wait until next March to have a special election to fill your office. They have to give candidates ample time to register and campaign."

Simon nodded. "Okay, that's not an issue. How are my children? Where are Tiffany and Alex? And why haven't you contacted them? Why aren't they here? Get Alex here immediately."

Howard touched his own face and sniffed deeply, and then leaned back in his chair. "Well, Alex and Tiffany have recuperated from their injuries, and are home, and trying to get their lives back together." Howard paused. "But, to be honest with you, Simon, I wasn't sure if letting them know you were alive was such a good idea. The reason I haven't contacted them was that my instincts were and are on edge about this. I just wasn't certain if I should let them know about you. For their sakes and yours."

"What? Why?"

Howard cleared his throat. "Well, there was an abundance of rumors surrounding the circumstances leading up to your accident, so, I decided to err on the side of being cautious. Until you regained consciousness, I was going to keep your status as discreet as possible. Even from your family."

Simon clicked the ice in his mouth. He rubbed his temples, and squeezed his eyes closed. "Even from my family? What rumors could possibly have been that devastating that they would cause you to make a judgment call like that?"

"Rumors that your death and the death of one of the leading drug dealers in the area might have somehow been connected. And if that was true, if you showed up alive, then you or your family might just be in danger."

Simon's eyebrows rose and his red eyes opened. "My family endangered. Me connected to a major drug dealer. Interesting." Simon folded his arms across his chest. "Who might this person be? And why would my life be in danger because of him? Because I'm the mayor?" Simon's questions were leading, and perplexed.

"A person going by the name of Moses was identified as the drug dealer," Howard said. "His real name was Edward Blanks."

Simon coughed and turned his head. "And he would be connected to me—how?"

"By coincidence and by circumstances," Howard said.

"You don't say? Hmmm. And this has been confirmed, I presume?" Simon asked.

"Indeed," Howard said, and nodded his head.

"Go figure. Edward Blanks a major drug dealer. Well, well, well, well. Ain't that something. Howard, that sounds like quite a story. And now, by what coincidence and circumstance is he supposed to be connected to me?"

"It's simple, Simon. There was a major gangland slaying and takedown of Moses' laboratory on the same night as your accident. Somehow, it's not hard to imagine that the same folks that took him down might've targeted you, too. Stranger things have happened, and I just didn't want to take any chances."

Simon closed his eyes and remained quiet while only the beep and click of his machines continued in the absence of conversation. "So, let me get this straight. Moses' lab was destroyed? All of it?"

"That's a fact," Howard said.

Simon whistled. "And this Moses was supposed to be a major drug dealer in the city?"

"*The* major drug distributor in the city."

"I see. And now he's dead, huh? Well. Isn't that interesting." Simon scratched his chin. "Is this your supposition, or is this what the newspapers are touting?" Simon asked.

"Both. But I take exception to some of the information that's being trumpeted. You know that I will always read between the lines. That's my job, and what I'm exceptionally good at," Howard said.

Simon struggled to sit up, and then rested on his elbows. "Well, Howard. I'm surprised. Part of me finds it extremely difficult to believe that you would ever swallow or regurgitate a cockamamie story like that. Bl—, uh, Blanks would never have the gumption to run any major operation. Someone is obviously not doing their homework." Simon shook his head and yawned. "Well, sir. I'm beginning to wonder if I gave you too much credit, Howard. I figured that if anyone would know the real deal by now, it would be you. Tsk, tsk, tsk."

Howard bristled, but refused to be challenged or intimidated by Simon. Especially not a sickly Simon. "You could never give me too much credit, Simon. Or should I say, Moses."

Simon shot Howard a flat look, but said nothing.

"Trust and believe, when you disappeared, I made sure that any connections between you and your alter ego also disappeared. And, as for the inquiring public, and the court of public opinion, they have digested the story without a second notion. It's yesterday's news. But for me, there are many holes that remain. Holes that only you and Moses can fill in. Holes that must be filled in before you ever resurface here in our fine city," Howard said.

Simon struggled to clap. "Bravo, Howard. I always thought that you knew but were just too polite to say anything." Simon squinted and motioned for Howard to adjust his bed.

Once Simon was sitting almost completely upright, he spoke again. This time his voice was stronger, and his words clearer. "Well, this kind of changes the whole scheme of things, now, doesn't it? I can honestly and truthfully say that I don't recall the specifics leading up to or of the accident, but I've got the gist of what happened beforehand."

"That's natural, Simon. You're probably suffering from trauma-induced amnesia. Your memory will come back, eventually."

Simon waved a weary, thin hand. "That's fine, Howard. I can handle that. All of this has changed my game considerably. Right now, I just need to get my house back in order. But, there's only so much I can do until I get better. And stronger. So now that we're on the same page, you can stop feeding me the bullshit. Tell me exactly why you haven't contacted my family?"

"Frankly, Simon, I don't know if they can be trusted," Howard said.

"Trust, huh? That's a big thing for me. And you say that you can't trust them, why?"

"It's a feeling, Simon. I read people very well, and let's just say that I don't like the text I've seen and heard from your son-in-law. And until I know for sure, I'd rather not involve him."

Simon paused for a moment. "I see. Well, it appears that I'm going to have to lean on you for a little while, Howard. Until we can figure this 'trust' thing out, I'm going to need your help."

"Understood, Simon. Understood," Howard said.

"We may need another set of hands. Do you have someone that I can trust?"

"I have an assistant, Royce, who seems pretty reliable. He's good for doing a little legwork. But don't worry. I'll have him do peripheral things for us, but I'll keep him on a short leash."

"Good. If you trust him a little, remember, I trust him even less. So let's get started. We've got a lot of work to do. I've got a lot of business to attend to. I know I'm not firing on all cylinders yet, but I've got enough firepower to make some headway. Now, I want to know what you know, and how you know it. And more-over, I've got to find out exactly what's going on. With my family. My estate. My memory. And my legacy. I know that I've crossed a lot of people in my past, and I need to use this time to figure out exactly where I stand. I want to know who's on which side of the fence, and who's straddling it. I want to know who's revealed themselves to be my friend. Or, God help them, my foe."

CHAPTER 8

A S SOON as Alex and Tiffany had departed for California, Lisa had moved out of the hotel and set up shop in their home. Thankfully, the throngs of reporters had vacated the premises, and she had arrived at their house with only one of her security agents.

With so many tasks at hand, she almost hadn't known where to begin. Methodically, she had taken the pieces of the puzzle that was Alex's life, mentally laid them out, and tried to fit them together. She had to get them together soon, especially since Alex had arrived back in town late last night.

Alex and his children were staying at Aunt Giselle's house, with a new nanny and a small security detail Lisa had provided. Alex had refused to even visit with Lisa at his old home, even though Lisa had rendered it "bug free." She'd installed her own elaborate security system, one that she said was one hundred percent confident could not be compromised.

From her command post in the Baxter's former dining room, Lisa reviewed Alex's schedule and her never-ending "to do" list. He was scheduled to close on his property later this morning, and then remove his personal belongings from his office at the District Building. She took a small silver tack and stuck the list on the wall.

Most of the walls were bare, except for the documents and papers she had tacked onto them. She leaned back in the leather ergonomic chair she had borrowed from Alex's office, chomped into a half-eaten Twinkie, and chased it with a swig of chocolate milk. She then placed her hands behind her head, and a frown crept across her brow. Though she tried not to show it, she was concerned that she was in way over her head. Nonetheless, she was determined not to let her friend Alex down. They had always been there for each other, and now was no exception.

Always battling her weight, Lisa knew that her nerves were getting wrecked. Her snacking was out of control, as evidenced by the contents of the mahogany dining room table. It was scattered with crumpled Snickers bar wrappers, greasy Big Mac containers, half-empty Pepsi cans, and red pistachio nutshells.

"I've got to get a grip," Lisa said out loud, and finished her cream-filled pastry with one swift bite. She was glad she was alone in her clandestine office. She checked her stainless-steel-and-gold Ebel watch and it read 7:15. Normally an early riser, Lisa was clocking fewer than four hours sleep a night, and it was beginning to show. She caught a glimpse of herself in the mirrored background of the china cabinet, and almost said, "Yikes."

Her bright red manicured nails were chipped, and she was outfitted in day-old baggy blue sweatpants and a burgundy Morehouse sweatshirt. Lisa was not looking her disco best. Fortunately, her asymmetric hairdo was laid as usual, and her facial features were not hard on the eyes. She was so glad that Pat, her hairstylist, had talked her into cutting her hair and waxing her eyebrows before she left Atlanta.

Lisa was exceptionally thorough when she conducted her business, and never let anyone see anything but the best from her. As a female in an extremely male-dominated profession, she had to have her shit together. Better than together. It had to be tight.

A size fourteen, she looked good in her clothes, and always beat her face when out in the public eye. She didn't play about that. But in her quiet moments, she would definitely let it all hang out. She wasn't one of those sisters who sit around in matching loungewear or wear frilly little pink slippers. She prided herself on being a real homegirl. One who relaxed and got down in sweats and a T-shirt. And if she had a man, then she'd don his boxer shorts. But since she was currently sans a man, she was left to her own devices.

And, despite her concerns, she was taking care of business. Over the past week, she had fired anyone that had been hired during the Mayor Blake regime. Scratched them off the list and then arranged for them to be tailed for at least a few weeks. That included the housekeepers, gardeners, and even the nanny. As Alex had requested, she had checked and verified that Aunt Giselle's house had not been bugged. Lisa had dismantled the extensive security system in the house, ridding it of the cameras and electronic bugs that had secretly invaded Alex and Tiffany's privacy since they had moved into the house. Lisa had been amazed at the intricacy of the devices that she'd found in the house and in both of their cars. Simon Blake had spared no expense in his quest to keep a watchful eye on his child and her husband. The whole thing creeped Lisa out, but she had to keep her perspective. Alex was a client now, and she had to stay focused and not get caught up in the personal details of the job.

Easy to say, but damned difficult to do. It was a fine line she was maneuvering along. Alex was her friend, but this case was intense. Lisa had fallen into the investigation field by accident, choosing to work in her family's insurance company in a department that was basically ignored. Lisa thought it was a challenge, and quickly found her niche. Always inquisitive and nosy, she had no problem taking on the insurance fraud cases. But now she was treading on perilous ground. She wasn't truly experienced as a professional PI, and the lives of one of her closest friends and his family hinged on her ability to accurately perform her job. The pressure was a bit much.

Lisa took another swig of chocolate milk and burped. She tried to regain her focus. She had made significant progress. Armed with Alex's power of attorney, she had sold Tiffany's steel gray Volvo, but had decided to keep Alex's midnight black 525 BMW to use as her mode of transportation. She hadn't mentioned it to Alex yet, but had arranged for him to use a rental until he picked out another car.

Lisa realized that a lot of Alex's actions and reactions were being driven by emotion, and if she didn't do some strategic thinking for him, he'd be in debt way over his head. Hell, as of today, he really didn't even have a job since he was part of Simon's select administration, and now that was no more. Fortunately, he had plenty of personal leave to exhaust, so he did still have income flowing. But he also wanted two new cars. And the houses he had been considering were pricey. They were averaging almost $450,000. Lisa understood how Alex felt, and she sympathized with his plight, but she wasn't about to let him do anything completely crazy. Like go bankrupt.

She had hired professional movers, who had packed their possessions and stored them in the basement. They were scheduled to pick up the items later in the week and move them into the Baxters' new home. In the interim, she had also changed their phone number, and put the service in the name of a bogus corporation she had established for them. Until she was sure that Alex and his family weren't facing any imminent danger, she wanted any and all activities to be routed through the Rextab Group. After managing all of those tasks, now the real job was at hand. And that was to start tracking the slick, wormy paper trail that constituted the remains of Mayor Simon Blake's life.

Sitting amid stacks of files and office equipment, Lisa sighed and rubbed her temples. The hard drive from Simon's PC had produced a detailed list of accounts in various countries. They were coded, and Lisa had hired an expert to decipher the coding; he'd promised to have it broken by the end of the week.

It was Wednesday morning, and Lisa was slated to go to the mayor's mansion and go through Simon's personal possessions. Though the property was secured, she had negotiated the search as a personal request of the Blake family. With Fortune supposedly watching the house since the mayor's disappearance, Lisa was relatively sure that no one had accessed the property, or removed anything. But she was going to make sure of it today. She'd leave no stone unturned when it came to sweeping Simon's house. She had decided to do it herself, trusting the actual task to no one else.

Lisa grabbed a thick file folder labeled "accounts," and after clearing an open space on the table, she laid the file open, and began reviewing its contents. The phone rang, and she jumped in her seat.

Startled, it took her a moment to find the cordless phone, and she finally answered it on the third ring. "Hello," Lisa said.

"What's happenin', doll face?"

The voice on the phone made Lisa bristle. "Fortune."

"Yeah, it's me," Fortune said, and then repeated his original greeting.

"Nothing's happening, Fortune. I'm just trying to get some work done. Like in job, you know, work—occupation. A foreign concept for you, I'm sure."

Fortune laughed. "Yeah, you right. That nine to five ain't for me, ya know. Anyway, I was callin' to let you know that everythang's quiet on my end. Nothin' to report."

Lisa sucked her teeth. "Why am I not surprised?"

"I'm just tryin' to offer my help. I know you need some."

"You don't know what I need."

Fortune sighed. "I know you a sista that can handle her business, no bout a doubt it. But, I also know you got your hands full."

"I'm okay," Lisa said. There was no way she was going to let the likes of Fortune Reed know she was about to lose it.

"Glad to hear it. You got any word on Big Boy yet?"

"Who?"

"What's-his-name. Fatty. I mean Foody. Alex's homeboy."

Damn, Lisa thought. She'd forgotten to check the morgue or the hospitals again. "I'm on it," she said. She grabbed a pen, and scrawled and underlined "FOODY" in big, bold capital letters on top of a manila folder.

"Cool. So when you plan on gettin' over here to the dark side? You ain't even been to the old man's crib yet. I thought you'da been there by now."

"What are you trying to do, clock me? If it's any of your concern, I planned on coming over there today."

"Good; when? I'll meet you there," Fortune said.

"What? Why? I don't need your help," Lisa said, and stood up. She knew that she'd have to get moving, especially now that she'd let it slip out that she was going to the mayor's mansion.

"I hope you don't plan on bringin' some of those simple, thick-necked dudes you got workin' for you. They ain't gonna be able to find nothin'. They probably won't even know where to look."

"Fortune, please. They are professionals, unlike you. But to answer your question, I planned on coming alone. I trust my men, but I want to keep this as close to my vest as possible. As if I owe you any explanation."

"That's smart. So, what time?"

"Two o'clock," Lisa said, lying through her teeth. She really intended to be there by eight-thirty. If Fortune did show up at two, hopefully, she'd be almost ready to leave.

"Cool. I'll see you then, lady," Fortune said.

AFTER TAKING A QUICK SHOWER, Lisa hustled herself over to the mansion. It was a bright and cloud-free morning, and she cranked WKYS on the radio, with the moonroof open. "MotownPhilly" by Boyz II Men blasted, and as Lisa sang along, she zoomed down the Rock Creek Parkway to make it to the Southeast estate. She made it there by eight-fifteen, and when she pulled up to the gates to pass through police security, a zealous Fortune stuck his head through the open roof.

"Good morning, luscious. You gonna let me in? You'd better be careful ridin' around with your top all open like this. Somebody might reach in here an' snatch you out."

The police officer, checking Lisa's identification, raised an eyebrow and fingered his gun holster. "Are you all right, miss?"

Lisa retrieved her ID and warily answered, "Yes, sir. I'm fine. He's, uh, with me." She unlocked the doors, and gritted on Fortune as if she wanted his heart to cease beating. He returned her glare by blowing her a kiss, and plopped down in the passenger seat.

Lisa pulled into the driveway, gnashing her teeth. His presence bothered her, but she had to commend Fortune. His hair was cut, he was shaven, cleaned up, wearing a white oxford shirt, and a pair of beige khakis. He even smelled as if he had showered recently. To the untrained eye, he actually appeared quite presentable. As though he could be relatively normal. She quickly dismissed that thought.

"Fortune, I wish you'd stop creeping up on me like this. My goodness. Can't you ever do anything normal? And what are you doing here, anyway?"

Fortune laughed, stuck his hand through the open moonroof.

"I figured you'd be here a lil' early. You gave up on the info a lil' too quick, you know what I mean? I figured you'd try to ditch me, so I hung out. And whaddaya know? Up jumps you." Fortune grinned, and his teeth appeared to have been brushed.

Lisa rolled her eyes and shoved the car into park. "Whatever. It's a woman's prerogative to change her mind. I had planned on coming later, but I, uh, decided to come early." She leaned into the backseat and yanked a medium-sized doctor's bag from the floor. She opened the car door and jumped out, then slammed it, leaving Fortune sneering in the car.

"Are you coming?" she yelled, not even looking back. She didn't want to see his self-serving expression.

"Yeah, I'm right behind you," Fortune said, his eyes riveted on her ample backside.

CHAPTER 9

A S SOON as they entered Simon's mansion, Lisa directed Fortune to the west wing. Standing in the two-story foyer, she pointed toward the winding staircase. "I wonder which one is the master bedroom," she said aloud. "Well, let's start up there. In the bedrooms," she said. She clutched her black bag, and headed upstairs.

"That's exactly what I was thinkin'," Fortune said.

"Whoa, easy, tiger. You take those rooms," she said, and pointed in the opposite direction from where she was headed.

They spent the next few hours carefully examining the four bedrooms and the master suite on the second floor. Using basic detective techniques, Lisa turned over mattresses and nimbly ran her fingers down the seams for any slots or compartments. She checked for false bottoms in dresser drawers and behind hanging pictures and mirrors. She held a listening device to her ear and tapped on walls as she ran the gadget up and down to check for hollow spaces. Loose floorboards, old cigar boxes, and even wrinkles and upturned edges in the wallpaper were scrutinized. Nothing.

Their search of the main level and basement didn't fare much better. In the next few hours, they checked every square inch of Simon's residence. They checked cabinets and under furniture and behind pictures, and even checked the frames for false backs. It was an exhaustive process, and Lisa and Fortune were each frustrated to the point that they even rifled through the pockets of Simon's clothing hanging in the closets.

Lisa, at first skeptical of Fortune's sleuthing capabilities, was rather impressed with his investigative skills. She had quietly observed him as he carefully checked for loose cinder blocks in the basement walls, while she went through rusty old file cabinets that were neatly lined up in the damp basement. He even checked in the utility room, crawling behind a commercial-sized washer and dryer, the hot water tank, and the furnace. Besides the due diligence he demonstrated by almost getting snapped by a mousetrap, and actually getting stuck on a glue trap, Fortune turned up nothing.

Despite their best efforts, their discoveries were minimal. All they were able to find was a standard wall safe in the library and a small fireproof box that was in Simon's closet. Lisa and Fortune met in the library, and went over their booty.

"Told you there wouldn't be nothin' here," Fortune said, while Lisa hoisted her black bag onto the desk. "Say, what's in the bag, gorgeous?"

"Tools," she said, and twisted open the latch on the bag. She removed a stethoscope and headed over to the wall safe, which was behind an original Jacob Lawrence painting.

"Umph, I likes that. A woman that knows how to really get down. You must be gettin' ready to go to work on that safe, huh? Where you get schooled like that at?" Fortune asked.

"Let's just say I'm a fast learner," Lisa said as she placed the plugs in her ears and listened intently to the lock as she turned it clockwise and counterclockwise. "And, to your point, you don't know what's here. Why don't we just wait and see, before you start making your slanted assumptions."

"Say, uh—"

"Shhhh, Fortune. I'm trying to hear the tumblers," Lisa said, and at the final syllable, she turned the handle and the door opened. "See," Lisa said, her voice brimming with pride. She hung the stethoscope around her neck, and stepped aside so that Fortune could see the stacks of papers and journals stuffed in the tiny vault. She crammed the documents in her arms, and took them to the middle of the room and laid them on the floor. Fortune reached for them, and Lisa smacked his hand. "Wait a minute, will you?"

Fortune snatched his hand away. "Well, all right then. I like a lady that likes it a little rough," he said with a little grin.

"Very funny, Fortune. And you know what? I wish you'd stop with all this sexual *entendre*. I don't have time for your little snide remarks," Lisa said. She sat Indian-style on the floor. "Now, pass me that strongbox and my bag."

Fortune picked up the items, and handed them to Lisa. "Um, Lisa?"

Lisa grunted. "I told you. This is not the time or the place," she said, and reached in her bag. She picked out a flat case of tools, ones that professional locksmiths use. She immediately went to work on the lock.

Fortune tried to get her attention again, and Lisa bit his head off. "What is it, Fortune?"

Fortune reached down and opened the lid of the box. "I was just tryin' to tell you that the box wasn't locked."

THEY TOOK TURNS going over every document from the two safes. There weren't any revealing documents. There were some old appointment books, a few bookkeeping journals, and a passbook account from Riggs National Bank. There were two odd-shaped keys, etched with DO NOT DUPLICATE, in a small, change-sized Riggs envelope. Lisa quickly deduced that they were safe-deposit-box keys.

Once again, Fortune reiterated his opinion that they'd find nothing of any value there, either.

"Well, we had to start somewhere. Hopefully, this will lead us to something more substantial," she said, and struggled to her feet. "These are keys to safe-deposit boxes."

"Sho' you right. I just know that he's got a treasure map in one of those boxes that'll tell you exactly where he's stashed his buried treasure. Maybe, just maybe, if you click your heels three times, yo' fairy godmother just might take you to the magical place with the magical boxes."

Lisa stood toe-to-toe with Fortune and poked him in his bony chest. "I've had just about enough out of you, Fortune Reed. Now, if you're just going to be bugging me with a whole lot of negative energy, then I don't need you hanging around. If you don't have anything positive to say or share, well, then you can take your dusty ass out of my face and get to steppin'." Lisa snatched some of the documents from the floor and shoved them back into the wall safe, and placed the keys in her pocket. She took the more important documents and crammed them in her bag.

"I'm sorry, Lisa. I just meant, well, I was just tryin' to let you know that although I know you know what you're doin', you got a lot of ground to cover, and we don't got a lot of time." Fortune shrugged. "I'm just tryin' to help."

Lisa gritted her teeth. "Okay. I accept your apology. And I'm probably just a little bit punchy by now. You're right. I've got like a year's worth of work to do, and with very little time to do it in. Especially with Alex back now."

"Word," Fortune said.

"Plus I'm getting hungry. And if you must know, I do get a little crabby when my stomach's empty," she said.

"I thought I heard it grumblin' a little while ago. So I tell you what. Why don't we go and grab a couple of fish sandwiches from Horace and Dickey's, and head back up to the crib? And really work somethin' out."

AN EXHAUSTED-LOOKING Alex arrived before Lisa and Fortune could leave. They were standing outside on the front stairs, when Alex pulled up in his rental car. They walked over to the car, and when Alex stepped out of it, Lisa handed Fortune her bags and the confiscated booty. She hugged Alex, and immediately asked him why he wasn't closing on his new property.

"I decided to wait. I spoke with Aunt Giselle, and Tiffany's doctor thought that a move to a new house may be too disruptive for her right now. She's already dealing with abandonment issues and feeling like she has no control over her life. If her home and what's most familiar to her is gone, and she hasn't had any input toward it, it may be too traumatic for her. So, I guess I'll have to deal with the old house for now," Alex said, his expression wary. "You're sure it's okay, right, Lisa?"

Lisa immediately thought about the mess she had created in their dining room, and answered slowly. "Yeah, it's clean," she said, making a mental note to have a cleaning company come through immediately. "I'll have the movers come back and put everything back to its original state, tomorrow." Lisa paused. "So, I suppose I'll be moving out, huh? I don't mind going back to the Four Seasons."

Alex shook his head. "Naw, you don't have to do that. There's plenty of room at the house. Plus, I need you around for moral support. But if you need some privacy, you can take the room over the garage. It's an efficiency, you know."

"Yeah, I saw it. That's cool. I can move my stuff there so it won't disturb you and Tiffany."

"Thanks, Lis. So, what's up, you two?" Alex said, and glanced at both Lisa and Fortune.

"Nothin' much, Alex. But you look like shit warmed over," Fortune said, and slapped Alex five.

"I feel like it, too. Did you find anything?" Alex asked, glancing over Lisa's shoulder.

Lisa reached in her pocket, producing the two keys. "Just these. There wasn't a lot in there, besides his personal items. And that stuff right there," she said, and pointed at one of the bags Fortune was holding.

She quickly ran down the day's events, and Alex tried to keep his composure. Things weren't progressing as fast as he needed them to, and he was getting anxious. Especially with Tiffany coming back next week.

"Lisa, these keys are nice, but what are they for? Where do they go?" Alex asked. "We've got to get moving. We really don't have a moment to waste."

THE THREE DECIDED TO MEET at Aunt Giselle's and strategize. After Lisa reluctantly accepted Fortune's help, she and Alex were able to map out a plan to get all of the loose ends tied up tight. Fortune would keep his eyes and ears open on the streets, while she handled the sleuthing and business intricacies. Alex would be relied on to scrutinize every document, from a legal perspective. It was a haphazard plan, but it might work.

IT WAS NOW A LITTLE OVER A MONTH since Simon had disappeared, yet his presence still dictated everything that Alex did. The next day, he and Lisa planned to comb through Simon's office in the District Building. They both figured that the exercise would be brief. Alex really wanted to clear out his own office, but Lisa strongly suggested that he leave it intact, so that no one would question his motives for clearing his office out so soon. It bothered Alex that now every action related to his life was always done for appearance' sake.

LISA ARRANGED to have Simon's personal effects tagged at his home, since she had been notified by the city council that they had consented to keep Simon's residence intact for at least another month. Lisa had inventoried everything and had the items packed for storage.

After minimal querying, she learned that part of the numbers on the safe-deposit keys indicated which branches the keys belonged to, and after a couple of phone calls, she discovered that the keys were from the New York Avenue branch.

EARLY THE NEXT MORNING, Lisa and Alex met and headed over to the bank. After distracting the bank administrator, Lisa flashed a fake badge and checked the sign-in log to see if any familiar names had been used to try to access Simon's safe-deposit boxes. Content that there had been no unauthorized access, Lisa directed Alex into the vault.

Once inside the secure area, Lisa pulled up a chair, while Alex paced. The first key opened a safe-deposit box that was stuffed full of documents and papers. It had Simon's last will and testament, his wife's will, numerous pieces of estate jewelry, and the couple's insurance papers. Lisa took a small palm-sized camera from her MCM bag, and took pictures of all of the items, while Alex provided a cursory assessment. Lisa nodded when he asked her if the pictures would adequately depict what was on the documents.

"Just like a Xerox machine," Lisa said.

"Time and date stamped?" Alex asked. His years with Simon had taught him to pay attention to details.

"Indeed," Lisa said. "We need to document every step we take, just in case."

THE SECOND KEY opened another safe-deposit box that was curiously bare. There was a set of keys, which appeared to be locker keys, and a small book that was filled with handwritten addresses and codes.

"Well, well, well," Lisa said as she handed those items to Alex. "It looks like we've finally found something."

Alex flipped open the notebook, and tried to decipher the lists of numbers and figures. "I can't make any sense of this, Lisa," he said, and ran his finger along the small pages.

"Don't worry. We'll figure it out," Lisa said, and pointed to the tiny notebook. "Now, be sure to take that with us. We'll return it once we get it decoded."

Alex shook his head. "No, I don't think so, Lisa. We better copy this thing, and leave it here. Just in case somebody comes looking for it. We don't want anyone to know that we might be on to something."

"Understood, Alex. But I think we'll be safe for a little while. Before we go, I'll speak to the bank manager and ask them to notify you if anyone tries to access the mayor's boxes. They'll think that it's just a precautionary measure, given the circumstances."

Alex reluctantly agreed to go along with it, after insisting that Lisa return the items as soon as possible. Given all that had happened, there was no way he was being overly cautious. Not when dealing with the likes of Simon Blake.

CHAPTER 10

S IMON'S HEALTH continued to improve, and he had gotten strong enough to sit up for longer periods of time. Eventually, he was able to stand, but his legs were weak and unsteady, and he was unable to take a step. Howard had brought him some hand weights to help him improve his strength, and brought in a set of parallel bars and a walker to help Simon regain his gait.

Not surprisingly, Simon was restless and frustrated that his health was not progressing as quickly as he had planned. He was sick of the stuffy, sweet, sickly smell in the attic, the sponge baths and the open-backed hospital gown he had to wear. Besides the fact that he hated depending on anyone for anything, Simon absolutely despised being subjected to these primitive conditions.

He rued the situation he was in, but Simon didn't have a lot of options. He was like a poker player holding five ugly cards and down to his last chip. With his right-hand man, Blinky, gone, there wasn't anyone else whom Simon knew he could trust, except for

Alex. And now, based on some of Howard's innuendoes, he wasn't sure about him. Yeah, Simon had some allies sprinkled around, but he wasn't even sure which players he needed because he wasn't sure of the game he was playing. Nor was he sure who had put him in this position. But one thing he did know was that he couldn't totally trust Howard. Relying on him was tantamount to trusting the fox to protect the henhouse, but Simon was stuck. Until he was fully recovered, Howard was his only link to his past, his present, and his future. He knew it, and Howard did, too.

Howard had him in lockdown. Whereas the attic was once a makeshift safe haven, now it felt like a prison. There was no telephone, no television, and no access to the outside world. There was only one window, small, dusty, and octagon-shaped, that didn't open and barely let in any light. And, there was a one-sided dead-bolt lock on the outside of the door, which Simon heard Howard open whenever he entered. When Simon questioned Howard about the lock, he mentioned that it had been for Simon's protection. Now that Simon was better, he knew he didn't need that much protection.

But despite Howard's flawed and questionable execution of his duties, his usefulness was essential, and Simon knew how to play him, just like Howard thought he knew how to play Simon. Simon's memory hadn't completely returned, but he recalled enough about his previous life to know that he was standing on shaky ground. And with Howard his only link to the outside world, "shaky" might be an understatement.

Simon had to first figure out why someone had tried to kill him. It didn't matter whether it was because of his political position or his illegal activities. He was insulted. Whoever it was had tried to deprive him of his legacy and his livelihood. It didn't matter. The *why* would determine the *who*. Or vice versa.

He scanned his memory over the names and faces of all who had a beef with him. It was an extensive list, but when he considered the level of intellect and resources it required to pull off such an attempt, the list would be shortened significantly.

In addition, he had to figure out how to protect what he had worked so hard to acquire. He had always taken second and third steps to cover his trail, but now that his organization was dismantled and he was severely infirm, he had no way of getting things back in order. Never one to write too much down, most of his incriminating documentation had been destroyed with the boat and his warehouse. He had funneled cash to offshore accounts and spread cash throughout the city. Only he and Blinky knew exactly where his drop boxes were, and he had committed those to memory as well as encrypted their locations in a little notebook that he had in his safe-deposit box. Which now might not be such a safe location for it.

It was clear. Until Simon could get his legs back, he had only Howard, and he was as slick as a snake crawling through Crisco. But Simon was not deterred. He'd use that snake to slither his bidding, until it came time to chop its head off. Simon laughed at the thought and picked up one of the five-pound weights. He had to get better, soon.

SIMON FINALLY GRILLED Howard about the circumstances of the boating accident, and about why Howard insisted that Alex's actions, after the fact, were questionable at best.

"Why do you think that?" Simon asked. "Alex would never do anything against me. I know that for a fact. I've been like a father to him."

"Well, Simon. I can't explain what happened, but all I know is that where Alex came ashore, relative to where the boat blew up, was quite a distance apart. And when he was admitted into the hospital, he had a knife in his possession."

"A knife?"

"Yes, a knife. Which I thought was odd. But then you show up, with knife wounds in your chest," Howard said, pointing a tiny, dramatic finger at Simon's bandaged chest. "Something just doesn't add up. Why would he want to kill you?"

Howard went on to say that there'd been a curious-looking young man at the hospital with Alex, who seemed to be quite protective of him. And Alex hadn't behaved too remorsefully at the memorial service, and then had whisked Tiffany and the children away to an undisclosed location. And in his absence, he had some female PI running his affairs. Now Alex was back and snooping around the mayor's mansion and offices. And Simon's things.

Simon held his head. He scanned his jagged memory and rubbed his temples. He had a lot of enemies, but he never counted Alex as one. "This doesn't sound right. Alex is probably just trying to TCB. He'd know what to do if he thought that I'd disappeared. But, Alex involved? No way. Remember, you said that you thought the demolition of my lab was connected to my being stabbed. That whole thing sounds like something someone with a lot more at stake was behind. I've crossed a lot of paths in my lifetime, but I don't think I'm off the mark. It was either Winnie Sutton or those Cavanaughs behind this."

Simon and Winnie had had a contentious relationship for years. Their last fierce battle had taken place over the stadium, and when Winnie weighed in against it, Simon decided to remove her from the equation. He had her husband, Jake, beaten and robbed to distract Winnie long enough to get the vote passed without her. Perhaps she had found out about it, and about the drug lab in one of her neighborhoods. Simon didn't put it past her to have orchestrated this whole thing. And he didn't have a hard time believing that she'd be angered enough to want to kill him. But then, maybe that was a stretch. Simon discounted her. Winnie was tenacious and out for his blood, but the Cavanaughs were truly cold-blooded killers.

"Yes, Howard. There's more to this than what meets the eye. There were some heavy players involved in this, and not just little

Alex. I've given it some thought, and my money's on those self-righteous Cavanaughs."

Howard shrugged. Being privy to the hushed circles of D.C.'s high society, Howard had known for years that there was bad blood between Simon and Howard's other benefactors, the Cavanaughs. Edgar Cavanaugh had had an affair with Simon's wife, Marjorie. And it was rumored, but never confirmed, that Edgar could, in fact, be Tiffany's father. The affair didn't sit well with Simon, and eventually the liaison was put to an end. An end caused by Marjorie's untimely and highly suspicious death. After all of these years, their affair and Marjorie's death were subjects that still drew the Cavanaugh's ire, and apparently Simon's also. Howard downplayed Simon's concerns, hoping not to incense him any further. Or draw any unwanted attention to the Cavanaughs.

"It may sound like it, Simon, but there's been nothing said or done by the Cavanaughs to substantiate your inclinations. However, it's funny that you should mention them. I'm not sure if you recall that before your accident, Harrison Cavanaugh had taken ill, and word has it that now his children are vying for leadership of the family."

"Hummph," Simon said. "See, there's even more reason. Taking over the family sounds like a lot of motivation for one of those spoiled brats, especially that damned ill-tempered Connie. I swear, if he had to stand on his own two big feet, that punk would fall flat on his face within two seconds. But he's an opportunist. Knowing him, he probably did do something to his old man, and then tried to take me out, too. They're notorious for that, you know. If they think you present too much of a challenge, they eliminate you. Whether you're in the family or not."

Howard snapped his fingers. "Well, you know what, Simon? You may be right. Connie just might have something to do with this. Just the other evening, something happened to two other— well, lesser-known syndicate types. Rumor has it that a hit was put out on them. Jury was blown to pieces; the other one, Dante's body has not been found. So, there may be a connection."

SIMON KNEW THEM WELL. Jury and Dante were a couple of young, reckless, hungry hustlers who were itching to make their mark in the game. They were greedy, stupid, and lacked home training, but Simon had considered them pretty harmless. But apparently, someone less confident had felt threatened by them. "So, someone's trying to make it seem like one took the other one out. Interesting. That was a smart move, but, I'm not buying that, Howard. That whole episode has *Cavanaugh* written all over it. It's them, Howard. I'm telling you. They want to eliminate all of the competition. Especially me.

"See, Harrison and I go way back. We had a gentlemen's agreement of sorts. We tried to keep our business and professional squabbles separate. Now, I don't like that son of a bitch, but he respected what was mine, and I respected what was his. But, trust and believe, I've always had a leg up on him. That's why I never considered him to be a very formidable adversary anyway. I just basically left him alone, as long as he didn't try to encroach on my territory. Then, we would've had problems. Big ones."

Simon chuckled and then sneered. He wasn't about to tell Howard the entire truth. The truth being that he only tolerated the Cavanaughs, and that he had been plotting revenge for Edgar's coveting his wife, and for the whole family treating him like he was a dumb southern bumpkin with the incorrect pedigree. Simon had vowed long ago to get even with them, and payback was something he never forgot.

Simon was an extremely vengeful man, but definitely not a stupid one. He had been patiently waiting until an opportunity presented itself where he could squash them all with one fell swoop. His beef was with anyone with the Cavanaugh surname, from the old man, Constantine, to that slick-assed Edgar, to Mr.

Politically Correct Harry, and even his condescending, elitist wife, Sylvia. Their offspring would just be bonuses. Although it had taken over twenty years, now was the time. And he had the goods on the Cavanaughs. He had what was probably more important to them than their damned touted reputation, and the beautiful part was that they were completely clueless about it.

Years ago, Simon had applied some well-placed pressure on the Cavanaugh's jeweler, Jules, and coerced him into copying their crowned ruby, that damned ostentatious *Il Rosso*. And Simon had switched it with the real one, unbeknownst to the mighty Cavanaughs. To cop that piece had been Simon's definitive score, but the coup lost its significance when Edgar hightailed it out of D.C. Simon's crucial issue with the Cavanaughs lost its priority, but Simon never forgot about it. But he never shared his secret with anyone, either. Not even Blinky. It was Simon's hold card, and though he had moved it around over the years, he had finally found a safe hiding place. It was hidden in the home of his daughter.

SIMON COUGHED and phlegm rattled in his throat, an unpleasant reminder that he still wasn't completely well. "But, anyway, back to those young bucks. I swear, they can't even spell *respect*. I'm thinking that maybe Connie and company did get to Alex somehow, since he was so close to me. Perhaps, he is in cahoots with them. I guess the new regime is anxious to take over."

Simon hacked again and scratched his stubbly face. He shook his head and frowned. "But, that's just speculation. I can't believe that Alex would've been involved with the likes of them. He could never betray me like that. But whoever has, I want to get down to it, Howard," Simon said, as he sat on the edge of his bed, raising and lowering his legs. Three-pound weights were strapped to his ankles, and he struggled with every effort. "Right now."

Howard, clad in banana yellow and kiwi green gym gear, and holding his bag, took his customary seat next to Simon's bed.

"Understood. I think I may have a way of finding out just who may be behind all of this. I bumped into Joey Cavanaugh at the gym today, and he may be a good candidate to extract some information from. He appears to be the one most amenable to keeping things respectable in his family, so I'll see what I can glean from him. And, if he doesn't work out, there's always Connie. I'm sure that I can get to him, too. Now, the real question is, and I know you don't want to think about it, but what if it really isn't the Cavanaughs? What if it's Alex?"

Simon shrugged. "I'll cross that bridge when I get to it," he said, and continued his strenuous leg lifts.

THE MEMORIES CAME CRASHING down on him as soon as he stood to rise. Sick and tired of using the bedpan, the prideful Simon had decided to take a few steps over to the Porta Potti, but ended up falling backward onto the bed.

"Alex knows." Blinky's crushing final words rang over and over in his mind like a broken record. That's how the warehouse got demolished. Blinky had followed Simon's instructions and detonated explosives that took the warehouse down and destroyed the evidence the night of the fund-raiser. Alex had initially tried to stop Tiffany from getting on the boat, but she'd stayed. And then Alex had showed up later, and Simon had drugged him.

Simon clutched his spinning head. "Son of a bitch," he said aloud. Every intricate detail came back to him.

So, it was true. Indeed, Alex was involved. Way back in the day, Alex's brother had been mistakenly killed by Moses' hit men. Simon had ordered a hit on one of his thieving runners, a smart-assed street kid named Fortune. It all made sense now. Perhaps it was Fortune who had resurfaced and hipped Alex to everything. Simon scanned his memory. Maybe it was that damned Fortune whom Howard had seen at the hospital with Alex. And perhaps the fait accompli was for Alex to have the assistance and backing of the Cavanaughs. It was obvious to Simon. How else did Alex find out about the lab? Who else besides the Cavanaughs would stand to benefit from Simon's demise?

Simon's bladder churned, and he remembered that he had to use the bathroom. The room turned crimson, and blistering anger heated up his entire body. Now that his memory was back, there was going to be hell to pay. For Alex and those damned Cavanaughs. For killing Blinky, destroying his business, and for trying to kill him, too. Simon forced himself to his feet and struggled to walk. With sheer vengeance as his motivation, and the walker as support, Simon persistently inched himself toward the toilet.

SIMON BEGAN WORKING out relentlessly, and the minutes turned to hours, which turned the light of day into a darkened night. When he realized the lateness of the hour, Simon was surprised that Howard hadn't returned. Simon was getting a little anxious. Howard had dismissed all of the nurses except a small, Honduran nurse's assistant, and she came only once a day. Simon was concerned. And he was getting hungry.

He was walking with great difficulty, but since he was locked in, he couldn't go anywhere. He waited out the night, until the morning, when the nurse's assistant came. He demanded to know where Howard was, but the young woman spoke only broken English.

SIMON WOLFED DOWN THE FOOD, and tried to prevent her from locking his room door. She scurried away from him, and slammed the door, and Simon heard the lock being latched.

For hours, Simon waited, but grew increasingly impatient. With no outside contacts, he was worried that he had battled and beaten death for naught. And now he was going to perish in Howard's dreary attic, without having the opportunity to avenge himself. He wasn't going to go out like that.

He studied the locked door. The hinges were on the other side, so he couldn't take them off. Furious, Simon grabbed his empty bedpan, and began banging it on the floor and walls. He banged for hours, until sweat poured down his face and back, until he reached the point of exhaustion.

Finally, Simon heard footsteps. He kept banging loudly, and yelled with his weakened voice. "Howard? Is that you?"

There was dead silence. Finally, a man responded. "No, this isn't Howard," he said. "Who are you?"

"It's none of your damned business who I am. And, I don't give a damn who you are, either. Just get something to open this door. Now!"

"Well, uh, I don't know about that," the man said, his voice hesitant and uneven. "Who are you? Howard didn't mention anything to me about this, so, I don't think I'm supposed to do that."

"I don't give a damn what you think you're supposed to do. Just open this goddamned door," Simon roared, and hurled his bedpan at the door.

The man mumbled something, and then quickly ambled away. Simon heard his descending footsteps, and for a few moments, there was complete quiet. Simon held his ear to the door, until he heard the sound of the man returning, with keys jingling in his hands.

After trying several keys, the man swore and muttered out loud. Eventually, the latch clicked, and he swung open the door to the room. When the slight, well-dressed man saw Simon standing there, his light brown face drained of color.

"Oh, my God. Mayor Blake? Is that you?" he asked, his hands shaking nervously, the keys clanging loudly. "What on earth are you doing here? Are you okay? I thought you were dead. Oh, my God. Howard hasn't kept you here since you disappeared, has he? Please, tell me that's not so." He was almost trembling.

Simon looked him up and down, and eyed him suspiciously.

"Who the hell are you?" Simon wedged his walker in front of the door, and glared at the fidgety young man.

"I'm, um, I'm Royce, sir," the young man said. "Are, are you okay?"

Simon blatantly ignored Royce's questions. "Royce, huh? Howard's assistant?"

"Yes, sir," Royce said.

Simon demanded to know where Howard was, and Royce replied that the last time he had spoken with Howard, he was going to meet with Connie Cavanaugh.

"Well, I guess you happened along at quite an opportune moment," Simon said, and then smirked. "It appears that you'll be working for me now, son," Simon said, and struggled back to his bed. "And you're in for quite a promotion."

"What? I don't understand what you mean," Royce said. "How, uh, I mean, I don't even understand what you're doing here."

Simon plopped down onto the side of his bed and exhaled. "In due time. In due time. Right now, what I need for you to understand is that I'm quite certain that your boss isn't coming back. And today's your lucky day. From here on out, I'll be the one that asks the questions. Everything you need to know, I'll tell you. And as long as you can keep your mouth shut and help me do what I need to do, then I'll let you live to be a very wealthy young man. You got that?"

Royce nodded, and assumed his position at the foot of Simon's bed.

"I want you to understand. I pay royally for loyalty. And you'll pay dearly for disloyalty, do you understand?"

ROYCE WAS IN QUITE A QUANDARY. He had been hired by the Cavanaughs to keep an eye on Howard, because despite their lengthy business association, they didn't trust him. During Royce's brief tenure with Howard, he'd never had any inkling that Howard was affiliated with Simon, outside of his pseudo public-relations job. Never would Royce have ever imagined that Howard had been harboring Simon. Now he had to decide if he was going to share this titillating news with his ghost employers.

It was evident that Simon had been gravely injured, but Royce had no idea to what extent. Simon was much grayer and thinner than before, and based on the appearance of the room, he had required a significant amount of medical care. Howard's peculiar behavior, as of late, had seemed even more erratic to Royce, and now it made sense to him. For the past month, Howard had restricted Royce's access in his house to his basement office, saying that he was planning some renovations on the upper levels.

Now the game had been escalated. Knowledge of Simon's existence would be of keen interest and extreme value to the Cavanaughs, and Royce had to carefully chart his course. He could work this situation to his full advantage. The Cavanaughs paid well, but if he could gain Simon's trust and confidence, there was no telling what riches would be in store for him. So, Royce decided not to tell the Cavanaughs about Simon or about Howard's disappearance. Not until he figured out if Connie had made Howard's elimination a matter for the family record.

The first thing Simon wanted was to be moved downstairs, into more proper quarters. He needed clothes, a cellular phone, a typewriter, and for Royce to run a few errands. The first errand was for Royce to retrieve a stashed package of Simon's, and bring it to him. Simon's initial requests didn't seem too outlandish, and Royce vigorously complied. He had suited up for a new team, and was being called in from the bench to play in a game that would have few winners, but Royce was determined to be one of the victors.

CHAPTER 11

ALEX RAN his fingers through his coarse, wavy hair, and when his wedding band caught, he concluded that he needed a haircut. He glanced down at his simple etched gold ring. The sight of it made his chest ache slightly. He was wondering just how strong that band of gold was going to have to be in order to weather this torrential storm. Alex looked and felt quite disheveled, and knew that he had to get his act together before Tiffany came back home. She was scheduled to arrive on Saturday, which gave him barely two days to regroup.

Lisa had done a remarkable job corralling the movers back to the house the day before, and she'd made his home look as if it had never been touched. As he sat behind the desk in his home office, Alex twisted his neck from side to side until it snapped, relieving his built-up tension. He sighed and tilted his head back, and then cracked the oak window blinds and spotted the blue, unmarked car of one of Lisa's security agents. He felt a chill creep down his spine. He hoped to God that he wouldn't have to live the rest of his life in fear, cloaked under guard and protection.

He stretched, then took a deep breath and exhaled, his lips purposely making a raspberry sound. Alex had taxed his brains over the last twenty-four hours, painstakingly reviewing the documents Lisa had photographed from Simon's safe-deposit box.

The contents of the safe-deposit box were surprising. The key item was Simon's will, signed and notarized three years ago, and it named Alex as the executor. There were trust funds set up in Alex's children's names; both in the amount of $25,000. Simon's estate cited a few real estate holdings, which were valued at approximately $300,000; his pension, money market, and other bank account statements, which totaled approximately $75,000. The bulk of Simon's estate was his insurance policies, with the most substantial one underwritten by the city, which was a term life policy valued at $1 million, and a personal burial policy, which had a face value of $25,000. Both policies would be doubled if Simon's death was ruled accidental. Alex and Tiffany were named the beneficiaries of those policies.

Although he didn't expect to find Simon's illicit funds included among his legitimate papers, Alex had hoped to find something. Something besides what appeared to be a clear motivation for him to kill. All of Simon's financial fingers pointed directly at Alex.

The one thing of interest that Alex did uncover was the will of Simon's late wife, Marjorie. He quickly turned to the last page, and checked the date, signature and notarization. Marjorie's signature, caught his eye. It was almost as elaborate as John Hancock's.

He also noted the date of the will, January 16, 1970, and that it was notarized by a J. Canty. For some reason, that name stuck in his mind. As Alex reviewed the will, he confirmed that Marjorie was the truly wealthy one, and her investments were the foothold of Simon's fortune. She had left numerous pieces of prime downtown real estate, acreage in Maryland, several valuable pieces of estate jewelry, and a life insurance policy that was valued at $750,000, at the time of her death. Since that was over twenty years ago, Alex estimated its value to be several millions now. Her entire estate was bequeathed to Tiffany, with the one stipulation that it be held in trust for her until she turned thirty. Simon, being the surviving parent, had been named the executor of Marjorie's estate. Apparently, he had been living extremely well off of Tiffany's money all of those years.

"That figures," Alex said out loud. "Simon was the master of illusion, and he didn't even have anything of any value."

He rubbed his eyes and thought about his own life. It was like scenes and acts in a complex, unfinished play. The actors were milling about, clutching bits and pieces of a senseless script, and no one knew the ending. And the master playwright, Simon, was MIA.

Simon's will would be held intestate until his body was found, or unless Alex petitioned the court to have him declared dead. At this juncture, Alex wasn't overly anxious to do anything. He wanted it over, and his wife well, but he didn't want to haphazardly force anything. He decided to wait until Tiffany got better, and then they could make some of these life-altering decisions together.

Alex locked his fingers behind his head and leaned back. He glanced around his office, eyeing the well-stocked library and the numerous pictures, degrees, and awards that hung on the wall. "What a sham," he thought.

He decided to take a stroll over to the efficiency, where Lisa had set up quarters. She had buzzed him earlier to say that the account information had come back from Simon's hard drive and that it corroborated the information in the files Alex had swiped from the file cabinets in Simon's warehouse. The most damning evidence was confirmed by the verification of Simon's intricate accounts and illegal corporations. Through this covert network, Simon had funneled over $5 million to offshore accounts, using his grandchildren's names.

THE MIDAFTERNOON SUN was high and hot, and the July humidity and stickiness slapped Alex in the face as soon as he stepped out onto his patio to walk over to Lisa's apartment. Barely able to breathe, Alex really gasped when he saw an ominous figure reclining in one of the patio's wrought-iron lounge chairs. He wanted to reach for a gun, but he wasn't wearing one. Thankfully, it was Fortune.

"Somethin's up, man," Fortune said.

"How'd you get past security?" Alex asked, and forced his heart back down his throat.

"What? Them rent-a-cops? *Please.* Give me a little credit. They might as well be security guards at the damned mall," Fortune said, and folded his arms. A slight smirk crossed his face.

Alex strolled across the patio, and took a seat at the glass-topped table near Fortune.

"What are you talking about?"

"I'm sayin', something is goin' on," Fortune said. "Jury and Dante's dead."

"Who the hell are they?" Alex asked. "Why are you telling me this? What do I care about them?" Alex shook his head, and glared at Fortune. "I don't have time for this nonsense."

"This ain't no nonsense, Alex. They gettin' killed ain't by no accident. Word on the street is that damned Connie Cavanaugh had somethin' to do wit' it. An' then, right after they gets iced, your boy Howard goes down to Hains Point, but he don't come back. Folks is droppin' like flies."

"What? You think that Howard's been killed?" Alex had wondered why Howard hadn't been snooping around or calling lately.

"I'm sayin', he goes in, behind some fake-ass police barricades, but he don't come out. But, guess who do? Connie." Fortune crossed his legs.

"Again I ask you—what are you telling me this for, Fortune? What do I care about Connie Cavanaugh and what he does? Damn. Don't I have enough to worry about? And why do you think that Connie would want to kill Howard?"

"Because of your boy—Simon. Think about it. Apparently, Connie's makin' some major moves by takin' out the competition. An' trust me, that'll flush Simon's ass out, if he's still around. He's too greedy not to be pressed about who might be takin' over his business. An' maybe Connie offed Howard 'cause he was close to Simon or 'cause he was their connection to Simon. As slick as he was, maybe he was tryin' to blackmail 'im. Either way, he probably knew too damned much."

"Knew too much about what? Simon?" Alex asked. He felt as if his head were literally spinning.

"Yeah, and about their business. That's what you got to find out," Fortune said. "See, with Blinky gone, an' Simon's ass in the wind, it figures that the Cavanaughs don't want nobody around that could dime them out or give them any static. Now they can run this town, and no one's in position to do or say anything about it."

Alex grunted, and looked out into the distance. It was difficult to imagine Howard doing something to offend the Cavanaughs, and ultimately signing his own death warrant.

"Face it, ol' Howard's usefulness was probably gone," Fortune said.

Simon, Howard, the Cavanaughs. Jury and Dante. What in the hell was going on? This drug game was far more complex than Alex had originally thought. "I've got to find out how the hell all of these people are connected, besides being criminals. I just don't see it now."

"I can't answer that for you, bro. But, somethin's up," Fortune said, and re-reclined in his seat.

"Something is up, Alex," Lisa said as she joined them from the side of the house. Her brown, wedge-style sandals clicked on the terra-cotta tile. She was wearing dark shades, and a provocatively tight red T-shirt stretched across her full chest, and some painted on Calvin Klein jeans.

"Day-um," Fortune said, as he caught a glimpse of her, and Lisa rolled her eyes. "My, my, my."

Alex held his hand up and shrugged. "Like what?"

"Believe it or not, every one of those foreign accounts Simon set up is linked back to you some kind of way. There's no connection to him whatsoever, and it looks like you were the one funneling large sums of money into those accounts. Simon made a veiled attempt to try to convolute things and make it appear like *you* were trying to cover your ass. But, all of those accounts are pointing right back at you. And your social security number. Every electronic transaction was made from an IP address from your office PC, and your virtual thumbprint is signatory on those accounts."

"Son of a bitch. So, what you're saying is that it looks like I was the one running everything. Like I was stupid enough to use my own computer. Jesus. I can't believe that I've been set up to appear to be some damned criminal," Alex said, his eyes widened in bewilderment. He jumped up from his seat, kicking his chair over in the process.

"So it appears, to the untrained eye," Lisa said, and picked up Alex's chair. She sat down in it and crossed her legs. "He probably had a computer in his warehouse networked to yours. That way, he could've sent anything from there and made it appear that it came from your PC. Face it, Simon's slick. And the only way we can disprove that is if we ever get those files Foody downloaded."

Alex grimaced. The chances of that happening without Foody were a zillion to one. "So, what you're saying is that I'm screwed."

"Pretty much. And if Simon took the time to make his paper trail lead back to you, then there's no telling what else he might've done."

A stunned Alex felt the invisible noose tightening around his neck, but he tried to calm his rapid heart rate. It was apparent that Simon had orchestrated these moves a long time ago, so that he'd have Alex as the fall guy if he ever got pinched. And the beauty of it was that he had used Alex's naïveté against him. Simon planned to win, even as he lived, and even if he died.

Alex paced, his arms folded. "That bastard has screwed me royally, hasn't he? Even if he's alive, if he wanted to, he could make me take the fall for him. And if he's dead, then anyone really snooping around could make it seem like I wanted to kill him. Or, that I'm a damned con."

"Well, yeah, um, civil servants don't normally have offshore accounts, now do they?" Lisa said, and then shook her head. "You mean to tell me that you never questioned Simon's source of income? That boat? His extravagant lifestyle?"

Alex nodded. "No, I didn't. I mean, he was an attorney. And I assumed that he received money when his wife died," Alex said.

"Simon ain't been right a day in his life," Fortune said. "I don't care if he was a lawyer or not. Remember, I told you 'bout how he had one of his clients killed so he could steal his loot."

Lisa looked at Alex with a puzzled expression, and Alex recounted the story Fortune had told him about Simon making his legal career by representing thugs and a major drug dealer named Julius. Eventually, Simon's greediness took over, and he had the dealer killed. And Simon assumed his business.

"This is some deep shit," Lisa said.

"And it gets deeper," Fortune said, barely taking his eyes off Lisa. He turned to Alex. "Simon was a piece of work, no doubt. But don't be so caught up about whether his ass is still alive."

"I know. I have to figure out how to make all of this shit go away," Alex said. "All of it."

"That might be easier said than done," Lisa said. "It's going to take more than a minute to undo the damage that's been done by him trying to set you up. You have to be very careful how you proceed, Alex. Anything you do from here on out could possibly incriminate you."

"No kidding. You think I haven't thought about that? That's why you need to make sure everything is returned to its proper place. Those keys, that book. Everything. Nothing can look like it's been disturbed. I don't want anyone getting wise to us."

Alex sighed. "I can't even sleep thinking about how much Simon has screwed up my life. He sacrificed me, my wife, and my children for his greed. He toyed with me like a pawn on a chessboard. He's controlled me and just about everything that I've ever done. He had me in a death grip while he lived, and even now that he's gone. Damn," Alex said, and walked to the edge of his yard.

He snatched a bloom from the rhododendron plant, and crumpled it in his hand. He punched his fist in his hand. "I've got to find some kind of way to prove that Simon was Moses and that he was behind this charade. That's the only way that I'll be free from him. And I know it's here somewhere. Simon was smart, but he wasn't perfect," Alex said, and rubbed the bridge of his nose. "With all the dirt he did, we should be able to see some of the grime he's left behind."

"Well, you still have some options, Alex. If we can crack the codes in that little notebook of his, perhaps we'll find some kind of connection that'll implicate Simon," Lisa said.

"Who's workin' on that? One of them eggheads you got?" Fortune asked. "If it is, then you better give that to me. Trust me, if there's some kinda code in there that Moses, I mean, Simon wrote, ain't no computer geek gonna crack that. Whatever's in that book is about the streets, and it's gonna take somebody like me to figure it out."

Lisa removed the tiny notebook from her back pocket and flapped it at Fortune. "So, I guess now I'm an egghead. I told you your mouth was going to get your ass in trouble."

"What you gonna do? Beat me? I'm not too sure if I'd like that rough stuff too tough," Fortune said.

"Let me see that, Lisa," Alex said, and Lisa tossed the book to him. "I appreciate the offer, Fortune, but I've got to try to figure this out myself. This is my life, and right now, I don't trust anybody to save me but me."

CHAPTER 12

UNFORTUNATELY, in his haste to prepare for Tiffany's arrival, Alex didn't have time to work on the notebook's code. Instead, he carried it around like a bible, and focused on making his family nest as comfortable as possible.

When he picked Tiffany and Giselle up from the airport, Aunt Giselle whispered to him that Tiffany was still prone to mood swings. To Alex, Tiffany did appear subdued and a little withdrawn, but when he greeted her with a dozen long-stemmed red roses, it made her smile. The doctor's prognosis had been favorable, but cautious. He had recommended that she continue therapy, and armed Aunt Giselle with Tiffany's medications and a list of specialists in the metro area.

Her mood brightened considerably when she arrived home and saw her children. Alex had made sure that they were the only ones at their home, and that things were calm and tranquil, so that Tiffany could get acclimated over the next few days. Lisa had even gone home to Atlanta for a long weekend, to give them a little time and space.

They retreated to the family room, where they sat on the over-sized taupe leather sofa and held the children. Despite the cozy family moment, it was a little awkward. The large-screen TV was on with *The Cosby Show,* but the sound was barely audible. Alex held Anya, and had his arm around his wife's shoulders, while Tiffany bounced their son on her lap. They sat closely together, each trying to allow the television to soothe the uneasy silence.

As the show ended, the children cooed and fought sleep, while Alex grappled for words. He was about to speak when Tiffany finally broke the silence.

"I really missed you and our children, Alex. I really did. So much has happened. But, I realized how much I love and need you in my life."

"We missed you, too, Tiff. And, God, I love you, too. You probably don't even know how much I love you," Alex said. "But I'm worried about you. How are you feeling? I mean, how are you really feeling?"

Tiffany sighed. "I guess I'm okay. I'll be okay. I kind of feel like my life is starting over. Or just beginning."

"Maybe it is a new beginning, baby. And I'm going to be right here with you."

"I hope so. I just don't know if I can take anyone else leaving me. I guess I really never thought about it before with my mother, but now that my father's gone, it really is an issue for me." She paused and looked at him. "Promise me you'll never leave," Tiffany said.

"I'll try not to," Alex said. He leaned over and kissed her ear, as Anya rustled in his arms. "But you know a Black man's mortality rate is a little higher than a Black woman's." Alex chuckled softly, but his humor went past Tiffany, who was still wrapped in her thoughts.

"And I have to believe you'll never fail me, too. I know it sounds stupid, but it's true. I mean, everything's kind of mixed up for me right now. I'm sad, and I'm hurt, but I'm kind of angry and disappointed. Like I keep getting shorted in my life. I'm trying to work on my feelings, but it may take me some time. Please don't give up on me."

Tiffany sighed. "Don't get me wrong, I'm thankful to have you and the children, but I kind of feel like ever since I was a child, something's been missing in my life. And though I may not have ever really understood how much my mother's death impacted me, I always felt disappointed that she wasn't there for me. And now my father's gone. And I don't know if I can take any more disappointment in my life," she said, and reached for her husband's hand.

Alex was at a loss for words. Tiffany was far too fragile for him to tell her the truth about her father, but what would he have told her if she weren't in such a delicate state? Hell, he had no proof about anything. And on top of that, all of the evidence suggested he was the criminal. But once he got some proof, would she still feel betrayed? He only hoped that one day, she'd be able to understand. One day, when she wasn't so vulnerable. One day, when he was more certain of their future.

So instead of speaking, Alex lifted her hand and kissed it, and then led her upstairs. Together, they laid their precious children down, and Tiffany caught Alex up on her weeks in therapy. "I've realized a lot of things about myself," Tiffany said, and then paused. "I guess therapy helped."

"I'm sure it did. And you're home now. I'm going to make sure that you're taken care of."

"I'm going to hold you to that," Tiffany said, and kissed his face. "And you can start tonight."

ALEX OBLIGED HIS WIFE by cradling her in his arms. He would have done so throughout the night, but at times she clung to him and at times she retreated to the farthest edge of their king-sized bed. Sometimes she'd pretend to be asleep, and other times, she would thrash about. Alex tried to rest, but his eyes popped open and he jumped at every one of her frantic movements.

The next few days were quite an adjustment for them. Alex had told Tiffany that Lisa was staying in the guesthouse because she was in town on business, and Tiffany didn't seem too bothered by it. She was putting forth an effort to be strong, and Alex appreciated the strides that she was making. By Monday, Mrs. Roberts, their new nanny/housekeeper, was on board, her credentials having been thoroughly scrutinized by Lisa. Alex felt hopeful, as though he and his wife were settling in and getting back to their routine, and regaining a sense of normalcy. It was only when Alex bolstered up enough courage to broach the subject of their future, and minimally, Simon's estate and Tiffany's inheritance, that he found she really didn't want to talk about her future. She only wanted to talk about her past. And mainly about commemorating her parents' legacy.

As they sat over breakfast, Tiffany laid out her plans. "Alex, I know I probably mentioned this to you before, but I really want to do something to memorialize my father. And even my mother, too."

"What'd you have in mind?" Alex asked the question, but was really wondering how he was going to keep his eggs and pancakes down after hearing Tiffany's plans to immortalize Simon.

"I was thinking about petitioning the city to have a statue of him created in front of the District Building. I think that since Dad is, or was, thought of so favorably, I shouldn't face too much opposition."

The irony was killing him, but there was almost nothing Alex could honestly say without upsetting his wife. "I, uh, see, dear. I think that's pretty noble of you. And I'm sure that you'll have no problem getting the support you need to make this happen."

Tiffany glanced up from her yogurt and fresh fruit. "What do you mean, Alex? I'm not trying to be noble. I just want my father to be remembered for the great things he did for this city. That's his legacy. And you should want that, too."

Alex exhaled heavily, and sought to choose his words carefully. "I didn't mean that. I meant to say that what you're trying to do is a good idea." He wanted to bite his tongue in half.

"And maybe I'll have something dedicated in my mother's memory at the Martin Luther King Library. She always had an incredible interest in literature."

Tiffany smiled, a slight, wistful one. "I think that I'm really going to take my time with this project. I have some vacation time at the agency, but I may just request a leave of absence. I'll see how my event planning goes, so I'm not going to rush back to work too quickly. I'd rather concentrate on this memorial and my family."

Alex reached across the table and caressed his wife's hand. "I think that's great. And eventually, we need to talk about your father's estate." He was going to mention her pending inheritance, but Tiffany cut him off.

She raised her hand. "I don't want to talk about this now, Alex. I know you're trying to handle our business, and I really appreciate it, but I don't want to deal with this right now. Not now." She stood to leave, and reached over and pecked Alex on the forehead.

As Tiffany wiped her lipstick from his brow, Mrs. Roberts brought in the mail. She handed the stack to Tiffany, who laid the envelopes and letters down on the table. "I don't want to deal with this, either," she said, and then noticed a large manila envelope addressed to her. She took a knife from the table and slit open the edge of the envelope. She peeked inside, and her eyes riveted on Alex, whose eyes were fixed on the newspaper.

"Oh, my God," Tiffany said, with a deep gasp. "Oh, my God." She clutched her chest and started tapping her foot. "What the hell is this? Alex?" Tiffany was speaking through clenched teeth, and her voice was rising with every syllable. Her body began shaking so violently that the papers rustled in her hands.

"What's what?" Alex asked, newspaper in one hand, and coffee mug in the other. He barely glanced up at her. He was reading a captivating article about a renegade FBI agent that had been killed overnight in a soured drug deal on a Baltimore pier. Alex immediately wondered if this incident was somehow connected to Simon, but he dismissed the thought. It was confirmation that he was truly getting paranoid about everything.

Tiffany took the contents and threw them in Alex's face, and they landed faceup in his breakfast. "These, damn it!"

Alex nearly choked on his coffee. They were the pictures of him and Stacey, a one-night stand that he'd had years ago. They were photographs of a sheepish, guilty-looking Alex, cavorting with his late brother's former girlfriend. It wasn't something that Alex was proud of, but it had occurred before he and Tiffany were even married. The time-and-date stamps proved that. The problem was that Alex had failed to ever mention it to his wife. In fact, he had all but forgotten about it. And now was the worst time for it to be brought to light.

"I, uh, I, don't know what to say, Tiffany," Alex said. He was honestly flabbergasted, and was incensed at his own stupid betrayal. Someone, who he later found out was Simon, had once tried to blackmail Alex with these same photos, and he should have known that they'd come back to haunt him. Alex should have told Tiffany back then. And now the disappointment and anger that covered his wife's face leveled him. "Let me explain."

"Explain what? How you have sex? I already know how that works, Alex."

"That's not what I meant." Alex stood up and faced his wife. "It's not what you think."

"Forget it, Alex. I don't even want to hear what you have to say."

Alex grabbed his wife's shoulders. "Listen to me, Tiffany. That woman in the pictures doesn't mean anything to me."

Tiffany snatched away. "Get your hands off of me! Get off of me!"

Her eyes had a wild look in them, and Alex immediately thought about her mental state. What the hell had he done? He couldn't push her, so he quieted his voice and said, "She didn't mean anything then, and she doesn't now. I swear."

Tiffany's eyes filled with tears, and her face became flushed. She was trembling, and her voice shook with every syllable. "Like you swore you'd never disappoint me? Yeah, that means a lot, Alex. There's absolutely nothing for you to say now. Not a damned thing. Except for good-bye."

TIFFANY LEFT THAT SAME DAY. She refused to even acknowledge Alex, or respond to anything he said. And he tried, but there was no talking or reasoning with her. Alex begged and groveled, but Tiffany was immune to his pleadings. She swooped up the children and left, telling him that she would send for their things.

A few moments after she left, he dialed her cellular phone, but the call went straight to voice mail. Within the hour, the recorded message said the number was no longer in service. Alex's father's advice about taking care of his wife played over in his mind. He'd almost lost her twice before, with her brush with death and her near breakdown. This just might be his third strike. This time, he might not be able to get her back.

Assuming that she'd sought refuge at her aunt's house, Alex placed a call. Aunt Giselle confirmed that his family was there, but when Alex tried to press her for some insight, she refused to get involved. "Tiffany's like my child, Alexander, and she's deeply upset right now. I don't know the specifics, but I suggest that you just give it some time," she said.

"But, I don't want her to think that I don't care, or that I'm not concerned about her and our children. I don't want her to feel like she's been abandoned again. Especially not by me."

Aunt Giselle, stoic as ever, responded, "It may be too late for that, but I will inform her that you called, Alex. But you must realize that your wife is going through a great deal at the present, and you'll have to respect that. Tiffany is a lot like her mother, and I know it's going to take some time for her to digest whatever has happened. And you must respect that. No, let me rephrase that. You're going to respect that."

Alex tried to keep pleading his case, but Aunt Giselle refused to elaborate any further. "Good evening, Alexander," she said, and the phone went dead in Alex's ear.

CHAPTER 13

THE COVER-UPS. The lies. The betrayals. Simon's secret life as Moses and his disappearance. Foody's probable demise. Simon's rivalry with the Cavanaughs. Howard's duplicity and now disappearance. Alex's link to millions of illegal dollars. The drug dealers' murders. Alex had mentally mapped these people, places, and things, but he just couldn't see the thin line that tied those entities together. Up till this point, Alex had thought that he was on the right path to making the connections. Until those damned pictures appeared, and were thrown into the quagmire.

He had spent days and sleepless nights trying to figure out who had sent Tiffany those pictures, and why. Once again, the only logical person was Simon. Or someone working for him. Alex quickly dismissed the thought that it could be someone who had just found them. What would be their motivation? If it was blackmail, the pictures would have been delivered to Alex, with appropriate demands. There was no other reason than vindictiveness. It was a masterful move to further complicate Alex's life. Anyone who knew him knew how important his marriage was, and someone had gone for his jugular. Since Tiffany's departure, Alex had been in a fog. She had been his anchor, and without her, he felt adrift at sea. Maybe that was the real motive behind the reappearance of the pictures. It was the best way to distract Alex from the evolving mystery of Simon's disappearance, and the seemingly unconnected events that had transpired ever since.

But Alex had wised up. It would have been easy to fall prey and focus on his marriage. While that was important, Alex was determined not to be so easily defeated. As emotionally unsettled as he was, he was still focused on the big picture. Who he was and what he was doing was making someone uneasy, and even though the specifics were unclear to him, he must have been on the right track. He couldn't get derailed now.

But, I'm not going to let them destroy my marriage, he thought. Alex had left several messages for Tiffany, but she hadn't returned his calls. Only a few days had passed, but his heart ached for her and his children. Since Tiffany had left, she hadn't even looked back. Alex would probably have felt better had she said something to him, cursed, kicked, screamed, or even clobbered him, but she gave him nothing. Nothing but sad, cold, empty, eyes. And her departure from his life hurt more than any cruel words she could ever say. He'd figure out how to get his wife back, if it was the last thing that he did.

But the most immediate thing he needed to do was put his personal feelings aside and concentrate on the documents he was reading. He was analyzing Simon's will, and everything seemed in order. It was correctly dated, notarized, scribed, and legally sound. There were no glaring errors or questionable inclusions, and Alex read and reread the document. It was perfectly sound, and just the right instrument to provide motive for murder. With Alex as one of the main beneficiaries, and the executor of Simon's estate, the implications were clear. Alex would be the prime suspect if Simon was ever murdered. Or if Simon wanted to stage his own murder. The picture was getting a little clearer for Alex. Simon had every base covered.

LATER ON THAT DAY, Alex, Lisa, and Fortune gathered in Lisa's garage apartment to update each other. Lisa had returned from the ATL only a few days ago, and her presence had been a major help to Alex. Alex finally told Lisa and Fortune the details about Tiffany's exit, and afterward, Fortune just grunted. Surprisingly, Lisa was a lot more vocal.

"Who was she?" Lisa asked.

Alex shrugged his shoulders. There was no way he was going to tell her it was Ivan's old girlfriend Stacey. Fortune would have a fit. "An old friend I ran across in a bar. Nothing special."

Lisa shook her head. "Although your little tête-à-tête happened before you got married, you probably still should've told her," Lisa said. "You two were all on that 'I've been with only you' tip, and I guess that was important to the old girl. I wouldn't know. I don't have those issues. But, the bottom line is that you just weren't honest with her, and I'm sure that's what she's pissed about."

There were many things that Alex hadn't shared with Tiffany since her father's disappearance, but he had never thought about those pictures coming back to bite him in his ass. And, now that they had, it could not have happened at a worse time. There was nothing Alex could say to Lisa, either. He just wanted his wife back.

"You could try some flowers, Alex," Fortune offered. "Chicks dig that kind of sentimental shit."

"How original," Lisa said, and rolled her eyes. She turned her attention to Alex. "Face it, Alex. You fucked up and now you just need to be a man about it. You apologized, right? So, just give her some time. You know that it's not only the unfaithfulness that she's dealing with, but other issues as well. Plus, you know she's kind of fragile now." Lisa whistled the theme from *The Twilight Zone.* "She's out there. But, once she works through some of that, I'm sure she'll come around. But face it. Girlfriend has been through a whole lot here lately. Right now, you need to give her some space, and maybe find out who sent those damned pictures. Especially if Simon's somehow connected. But, first and foremost, you have to make sure you can get yourself out of this shit Simon's got you in. That may help."

"Oh, it's on now," Alex said. "I've got to get some insurance against Simon's setup, or I stand to lose my wife and my freedom. But it's tricky. If I do too much to implicate Simon, it might push Tiffany further away. She may never forgive me if she thought I was trying to disrespect her father's memory." Alex sighed. His choices were either *not so good* or *even worse.*

Lisa said that there had been no confirmation of Foody's death, and the verification of the unidentified bodies and human remains had been given the lowest priority by the overtaxed, understaffed city medical examiner's office. When Lisa suggested that Alex might have to accept the fact that Foody was gone, it barely fazed him. It was just another loss suffered because of himself.

Even as he tried to focus on combing through various pieces of Simon's deceptive paper trail with Lisa, Alex just couldn't concentrate. He had given Simon's little code book to Fortune, who wasn't having much success with deciphering the cryptic notations, either.

"I just don't get it," Fortune said. "What the hell is a 3WG6C4R16-A1425/F3/A6?" He flipped the pages of the small book, and almost tossed it aside.

Alex had barely glanced at the book before, and when he had, he only recalled that each page was headed with a code, and then there were a number of entries below. When Fortune read off the sequence of numbers and letters, something clicked in Alex's mind.

"Say that again, Fortune," Alex said, and pressed his index fingers against his temples.

Fortune repeated his statement, and stared at Alex, with a curious expression on his face.

Alex snapped his fingers, and shook his fist. It was all coming back to him. Those codes were taken directly from a D.C. map. The kind of grid maps that the municipal agencies used. And Alex recalled where he had last seen one of those maps. Full of push-pins, hanging on the wall of Simon's former warehouse offices.

"3W? That's Ward 3," Alex said. "That slick son of a bitch. G6? Grid 6. What was the rest?" After Fortune repeated it again, Alex cracked the code. "C4, R16? Column 4, Row 16. If we look on the map, that gives us a specific street location." Alex paused, and scratched his chin. "The rest, I'm not too sure about."

Lisa chimed in. "It's probably the address. Look, A1425 probably means—"

"Number 1425," Fortune said, jumping in. "F3 probably means the third floor, and A6's the apartment. Cool, that shit makes sense now. I swear, Simon's a slick son of a bitch."

Fortune began rattling off the rest of the codes, and suddenly a light, a bright light, had turned on. Perhaps things weren't as dismal as Alex had thought.

"You guys have to get a municipal map and find these addresses," Alex said, feeling a sudden burst of optimism. "And get this book back in that safe-deposit box today." Finally, the gods were looking down on Alex with some degree of mercy. Lisa and Fortune could track down these locations, while he could focus on winning back Mrs. Tiffany Blake Baxter.

AS SHE SAT IN FRONT of the vanity, preparing to brave the world as a single woman, Tiffany's stomach twitched. She applied her eyeliner and thought about how far she had come in the two weeks since she and her children had arrived at her aunt's.

When she first arrived, Tiffany was a crying, jittery mess, but Aunt Giselle helped her to calm down. Thankfully, the children were asleep, and after Aunt Giselle laid them down, she gave Tiffany a Valium, and put her to bed.

The next morning Aunt Giselle quietly entered Tiffany's room, holding a tray filled with Tiffany's favorite breakfast: French toast with caramel and hazelnuts, crisp bacon, and hot chocolate. Aunt Giselle even garnished the plate with an orange slice and a sprig of parsley. The sight of the meal immediately perked Tiffany up.

"Thank you, Auntie," Tiffany said. She yawned and stretched, and looked at the window. The blinds were drawn, and the dark floral drapes covered any hint of light. "What time is it?"

"It's almost one. But, don't worry. Everything's been taken care of," Giselle said, and placed the tray down on Tiffany's lap. "The children are fine, and you will be, too."

Tiffany sighed. "I don't know if I will be, Auntie." It was difficult facing the fact that her marriage was a lie. And she didn't know how to talk about it. Especially with her aunt.

Giselle walked over to the window and pulled back the drapes. "Sure, you will, my dear. Now, when you arrived here last night, you were a bit out of sorts, and I didn't quite understand what you were saying. The only thing I caught was something about Alex betraying you, and you didn't know what to do. Do you feel like talking about it now?"

Tiffany nibbled on her toast. "Yes, I do, but I don't know what to say. I don't want you to think badly of us."

Aunt Giselle rested on the bed beside Tiffany, and rubbed her leg through the thick comforter. "I'd never think that. But, I'd understand if you didn't feel comfortable talking to me. Maybe it's something you should broach with your therapist."

Her therapist. Tiffany hadn't even scheduled an appointment with the therapist her doctor in California had recommended.

"I'll do that, but right now I need to talk to you. And for you to please listen to me." Tiffany took a deep breath. "Let's just say that I found out that Alex has been deceitful in our marriage. And, he cheated on me."

The corners of Aunt Giselle's mouth dropped, and she peered over her reading glasses at Tiffany. "Are you sure?" Tiffany nodded, and kept nibbling on her breakfast.

"Well, Tiffany. Betrayal is a devastating thing in a relationship. Especially in a marriage."

Tiffany placed her fork down, and tears formed in her eyes. "I just don't know. I guess I had some picture perfect idea of what marriage was supposed to be like, and now I feel stupid. I'd always hoped that I'd have a perfect marriage like my parents."

Giselle bit her lip and stroked Tiffany's hand. "Tiffany, dear heart. Nothing is perfect."

"What do you mean? My parents' marriage wasn't perfect?" Tiffany sniffed, and her eyes questioned her aunt.

"No marriage is without its challenges. That's a fact of life."

Though she was almost thirty years old, Tiffany suddenly felt like a child who had just found out that there was no Santa Claus. Her foundation was crumbling. Her parents' marriage was her ideal. And, now her aunt was threatening to make that a sham, too. "No, Aunt Giselle. But you said, well, my mother always seemed to be so happy with her life. How can that not be true?"

Giselle took a napkin from Tiffany's tray, and wiped her niece's face. "Your mother was happy with her life. Don't think for one minute she wasn't. She was a beautiful, vivacious spirit who took life by the reins and rode it like it was a thoroughbred. I really admired the way your mother lived her life. So unlike me." She cupped Tiffany's chin with her hand, and sighed. "All I'm saying is that human beings aren't perfect. We're all capable of making mistakes. Especially when it pertains to matters of the heart. But, don't worry. Your mother firmly believed in being happy. And if she wasn't happy, it was only momentarily. She found a way to make herself happy." Aunt Giselle kissed Tiffany's forehead and said, "As you should also."

TIFFANY CAREFULLY OUTLINED her lips with the dark red lipstick. She was nervous, but determined, as she rode with her cousin Lily down to the hottest club in D.C., The Ritz. The Ritz was a posh, multilevel club where all of the movers, shakers, and wannnabes hung out. It had a waiting line that rivaled the one at the famed Studio 54 in New York in its heyday. Only the best-dressed and most important were selected to enter. Tiffany knew that she would never have a problem getting in.

She touched up her makeup for the umpteenth time as WKYS-FM jammed Guy's "I Like." Tiffany was ready to throw down, just like the good old days. The only thing missing was a hit of coke, but she wasn't trying to go that far back.

The week before, after Aunt Giselle raised an eyebrow when she asked her to watch the children, Tiffany and Lily had ventured down to the club. But Tiffany was too tense to really enjoy herself. It had been a long time since she had been in the party scene, and the first time in years that she had done it without her significant other. *To hell with him,* Tiffany thought.

But, it was easier said than done. Though she ran into many people that she knew, it was Lily who was far more comfortable working the crowd. Tiffany was actually a little intimidated. Every guy she saw looked, said, or did something that reminded her of her estranged husband. She tried to drink away the painful recognition, and found herself blindly talking to gold-toothed, gold-chain-wearing bamas who had obviously paid dearly to gain entry. Lily had had to rescue her from going home with one of those clowns.

But tonight was going to be different. Tiffany could feel that in her bones. She was on a mission, and was going to be about the business of meeting every decent brother she could.

Now was the time for her to get her life. Alex had crept and slept on her, and had had her foolishly thinking that he was always hers. The lies and the deception. It harped on her mind like a dusty needle on a broken record. She constantly wondered about what else he had kept from her.

Lily valet parked her eggshell-colored Porsche 911, and the striking kin turned heads as they cut the line and headed straight to the front. Lily was on the VIP list, and was a welcomed regular on the Friday night party scene.

Outfitted in their brightly colored minidresses and matching three-inch pumps, they got wolf whistles, approving nods, and winks from every guy they passed, and eye and neck rolls from every woman. The outpouring of adoration and envy bolstered Tiffany's confidence, and put an extra "umph" in the sway of her curvaceous hips. She knew she had it going on.

LILY GRABBED TIFFANY'S HAND, and they weaved their way up to the most popular R&B floor of the club and over to the velvet-roped area of the coveted VIP section. The burly bouncer air-kissed both of Lily's cheeks, and then promptly seated them at a small booth, facing the luminous dance floor. They sat next to each other, which left the ends of the U-shaped booth empty.

"Girl, isn't this great?" Lily said, and adjusted her dress. She craned her neck so that she could see better. "This place is packed tonight."

Tiffany licked her teeth, and smiled broadly. "You're right, Lily," she said. The room was packed with some fine men, and she was ready to get her groove on. "I'm ready for them tonight, cous."

She and Lily grooved in their seats as the deejay pumped the crowd up. A tuxedoed waiter came over, and Lily ordered a White Russian, and Tiffany ordered a glass of champagne and an order of fresh strawberries. She was definitely going to take it easy tonight.

"Why did you order strawberries?" Lily asked.

"Because I can look really sexy biting into them," Tiffany said with a wicked laugh.

"I know that's right, girl," Lily said, and then made the peace sign. "Make that two orders of strawberries, please," she said, and winked at the waiter. She and Tiffany giggled like naughty schoolgirls.

AFTER A FEW MUSIC-FILLED MINUTES, the waiter returned with Lily's drink, a large plate of plump, ruby red strawberries, a long-stemmed flute, and a chilled bottle of Perrier-Jouët.

"I didn't order this," Tiffany said, and pointed at the fancy flowered bottle as if it were poison.

"It's compliments of the gentleman seated by the bar," the waiter said, and motioned toward the crowded bar area. He popped the cork, poured some into the flute, and then handed the glass to Tiffany.

Tiffany crossed her killer legs, and her eyes trailed over to the bar area, but she couldn't tell which man the waiter was referring to. She smiled demurely, and tried not to appear caught off guard. She merely leaned toward Lily, and they keekeed.

"I wonder who sent it," Tiffany said, trying to be discreet, and also trying to be heard over the thumping wall speakers. It was not an easy maneuver.

"I don't know, but whoever he is, he either has good taste or a lot of money. Either one is not a bad thing," Lily said, as she reached for her glass.

"Both would be better," Tiffany said, as she smiled at her witticism.

"I'll drink to that," Lily said, and she raised her glass, and clinked it with Tiffany's. Both cousins picked up a piece of fruit, and seductively bit into it.

"GOOD EVENING, LADIES," the short, nappy-faced brother said, with a grin. In Tiffany's mind, there was nothing worse than a man with a nappy head, and the same nappy hair and razor bumps on his face. They were called "nappy-faces" or "napfas" for short.

"Good evening," Tiffany said dryly, as she nudged Lily under the table. "Napfa," she said under her breath, and Lily giggled. She then eyed the bouncer at the entrance, and he promptly escorted Napfa away from the area.

The girls laughed at their good fortune. They were so into their fruit nibbling and conversation that they didn't notice the gentlemen that had approached.

"Ladies. It looks like you could use your own private body-guards," one of the men said.

He was a tall, dark brown, hunk of a man, with smoldering eyes, and an awesome body. He had a fade, and was wearing a dark suit with a white silk muscle shirt, and had a thick, gold rope chain around his neck. His voice was deep, with a strong New York accent, and when Tiffany glanced up at him, she nearly gasped.

He looked vaguely familiar. "Excuse me?" Tiffany said, as she touched her wide, flat, herringbone chain.

He extended his huge, muscular hand. "Please, allow me to introduce myself. My name is Vincent. And this is my buddy Alan." Vincent nodded toward a tall, thin guy who was standing next to him.

"Hello," he said. "Would you like to dance?" Alan asked Lily, and they headed to the lighted dance floor.

"Would you mind if I sat down?" Vincent asked, and the bouncer automatically unhooked the rope and ushered him in. "I just had to say hello to you, and I hope that you don't mind that I sent you something to drink." He smiled slyly.

Tiffany tried not to blush, as she scooted over so the massive Vincent could sit down. She noticed he had a tail, which she really didn't care for, but she decided to let him sit down anyway. "I don't mind. I think that you have very good taste," Tiffany said. "Would you like some?"

Vincent leaned back in the booth, close enough to Tiffany that she could get a whiff of his cologne. "Naw, I'm much more of a gin-and-juice type of brother, myself." He signaled for the waiter to bring him a Bombay Sapphire and orange juice.

They laughed at Vincent's joke, and interestingly enough, Tiffany didn't have a difficult time making conversation with him at all.

Over the course of the evening, they danced, and sipped their drinks, and had great dialogue. Vincent was a native New Yorker and was visiting family in the area. He had attended Parsons School of Design, where he had studied art, and was a professional sculptor.

"Very interesting, Vincent. I was just in the process of planning a memorial for my parents. I was actually thinking of doing a sculpture." She ran her manicured nail around the rim of her glass.

"You'd be surprised what I can do with a knife and the right subject matter to work with," he said, with a wink. He removed a small knife from his breast pocket, and picked up a strawberry. He expertly carved it into the shape of a flower, and presented it to Tiff with a flourish.

Tiffany placed a gentle hand on Vincent's arm. "I'm impressed. Hmmm. How fortunate it is that we've met."

Vincent smiled, his sleepy eyes and long lashes nearly closed. "Yeah, it's real cool that we did. And to think, I was going to offer to show you my portfolio before. Now, I guess I really have to produce one, huh?"

Tiffany was instantly intrigued by the playful, somewhat, brooding artiste. He kind of reminded her of her first boyfriend, Sidney. He was a muscular, confident, self-assured New Yorker, too, but definitely not as cultured as Vincent appeared to be.

While Lily had exchanged dance and conversation partners several times, she often came back and shot Tiffany one of those

"Don't spend all night with the same dude" looks. Tiffany played her off, because she was quite content to spend the evening conversing with Vincent. This dating thing might not be too bad, after all, she thought. And when he mentioned that his last name was Cavanaugh, it all made sense. Vincent did resemble one of the Cavanaugh brothers, Conrad, but appeared to be much more attractive than he was. Tiffany had hit the jackpot on her second time feeding the dating slots. She could almost hear the bells ringing in her head. She had triple-barred herself with one of the infamous Cavanaugh relatives, and she knew that her streak of good luck was only beginning.

CHAPTER 14

W HAT'D YOU SAY?" Simon said, as he nearly bit Royce's head off.

"I said that I understand that the Cavanaughs have company in town. It seems that Edgar, his son Vincent, and their entourage have almost taken over a floor down at the Grand Hyatt."

Simon dropped his leg weights and stared at Royce. "This certainly changes matters, doesn't it?" he said.

Almost fully recuperated, Simon's body was coming together, but his mind had never faltered. Despite his brief bout of amnesia, Simon was mentally fit and never doubted his mind's capacity. Royce's disclosure was proof positive that the Cavanaughs had indeed had something to do with the taking down of his enterprise. But now that Edgar was back in town, the game was elevated to a whole other level. It was definitely time to settle his old score. Simon had to accelerate his carefully crafted plans, which was going to be tricky.

Royce had proven a faithful if not completely trustworthy subordinate, and Simon had directed him to run some critical errands. The first was to retrieve some cash and photographs from one of Simon's drop points. Royce then arranged for the pictures to be delivered to Tiffany, and the events that had ensued were right on time. Simon figured that Tiffany would kick Alex out of the house, which would make Alex extremely vulnerable. But Royce reported back that Tiffany had taken the children and left, which put a slight kink in Simon's plans. He had counted on Tiffany's being there, so he would have unchecked access to the house. But, with Alex there, he'd have to revamp his plans. One of the things he had to do was get in touch with the woman in the pictures. She might come in handy, but he didn't have time for that right now. Getting back on the scene was imperative. And the only way he could reappear now was to use the amnesia ruse. Otherwise, he'd have no defense for his actions against Alex, and it would help disassociate him from his alter ego Moses.

An overly eager Royce nodded his head. "Yes, I'm sure this does change things significantly. What do you need for me to do now?" Royce's eyes lit up as if he were seeing dollar signs.

Royce's question made Simon think. Simon's eyes riveted on him, and he quickly weighed his options. Now that all of the players were back on the board, there wasn't much else Royce could do for him. Perhaps Royce had outlived his usefulness. He was just another loose end that needed to be snipped. And Simon was quite adept at cutting.

Simon picked up the ten-pound barbell he had been doing bicep curls with earlier, and motioned for Royce to move closer. "I've got one thing you can help me with, Royce. I don't think I've been doing those curls you showed me correctly," Simon said. "Perhaps you can show me how it's done."

"Sure, Simon. That's no problem," Royce said, and he stepped in Simon's direction.

When Royce was within arm's reach, Simon positioned himself in front of him and pretended he was going to begin the exercise. Instead, he brought the weight down on the center of Royce's cerebral cortex, caving his skull in with one forceful blow, splattering blood, skull, and brain matter on the walls and on the floor.

"WHERE ARE YOU? Are you driving?" Lisa's voice nearly screamed from the phone. Alex could tell she was shouting into her speakerphone, and he immediately turned down the volume in his receiver. Alex was driving his car, contemplating whether he could face the embarrassment of riding to Aunt Giselle's house to try to talk to Tiffany.

"Yes, Lisa. I'm driving," Alex said.

"Well, pull over," she said. "I've got something to tell you."

"Yeah, we got a lot to tell you," Fortune said, his voice echoing in the background.

Alex wasn't about to get caught in Lisa and Fortune's spy-versus-spy tactics. He kept right on driving. "I pulled over," he said, and mashed his accelerator as he sped up Massachusetts Avenue.

"Simon's back!" Lisa screamed, and Alex nearly rear-ended a white panel van in front of him. He quickly put on his hazards, and double-parked.

"What? You've got to be kidding," Alex said, his heart hammering through his chest. "How can that be? How do you know?"

Lisa said that the details were sketchy, but evidently, Simon had survived the explosion on the boat and had floated to a rural part of Virginia, where some family, who declined to be identified, had nursed him back to health. When he had recovered enough, they dropped him off at a local hospital, from where he was medevaced up to Walter Reed Army Medical Center. It was also mentioned that the mayor was suffering from a severe case of amnesia.

"Oh, shit," Alex said. "You've got to be kidding. That's not

even possible. Why would anyone keep Simon without ever saying anything? Lisa, did you verify all of that?"

"Yep."

"Are you sure? I just don't believe it," Alex said.

"Believe it, slim," Fortune said. "He's back, but I ain't diggin'
that memory loss shit, either. I say we go to that hospital, an'
whack him in the head to see if his memory comes back." Fortune
laughed at his own joke.

"Very funny, Fortune. Alex, I know that it sounds a bit incredible, but stranger things have happened," Lisa said. "Face it, this
puts a different spin on things."

"I'll say. Whether Simon actually can't remember anything or
if he's faking, it still doesn't let me off the hook, Lisa. From where
I sit, he still has me by the balls. If he remembers, he's going to
want to either kill me or frame me for what happened, and if he
doesn't remember, then he'll think that I'm here to still be his
lackey again. And, that's not going to happen."

"You better bet it," Fortune said. "Don't let that fool try to run
game on you again, naw-uh. He ain't never gonna hurt you again."

"I agree, but you may have another consideration, Alex. You
still need to clean up what you can. Because, if you can prove his
culpability, maybe that'll let you off the hook. And then, you can
pursue getting him prosecuted for his actions. Isn't that what you
really want, anyway?" Lisa asked.

Alex had to think about it. Although he had never believed that
Simon was actually dead, he'd never really thought about what
would happen if Simon was actually alive. "I don't know Lisa. I
just don't know."

Alex didn't have much time to think about the question. He
left Tiffany a voice-mail message, swung his car around, and
headed across town, to where Walter Reed was located. Though he
didn't want to go, he knew that was what was expected of him.

After wading through a flurry of news media, Alex was able to access the secure compound. He entered the building where presidents and congressmen were regularly treated, and headed toward the fifth floor.

As he stepped off the elevator, he saw Tiffany, and his breath nearly left his body. She appeared as radiant and as beautiful as ever, and though she was crying, this time it was evident that they were tears of joy.

Tiffany was sitting with Aunt Giselle and Simon's last lady friend, Elaine Bidwell. Aunt Giselle leaned over and whispered in Tiffany's ear. Tiffany glanced up and saw him, and her face froze. Surprisingly, she stood and walked toward him.

Alex wanted to run and sweep her off her feet, but the tight expression on her face said otherwise.

"Alex," she said, her voice cold and distant.

"Tiffany. How are you? How are the children?" he asked, and instinctively reached for her hand, but she pulled away.

"Don't touch me," she said, her lips barely moving. "And your children are fine."

"I don't like the fact that you're keeping them from me, Tiffany. I shouldn't be denied access to them because of—"

Tiffany flipped a hand in his face. "Fine, Alex. You can see them tomorrow evening if you'd like, because I have something to do anyway. And if you want a more formal schedule, then, we'll work something out. Is that appropriate?" She rolled her eyes at him.

"So, now that we've dispensed with the pleasantries, let me tell you something. I'm not here for a social visit, and neither are you. I want you to know that the only reason you're here is because my father has always thought of you as his son. His physicians don't know that we aren't together. So, for my father's sake and for appearance' sake, please keep that fact between us."

Tiffany suddenly stopped speaking when Simon's doctor approached them, but Alex's mind fixated on her statement about her having something to do tomorrow evening. He wondered if she was trying to make him jealous. Alex tried to dismiss the thought when he realized that he wasn't paying any attention to the doctor.

"Mayor Blake's overall prognosis is positive. He has traces of a deep infection, and we want to treat it aggressively, with intravenous antibiotics," Dr. Riley said.

"I see," Tiffany said.

"And as part of our routine evaluation, we also want to perform some extensive testing on the mayor's neurosystem, especially his brain, since it appears that he has both antegrade and retrograde amnesia."

"What does that mean?" Alex asked.

"That means that he can't recall events from either before or after the trauma—the accident. We still need to determine just how much memory has been lost, but we're estimating that it's essentially the last twenty years of his life."

Alex tried to keep a straight face, but he couldn't help thinking how convenient it was for Simon to have amnesia. But why twenty years? There had to be something significant about that time frame.

Dr. Riley scanned their faces. "Any questions? Okay, then. My plan is that once the mayor's wounds have sufficiently healed, he'll be moved to the compound's rehabilitation center. There he'll receive therapy to assist him with his mobility and other aspects of his recovery. Our concern is where His Honor will go when he's released from our care. And I'm estimating that will be in a few weeks. His convalescence and any hopes of his regaining his memory will be dependent on him being in a loving, stable environment."

Alex cleared his throat, and Tiffany cut her eyes at him. "Tell us what you think is going to be best for him, Dr. Riley."

"I was thinking that the mayor would probably best recuperate with you in your home. Not until he completely recovers, but at least until his memory becomes more current, and he's able to manage better on his own. He has been told that he's the mayor, but he has no recall of that aspect of his life."

"Most definitely, Dr. Riley. We'd have it no other way," Tiffany said. She reached for Alex's arm, and dug her nails deeply into his skin. "Right, dear?"

"Right, Tiff," Alex said, with a wince. He pried her fingers from his arm and tried to mask his skepticism. He suspected that Simon was lying, but why would he go back twenty years? That was before he became mayor and got as deeply involved in his drug activities. There had to be a reason.

DR. RILEY COMPLETED HIS DISCUSSION with a few more minor details, which Alex barely heard. It wasn't until Tiffany spoke that he began listening again.

"I've been in to see him, and he remembers me, but only as a child. But, he also thinks that my mother just died." Tiffany sighed. "I've tried to take things slowly for him, and I told him that I was now twenty-seven, and that I was married with twins. He's asked to meet you, and you should see him. But, don't think that there's anything else here for you," Tiffany said, her words and her eyes cutting through him like a saber.

The last thing Alex wanted was to see Simon, but maybe he could see through Simon's guise; so he fortified himself for the confrontation.

ALEX ENTERED SIMON'S BRIGHT, sun-filled room, with Tiffany close behind. He was surprised to see Simon, propped up on several pillows, playing solitaire. Alex searched his face to see if he would reveal anything, but there was nothing. Simon actually looked happy to see him.

"You must be Alex," Simon said, and spread his arms wide open. "How are you doing, my boy?"

Alex's tongue stuck to the roof of his mouth, and his size twelves refused to move. Tiffany jabbed him in the back. "Simon," Alex said, squelching the feeling of nausea burning in his throat. He slowly pushed his feet toward Simon's bed. "It's, uh, it's good to see you."

As Simon warmly embraced him, the memory of their fight in the river flooded Alex's mind. He sought some vibe from Simon that indicated his resentment or discomfort, but Simon didn't flinch or waver one iota. He was his same old beguiling self, and when he started talking, he kept apologizing while he asked Alex and Tiffany a lot of mundane questions.

"So, how are you two doing? I must say, you make a good-looking couple. You'll have to forgive me, but now how long have you been married again?"

"Over three years, Dad," Tiffany said.

"Three years, huh? Why didn't you answer, son? Cat got your tongue? You haven't been married long enough to be henpecked yet," Simon said with a wink.

Alex forced a chuckle. "No, sir. I'm definitely not henpecked."

"That's good to know, Alex. And I was only joking. My wife isn't, I mean wasn't, like that at all." Simon quickly shook his head. "It's going to take me a minute to keep these things together."

"We understand, Dad," Tiffany said, and rubbed Simon's shoulder. "You just have to try not to overtax yourself. You've been through a lot."

"I know, but relaxing has always been difficult for me. But I know it's best that I take it easy. I've got to get out of here so that I can get back to work. My practice isn't going to wait forever, you know. What's your line of work, Alex?"

Alex answered and tried to be pleasant, but while his lips were moving, his mind was reeling in another direction. He couldn't help thinking that if this was a game, Simon was playing it masterfully. But these stakes were mighty high, and one false move or an inept step would ruin everyone's lives. The cruelty of that possibility was only overshadowed by the disheartening possibility that Simon might actually have amnesia. Either offered unpleasant repercussions across the board.

And when Simon laughed, a modified variation of that infectious laugh Alex had been hearing for almost ten years, it made Alex's skin crawl. The only thing missing was Simon's favorite adage "always remember that." If he heard that now, Alex would probably have a stroke and be rushed to the ICU.

This had to be a fate worse than death, Alex thought, as he spent an angst-filled hour in Simon's hospital room. When there was a slight knock on the door, Alex thought that it was Aunt Giselle.

The door opened, and Elaine Bidwell entered, holding an exquisite arrangement of tropical flowers. Mrs. Bidwell had been Simon's companion for the past several years, and her face was a mixture of relief and concern.

"Simon? Hello, darling," she said, as she approached his bedside. "Hello, Tiffany. Hello, Alex," she said, clearly as an afterthought.

Alex and Tiffany responded, and Tiffany stood from her seat, and joined Alex near the window. Alex fixed his eyes on Simon, whose face registered no recognition of Mrs. Bidwell.

"Uh, hello," Simon finally said, and extended his hand toward her.

Mrs. Bidwell's face collapsed. "Simon? It's me, Elaine." She placed the arrangement on Simon's nightstand, and grabbed his hand.

Simon's face twitched with embarrassment. "Elaine? Oh, sure, Elaine." He shook her hand, and then shook his head. "I'm sorry, Elaine. I don't know who you are."

"It's okay, Dad," Tiffany said. "You and Mrs. Bidwell have been seeing each other for the past few years." Tiffany rushed back to her father's side, and rubbed his forehead. "Your memory will come back soon, and you'll remember."

Mrs. Bidwell maintained her decorum, but Alex was unimpressed when Simon failed to recognize her. It was clear that her feelings were hurt, but she tried to carry on as though it didn't matter. Mrs. Bidwell had been in the room for only a few moments before the nurse came in, and administered something to Simon that made him drowsy and less coherent. Alex was more than relieved to escape, and he was certain that Mrs. Bidwell also appreciated the gracious opportunity to exit.

BEFORE THEY LEFT THE HOSPITAL, Tiffany outlined the terms and conditions of her returning home if Simon's memory hadn't returned before he was released from the hospital. She stipulated that it would be only for Simon's sake, and that it changed nothing between them. To keep up appearances, they would act like a loving, married couple in his presence, but in reality, she would continue to lead her separate life. She had no intention of deluding Alex into thinking that she would discuss what happened between them, yesterday, today, or anytime in the near future.

Alex wanted to grab his wife and shake some sense into her, but thought better of it. Tiffany had to be reeling from Simon's reappearance, but she refused to talk to him about it. He could tell that she was anxious and probably a bit overwhelmed, but she defied any of his efforts to reach out to her. He only hoped that she was still in therapy and could at least discuss it with her doctor.

Alex never verbalized that he'd agreed to her terms; he knew that there was no way he could stomach living like that. With Simon back, the stakes in this game of die or survive, life or death, had been raised even higher. Alex absolutely had to do something to get control of his life back. Now, more than ever before, he had to prove Simon's guilt, and his own innocence.

CHAPTER 15

TIFFANY HAD just returned from a long visit with her father and was back at her aunt Giselle's house. She had a lot on her mind, for Simon had been moved to Walter Reed's rehabilitation center and was going to be released next week. His memory hadn't returned, and now she was going to have to make provisions for him to stay with her. Her and Alex in their faux happy home. It made Tiffany's stomach hurt to even think about it.

Though she was happy that Simon was alive and nearly well, her promise to have him come stay with her was really putting a kink in her plans to move on with her life. Although she wasn't completely set on ending her marriage, she was determined to have as much fun as she could before she decided what she was going to do. And having to play happily married just wasn't in her immediate plans.

Upon her return from Walter Reed, Tiffany had spent some time with her children and had plans to meet with Vincent

Cavanaugh later on that evening. He had invited her over for dinner at his suite at the Grand Hyatt, and then they were going to catch a movie.

After she laid the children down for their afternoon nap, she decided to try to locate an appropriate picture of her mother for Vincent to use as a model for his sketches for the memorial. Although Aunt Giselle had a beautiful portrait of her mother on her wall, Tiffany decided to take a long-put-off stroll back down memory lane. As she sat at the dining room table, she flipped through a dusty photo album. About six others were stacked in separate piles in front of her. She lingered on each yellowing page of the book, lovingly fingering each of the aged images.

She really hadn't known her mother very well, for she had died when Tiffany was only six years old. As she perused the cracked photographs, she saw numerous pictures of her mother, from a chubby-cheeked baby, to a stunning grown woman. Marjorie was a real knockout. Tiffany touched her face in one of the photographs and outlined the bridge of her nose. She could see her resemblance to her mother. It was something in the manner in which she smiled, and in her eyes. Radiant and vibrant, Marjorie had long, wavy, jet black hair and deep-set eyes. Tiffany could almost feel her energy as her fingertips touched her photos. She really wished that her mother were here.

Tiffany kept flipping through the book, and an old, torn Red Cross blood donor card fell out: MARJORIE NEWTON—BLOOD TYPE A, but the rest was torn off. Marjorie's florid signature was etched across the bottom of the card, and Tiffany smiled as she lifted the page lining and reinserted the card under it.

There were pictures of her mother attending youth cotillions, where she was dressed up in her frilly gowns and mini-tiaras. Marjorie's prom pictures. Her high school and college graduations, complete with bouffant hairstyles. Tiffany, a fashion buff, could see that her mother was a true clotheshorse, too. And then there were the college years, and pictures of Marjorie with her sorority. There were pictures of college coed Marjorie and a nattily attired young Simon in his frat gear, and Marjorie with a few other handsome young men. Mom had quite a life, Tiffany thought. And then she thought about the present state of her own life, and just what her mother would have to say about it.

Tiffany was spending every available moment with Vincent, and she was really enjoying every minute of it. He was fun, strong, and a manly man. A true departure from what she had become accustomed to. Yes, she still loved Alex, and their relationship had evolved from an innocent friendship to a torrid relationship to a loving marriage. And her father absolutely adored him. But, they had been so young when they hooked up. And perhaps she had missed out on something. Like fun. Alex could be too serious at times, and too work oriented. She admired that quality about him, and it made him a wonderful husband and provider, but somewhere along the line, after the marriage and responsibilities of child-rearing kicked in, they had forgotten the magical, impulsive thrills they used to have when they were just dating.

The spontaneous sex in the parks. Making out in public places. Quickies in restaurant bathrooms. Tiffany sighed. The spark was missing from their relationship. Perhaps, they had just married too soon.

Prior to Alex, Tiffany had had a few boyfriends, Evan in high school, and Sidney in college. But she was making up for lost time now. Getting to know Vincent was both a release and relief for her, and she thought that he had the potential to be someone special in her life. That is, as soon as she figured out what she was going to do with her life.

She had told Vincent all about her marriage, and he was supportive and understanding. He let her know that he was dating others, and really didn't press her for anything sexually. He had only kissed her on the cheek and grazed his lips across hers a time or two. But Tiffany could tell that there was a beast of a man lurking underneath that chiseled chest and those bulging thighs of his. And she had to admit, she was extremely bewitched, and curious about what it would feel like to be with him. Especially since she had never slept with another man besides Alex. She alone had been truthful about that, and it burned her that Alex hadn't told her about his tryst. Who was she? Why did he sleep with her? Was this mystery woman better in bed than she was? It was all so frustrating.

She tried to squash the annoying thoughts, but she was still vexed about her marriage. She didn't know if she could ever forgive Alex for not telling her the truth, even though they hadn't been married when it happened. It didn't matter. Hurt was hurt, and lies were lies. If Alex lied about that, what else was he hiding?

Then, she thought about her precious children. She felt bad about keeping them from him, and made herself promise that she'd allow him to see them more often. On the night that she and Vincent went to the Corcoran, she'd made it a point to let Alex see her, dressed in her form-fitting evening wear, and dripping in jewels. She could see the hurt in his eyes, and for a moment, she pitied him, but the feeling quickly passed. Alex deserved to suffer, long and strong.

Tiffany came across a picture of her mother and a very nice looking man. There was something in the way the man looked at her mother that made her want to find out who he was. Tiffany immediately took the book and went into the kitchen where Aunt Giselle was preparing tea.

"Auntie, who's this with my mother?" Tiffany asked, and held the picture up so that her aunt could see.

Aunt Giselle nearly dropped the pot. She pushed her reading glasses up on her nose and shook her head. "I'm not too sure, dear."

"Look closely, Auntie. There are several pictures of him with Mother."

Aunt Giselle peered down her nose and frowned. "I can't really say. Just an old friend of your mother's, that's all. Someone she used to date."

"No one special?"

"Not at all," Aunt Giselle said. "Now, how would you like your tea?"

The man appeared vaguely familiar, but Aunt Giselle's curt response and abrupt change of subject didn't faze Tiffany. She knew that her aunt was quite opinionated when it came to men. That was why Tiffany hadn't told her that she was dating someone. Although Aunt Giselle probably wasn't a virgin, she more than likely wasn't far from being one. She was quite conservative and would never even speak about her sister dating anyone but the man she married.

And that's how her aunt was handling Tiffany's situation. Discreetly, with minimal verbiage. Tiffany knew that her aunt would more than likely be supportive of her, and she had even deviated from her normal reticence and expressed some disappointment at Alex's behavior, but she reminded Tiffany that Alex was her husband. And, the father of her children. And, to Giselle, that was all that mattered.

Tiffany closed the albums when she heard one of her children cry. Though Aunt Giselle and the full-time nanny were always there to help, Tiffany didn't like the challenges and responsibilities of single-parenthood. But it was a small price to pay for her wounded pride, and the price was escalating every day.

But Tiffany was a true survivor, and she was going to make it. And tonight just might be the night when she crossed another threshold in her life. She ached to be held, to be touched, to be caressed, and to feel the strength of a man on top and inside of her. Tonight she might take her relationship with Vincent to another level.

CHAPTER 16

THEIR CHAMPAGNE glasses clinked, with the heavy sound of good crystal. Tiffany wasn't sure what she found more intoxicating: the view or the bubbly. The view from Vincent's penthouse suite was breathtaking, and with the lights glimmering across the city, she felt as if she had been swept up into some kind of fairy tale.

Their meal had seven sumptuous courses, all served by the Hyatt's tuxedoed waiters carrying domed silver trays. The fireplace was glowing, and as the steaming lobster thermidor was being served, Tiffany knew without a doubt where she would be waking up the next morning. She'd be soaking up the view when the sun was shining, with a flute full of mimosa.

Vincent was both attentive and accommodating. After dinner, they had retired to the sitting area, which was adorned with several lit candelabras, and the room was centered with a blazing fireplace.

There was something extremely seductive about a fire in the fall. Quite.

After they'd finished the bubbly, Vincent poured an aperitif. She nestled in the crook of his broad chest and arm, and they sipped Drambuie. It was a little heady for Tiffany, but she wanted to hang. Dressed in a sheer black, strapless dress, she knew she looked good and smelled great. The subtle fragrance of Coco by Chanel mixed with Vincent's Paco Rabanne, and it was smoldering. Tiff had even purchased a seductive set of La Perla lingerie for this special evening.

Vincent kissed her cheek, and then turned her face toward him. She caught her image in his eyes, and suddenly felt confused, and her stomach jumped nervously.

"I think I better go freshen up, Vincent," she said, and pried herself away from his grasp.

He took her snifter, and stood. He pointed down the hallway. "The bathroom's right over there, Tiffany. Hurry back."

Tiffany went into the gold marble bath, and collapsed against the door. Now that the moment of truth had arrived, was she really ready to have sex with another man?

She checked her reflection in the mirror and straightened out her hair. She was flawless on the outside, but on the inside, she felt like hell. She reapplied her makeup, and took a long look at herself. Was she going to cheat? Was it really cheating? Hell, Alex had cheated. Vincent was sexy and strong, and made her feel like a desirable woman. How difficult would it be to lie down with him?

Tiffany didn't want to spend too long in the bathroom, and by the time she decided to vacate it, she had prepared herself to be with Vincent. When she came out, she overheard Vincent talking to another man. They were standing in front of the fireplace, and Tiffany barely caught his face.

"Tiffany, I'd like you to meet my father, Edgar Cavanaugh. Father, I'd like for you to meet Tiffany Baxter."

Edgar grabbed Tiffany's hand and held it warmly. "It's a real pleasure to meet you, dear." Edgar smiled broadly, and his eyes flashed with a hint of mischievousness. "You are quite beautiful, I must say. My son has exceptional taste in women, but you are simply exquisite."

Although she had never met Edgar before, she felt as if she had seen him somewhere. Vincent resembled his father, but not to that extent. Then it dawned on her. He was the man in one of the pictures she had seen earlier that day. The handsome man with her mother. Though the years had creased his face and thinned his hair, he still looked great.

"Oh, my goodness, Mr. Cavanaugh. It is you. I just saw your picture earlier today." Tiffany dropped her hand from his. "You knew my mother. Marjorie Newton Blake."

THE EVENING DID NOT GO as either Tiffany or Vincent had planned. Instead, Edgar stayed and sipped cognac with them, while they talked about Tiffany's mother.

Tiffany was ecstatic to learn so much about her mother, and Edgar was more than willing to reminisce with her. He talked about how he knew Marjorie from their junior debutante days, and how vibrant and outgoing she was as a young woman. They had dated until she went off to college, where she met and eventually married Simon Blake. Their friendship was rekindled after Marjorie and Simon returned to D.C., and they were friends until her death. Tiffany and Edgar talked until the wee hours of the morning, when Tiffany finally decided to leave. Though she was disappointed that she hadn't gotten one desire fulfilled, she had unexpectedly addressed an unspoken need, and was satisfied with that. Especially since the opportunity had never presented itself before, and it might not ever again. She was certain that she and Vincent would have another chance to spend some quality time together. Real soon.

• • •

THOUGH HE DIDN'T WANT TO DO IT, Alex reluctantly allowed Simon into his home, under the pretext that it would aid in Simon's healing. He would've preferred to set Simon up in the garage apartment, but Lisa was still there. He didn't want her to leave, but he knew that Tiffany would never entertain the notion of Lisa staying in her house, and Alex needed her close by.

Despite Alex's trepidation, Tiffany remained true to her word, putting her best face forward, when she and Simon arrived home from the rehab center.

Alex was glad to have his family back and intact, but every moment with Simon was agonizing, even though Simon was nothing short of charming and supportive. Just as he had been before, except without the edginess.

Simon had always been larger than life, with a magnetic personality that consumed you and a determination that was infectious. He had a gift of forcing others to rise to his level of play, and Simon had cultivated that same spirit in Alex.

Simon had challenged Alex, and instilled confidence and assuredness in him. Simon had been Alex's taskmaster, guru, adviser, and most vocal cheerleader. That's why it had nearly destroyed Alex to find out who the real Simon was.

But that Simon was an accomplished man, not the Simon Alex was dealing with now. Simon was still driven, but he lacked the glibness that Alex had come to know. It was different, yet somehow the same. But then a man with an ego the size of Simon's might be humbled, especially if he really had the handicap of a memory loss. But the way Alex was thinking, twenty years ago Simon would still have been into illicit activities, so he needed to be watched like a hawk now. Both Lisa and Fortune agreed, and went about making sure that Simon had eyes on him 24/7. It was an easy task for Lisa, because either she or her agents could keep Simon on lock, without drawing any undue attention.

Simon continued to feign lack of memory, and was pleasant and charming to Alex. Tiffany spent time with him, trying to refamiliarize him with the events of the last two decades, while Alex waited skeptically on the sidelines, watching for Simon to trip up. It was an exhausting game.

But Simon didn't slip. He remained congenial and affable, and when they watched television, he seemed genuinely appalled at the offerings of cable television. Everything associated with modern times was a mystery to him. Cell phones, CDs, and SUVs were a few of the items that made Simon's jaw drop. It was a noble effort, but still, Alex wasn't convinced.

It was even more difficult for Alex to share living space with Tiffany but not her life. Once Simon had gone to bed, Tiffany would usually leave the house, while Alex sat there and stewed. He felt helpless, trapped in a marriage of convenience.

They ate meals together, and generally tried to keep Simon's environment happy and tranquil. But the arrangement was tearing Alex up inside. He was a prisoner in his own home, with no parole in sight. Simon, even in his alleged state of amnesia, still controlled Alex's life. Whenever Simon wanted to go somewhere, he asked that Alex take him. He was full of suggestions and innuendo as to how Alex should manage his family and his career. He was more subtle than the Simon of old, but just as manipulative.

Alex was expected to be attentive and kind to Simon, who used any pretext to hold conversations with him. Whether the topic was sports or politics, Simon always made sure that he weighed in with his opinion.

Alex's only reprieve was having Lisa around. Alex could venture off to her apartment, and they could discuss the current status of their investigation of Simon. Lisa and Fortune had located Simon's drop locations, and while they contained substantial amounts of cash, there was nothing to directly link Simon back to its source. Alex's options were fading.

Although the calls from reporters died down, Simon's faithful constituents flooded the house with get-well cards and visits, hoping to get a chance to meet with Simon. Though Simon still showed no memory of his years as mayor, he was very intrigued with politics and reveled in conversing with his allies and supporters.

One day, when Simon returned from a stroll through the National Zoo with his nurse, he cornered Alex in his home office. Although his door was closed, Simon knocked once and came right in.

"How are things going, Alex?" Simon asked, and sat down in the chair that faced Alex's desk.

"Fine, Simon. How are you?" Alex closed the *Forbes* magazine he was reading and clasped his hands.

"I'm well, I'm well. I had a great walk through the zoo, and I ran into a number of my constituents." Simon leaned forward and stared at his son-in-law.

"We had an impromptu meeting of sorts, and they were extremely supportive of me and my work here as mayor. I was flattered that they didn't treat me like an invalid, but I had to tell them that given my present state, there was no way that I could effectively resume my position as mayor. They were quite disappointed by my revelation, but then inquired as to whom I would support in the special election."

"That's interesting, Simon. Your deputy mayor is a logical candidate, wouldn't you think?" Alex asked.

Simon shook his head. "Mister, what's his name? Mr. Smalls, would probably be good, but I don't know him. Not like I know you."

"What do you mean by that?"

"I was wondering if you'd consider running for mayor." Gone was Simon's subtlety.

"Me?" Alex asked.

"Yes, you," Simon said, and placed his fist on Alex's desk. "It occurred to me that you'd be a prime candidate for this illustrious position. And who would be better than you? Or a more prudent choice? Especially with me in your corner. If I'm going to endorse anyone, it would be you, son."

It was an idea that Simon had conveyed to Alex before his deception was revealed, but now, it was much more significant. Alex's instincts told him that Simon was up to something.

"Well, since I followed through with my political aspirations," Simon said, "I must've been a pretty good leader. At least that's what they tell me. And from what I've been told, I had a number of things on my agenda. Statehood. And a new stadium. So it stands to reason that since I was mayor, or so you all tell me, I may be able to help you get in. And, of course, that means that you can help see that some of my agenda is accomplished. Who knows? It may even help me regain my memory, getting back in the thick of things."

When Simon mentioned the stadium, Alex fumed at his hypocrisy. After all, if Alex hadn't been out scouring for sites, he would never have happened upon Simon's warehouse. It took all Alex had not to leap across the table and choke Simon, but he refrained. Instead, he played the game, and focused on downplaying Simon's supposed goodwill. "Well, I'm flattered, Simon, but there are men far worthier to follow in your footsteps than me," Alex said. Men just as dirty as you are, he thought.

Simon steadfastly argued his point. "You have to look at the big picture, Alex. Running for mayor might be the best thing for you to consider. You have the experience and the intellect. And nothing makes a woman happier than to be married to a powerful man. Trust me—if Tiffany's anything like her mother, well, then she'd really be partial to that, I'm sure." Simon leaned back in his seat and winked. "You should honestly give it some consideration."

There was clearly a hidden message in Simon's words, but Alex was stymied. But he did realize that if Simon put it out that he wanted Alex to push his agenda, then that was only part of the deal. He sensed that Simon was trying to lull him into some kind of trap, but Alex wasn't falling that easily. He decided to beat Simon at his own game.

"Thanks, Simon. I'm really flattered that you think I'd be a good candidate, but I'm not so sure. But, I will think about it."

LATER, DURING DINNER, when Simon mentioned it in front of Tiffany, his words of wisdom proved true. Tiffany's eyes lit up at the possibility, and she smiled, in a way that Alex hadn't seen in a long time. She was even cordial to him during the meal, which was a pleasant thaw, compared to the icy treatment she normally gave him. Alex continued his charade while he watched Simon's every move. With one conversation, Simon had made it possible for him and Tiffany to reunite. But the real question was, what did Simon really want from Alex if he became mayor? What would Alex possibly stand to gain from it? Or lose?

CHAPTER 17

THE COOLER fall weather was evoking the notion of winter hibernation, and like squirrels storing nuts, the eminent Baxter-Blake family was preparing for a long and bitter winter. Stocking up on essentials.

Over the course of the next month, Alex saw his life take on a different hue, like the autumn foliage. No matter what Alex tried, Simon didn't slip up once. Alex tried to mention recent things, in casual conversation, but Simon remained poker-faced, and effectually dumbfounded. Eventually, Alex found himself considering the possibility that Simon actually had amnesia, much to Lisa's and Fortune's chagrin.

Simon was also interested in getting some structure back in his life. He was a licensed attorney and had mentioned going back into practice. Alex thought that Simon would go for his stashes. Now that he was formally unemployed, he was concerned about his future. He had requested that Tiffany and Alex get him an assistant, someone that he could have on his personal payroll who would help him manage his personal and business affairs.

And the kinder, gentler Simon was definitely committed to motivating Alex to run for mayor. Sticking to his own plan, Alex glossed over the suggestion, but the idea began to take on a life of it's own. Everywhere they went, whether it was to the barbershop on Rhode Island Avenue, Eastern Market, or the Georgia Mile Grill, Simon chatted up the prospect of Alex taking his place. The wheels of the rumor mill were greased, and Simon's allies began aligning themselves behind it. And it was, as Simon had said, a matter of keen interest to Tiffany.

Though their living arrangement was less than idyllic, Alex and Tiffany managed to keep it together for the sake of their family. It bothered Alex that Tiffany, although she was being discreet, appeared to be dating, but he refused to allow Lisa to put a tail on her. He appreciated Lisa's help in dealing with Simon, but he wasn't going to push the envelope and get her involved with what was happening between him and his wife. That was just TMI— too much information—for Lisa to have, so he tried to keep it to himself.

But holding all of that inside was killing Alex, and one day, while Simon and the children were napping, Alex blew his cool.

Tiffany was folding and putting away the children's clothing and preparing an overnight bag for herself. Evidently, when she left their home, she went to Lily's house, or so Alex hoped. At least that was what she claimed.

"Tiffany, I need to talk to you," Alex said, as he stood in the doorway to their bedroom. He walked in and closed the door behind him, and then removed a cotton diaper from her hands.

"What do you want, Alex?"

"We need to talk. How long are we going to go around here acting like we don't have a problem? You're my wife, damnit, and if we're going to stay married, then something's got to change."

Tiffany slowly blinked her eyes, as though she couldn't believe what Alex was saying. "Look, Alex. You made a promise that you'd be here for my father. And I appreciate that. But, I told you from the start that this little arrangement didn't have anything to do with you and me." She snatched the diaper from his hand, and went back to folding clothes.

The mounting pressure from playing amateur detective and Tiffany's inability to forgive him was driving him mad. "You don't get it, do you? I never said that I was going to live in purgatory for the rest of my life. We took vows, and we made a commitment that was for better or for worse, remember?"

Tiffany flung the clothes onto their bed. "And did our vows include lies that would tear us apart? Tell me, Alex. Since you insist on bringing this up, how many more lies have you kept from me? Huh? Any half-truths? Any little omissions or departures from fact?"

She pointed a manicured finger in his face. "I'm furious with you, Alex. Our whole marriage was based on a lie. The whole damned thing. Imagine how I felt when I saw those pictures. And then, it had to be at one of the most vulnerable times of my life. I should thank you, because now I know how strong I am, because I could've lost my mind because of you." She paused, her chest heaving. "Imagine that." Tiffany's voice elevated. "But, you know what? I don't even care anymore, because you'll never understand how I feel."

He reached for her, but she jerked away. "Tiffany, baby, you're right. I was wrong for not telling you. And, I'm sorry. But you didn't even let me explain. It happened before we got married," Alex said. "Way before." Tiffany met his words with stone-faced indifference. It was becoming painfully obvious that he was losing his wife.

He grabbed her shoulders, but she snatched away. "Don't touch me."

"Why won't you listen to me, Tiffany? After all we've been through? Why won't you give me a chance to explain?"

"We've had this conversation before. There's nothing for you to explain. Not unless you want to tell me how you had sex. Or why? The sex is only part of the betrayal, Alex. The other part is why you never told me about it."

"I was wrong not to tell you, but it just, it just happened. It wasn't like I went looking for her, but she was someone from my childhood."

"I thought you didn't date anyone when you were younger? Or, was that a lie, too?"

"That wasn't a lie, Tiff. I didn't date her. She was my brother's girlfriend."

Tiffany threw the clothes she was holding down on the bed. "Oh, my God. That is utterly disgusting, Alexander Baxter. Don't tell me anything else. I can't believe you slept with your brother's girlfriend." She folded her arms across her chest. "You make me sick!"

"I'm not proud of it. But it happened. We both needed closure, and I never realized how much I needed it until I saw her. I gave her a ride home, and one thing—"

"What? Led to another? Bullshit. You lied to me. You betrayed me. You had me thinking that I was your only lover and that meant a lot to me. And you pretended like it meant something to you, too."

"I know. And I'm sorry." Alex's hands fell heavily down to his side.

"How would you feel if you found out that I had slept with another man before we got married?" She paused, and held her hand up to her neck. Her three-carat diamond wedding ring reflected in Alex's eyes. "Or, what if I told you that I was sleeping with someone now?"

Alex's heart felt as if it had been hit with a sledgehammer. He stared at her and wondered who this woman was standing before him. Had Tiffany always been so unforgiving and he never noticed it? Rage boiled in his veins, and he suddenly found it difficult to breathe. That had to be the most hurtful thing he had ever heard from his wife's mouth.

Alex raised his hands, and then dropped them by his side. "Have you? Have you slept with someone else?" Alex flexed his fingers, while Tiffany stared at him defiantly. "I think that's called adultery, Tiffany. But, you know what? I don't even want to think about it."

"I'm sure you don't, Alex. But you know what? You will. Just like I think about what you did. Every day."

FROM HIS BEDROOM, Simon eavesdropped on the marital discord with mild amusement. He had figured that when Tiffany saw the pictures, she'd be a little angered by it, but he was surprised that she had carried her vendetta this far. He had wanted Alex vulnerable, but not on the verge of a divorce. That would ruin Simon's long-range plans. He'd have to come up with another way to cool Tiffany down besides enticing her with becoming the first lady of the city. She was on the verge of inflicting too much pain on the dear boy, and that wasn't what Simon wanted.

Simon knew Alex had been trying to trip him up, but he was much too smart for that. And Simon had decided that Alex was of much better use to him alive than he could ever be dead. It was fun running game on his bookish son-in-law, and watching him squirm. And if Simon had his way, the fun would never end.

If he could coerce Alex into running for mayor, the deed would be done. Simon could have everything he had before, and then some. His drug business, control of the city, and complete protection because he'd have the mayor in his front pocket. The risks he had taken before were now a thing of the past. D.C. was his for the taking and, the beauty of it was that Alex was going to hand it to him on a silver platter.

When Simon heard Alex storm out of the bedroom and then out the front door, Simon seized the opportunity to stir the pot a little more.

His knuckles barely brushed the wood as he knocked on the open door to Tiffany's bedroom. "Dear?"

Tiffany was sitting on the edge of her bed, holding one of the children's T-shirts. Her eyes were full, and she looked as if she was about to cry.

"Yes, Daddy," she said, and wiped the corners of her eyes. She turned toward him and forced a smile.

"Are you okay? Is everything all right?" Simon asked, and sat down beside his daughter.

"I'm, um, we're okay," she said, through her put-on smile. "I, uh, I have your assistant lined up. Actually, there are two candidates. I've seen both of their credentials and spoken to each one on the phone. But I'd like for you to meet with them tomorrow. And whichever one you feel better suited with can start the next day."

Simon grabbed her chin, and stared into her eyes. "That's nice, dear. And, I appreciate you taking care of that for me so quickly, but, you know that's not what I'm asking you about. You don't seem all right. Plus, I overheard you and Alex. Is there something you want to talk about?"

Tiffany sighed, and Simon put his arm around her. "Daddy, I'm not supposed to bring any stress into your life. But, there's so much that you don't know, or that you can't remember. I just don't know what to do."

Simon patted her shoulders. "I may not remember, but you can always talk to me about what's going on with you."

Resting her head on Simon's shoulder, Tiffany sighed again. "Alex and I are having problems. And, I've been trying to deal with it with my therapist, but it doesn't seem to be helping. I found out that he lied about something that he knew was extremely important to me. And when I found out about it, I wasn't in the best frame of mind to deal with it. And, I don't know if I can ever forgive him. I think I still love him, but I just can't trust him."

"There, there, dear. I'm going to step out on a limb and say that this must involve something along the lines of infidelity, am I correct?" Tiffany nodded, and Simon continued. "Well, since I am an attorney, I need to know something—do you have all of the facts?"

Simon's question was met with an awkward silence. "I see. Well, Tiffany, I know that matters of the heart aren't always so cut-and-dried, but unless you know everything about a situation, you really can't take rational measures. For every action, there is a reaction, and I'm sure that Alex knows the depth of hurt he has caused you. But, you need to examine your feelings for him, and what your marriage means to you. Only you can answer that."

Tiffany sniffled, and buried her head in her father's chest. "That's part of my problem, Daddy. I'm confused. I still love and care for Alex, but I just don't know if I can ever trust him again. And since we've been on the outs, I've met another man that's kind of taken my mind off my marital issues."

Simon stopped patting his daughter for a moment, and after a few moments, he continued with his parental comforting. "Really? And who might that be?"

Tiffany raised her head, and looked into her father's eyes. "His name is Vincent, Daddy. And he's absolutely wonderful. He's a talented artist, and he's only been in town for a little while, but he's thinking about making D.C. his home. Right now, he's staying down at the Grand Hyatt with his father." Tiffany smiled broadly. "And, Daddy, he comes from a really good family, too. You know them. The Cavanaughs. His father is named Edgar."

Simon's face dropped, and his eyes reddened. Cavanaugh? This was not supposed to happen, and Simon would be damned if his daughter would ever get involved with the likes of a Cavanaugh. Not even over his dead body, he thought, but his voice betrayed none of that turmoil.

"Well, dear. I understand that you're probably attracted to this young man, but you have to be mindful of the fact that you are still married.

"Alex seems to be a good man, and a good father. That's not easy to find, and can be even more difficult to duplicate. And he can provide a good future for you, too. He has goals, and aspirations, and would probably be a damned good mayor one day. I know you'd be a damned good first lady," Simon said with a wink.

Tiffany tried to smile, but couldn't. "I hear what you're saying, Daddy, and I believe you. But I can't help feeling like I do," Tiffany said.

"But you can help *what* you do, Tiffany. And if you're confused about where you are, my advice is not to do anything at the moment. Take no steps in either direction. Focus on you, your children, and your career, and see where that leads you." He kissed her forehead. "Now, you're going to listen to your old man, aren't you?"

"Yes, Daddy. I'll try. I'm sure you're right. I do have some very productive things to do. I don't know if I mentioned it to you or not, but I'd like to dedicate a memorial at the MLK Library in mother's name."

"What? Why would you do something like that?" Simon asked, before he realized that he had spoken.

Tiffany looked at him with a quizzical expression. "Why wouldn't I, Dad? I think she deserves to be remembered, don't you?"

Simon rubbed the bridge of his nose. "I'm sorry, dear. You'll have to forgive me. It's just that sometimes I forget that she's gone," he said, and he forced himself to sound weak and remorseful.

Tiffany rubbed his hand. "I understand. I'm sure that it must be difficult for you. I just want you to know that I realize that I should be channeling my energies elsewhere. I'm also trying to get refocused on my event-planning business. I even have an appointment with Sylvia Cavanaugh later on this week. She's interested in contracting my services for her annual holiday celebration."

"That's excellent," Simon said, as he continued holding his

daughter. Those damned Cavanaughs, he thought, and his mind jettisoned images of his wife and Edgar cavorting around behind his back. They tried to make a fool of him, and while Marjorie had paid her price, Edgar had gone free. But, no longer. Simon's anger was fueled to the point of near explosion, and he knew that it had to come to a flaming head. And this time, it would be Edgar's head that rolled.

CHAPTER 18

Thanksgiving at the Baxter residence was tense and a bit forced. It was as if all of the attendees didn't really want to be there, but had no place else to go.

Alex's father and Mrs. Owens joined Simon, Tiffany, Aunt Giselle, and Alex for a quiet dinner. Lisa had gone home to Atlanta for the holiday, and Fortune was in absentia. Alex had invited him, but was relieved when Fortune declined. It saved Alex from having to explain who he was to Tiffany. He really couldn't trust Fortune to be in Simon's company, whether Simon was incapacitated or not. Alex could envision Fortune carving the turkey, and then slicing Simon's neck.

Gerald didn't fare too much better in Simon's presence, since he blamed the man for the death of his eldest son, and the near death of Alex. Gerald was guarded, but kept a respectful distance between them. He and Mrs. Owens spent most of their time with the children, who, at almost seven months, were now raising their heads and trying to turn over. Gerald gave Simon little or no conversation.

As Tiffany had promised, she had curtailed her involvement with Vincent, but still hadn't warmed up to Alex. By the time dessert was served, Alex was more than ready to leave. But then the phone rang, and he was literally saved by the bell. He grabbed the cordless phone, and scurried into the privacy of his office. It was Lisa, breathless and extremely excited.

"What's up?"

"I've got the best news. Guess who called?"

"Look, Lisa. Get to it with a quickness, okay? I'm in no mood for the guessing game, you know what I mean?"

"Well, who peed on your turkey?" Lisa quipped, but Alex didn't even respond. "Anyway, it's Foody!" Lisa squealed. "He left me a message at my office, but it was really staticky. And it cut off before he could finish."

The blood rushed from Alex's head, and he dropped into his chair. "What? What do you mean?"

Lisa went on to explain that Foody had spent the last few months on a cargo ship, headed to the South Pacific. He had barely escaped the fire, and had managed to get out of the building before it collapsed. His leg had been hurt, but he was able to get farther down the docks, where he passed out on a ship. By the time he woke up, it had set sail for parts unknown, and he was considered a stowaway.

"He was on the water for weeks on end, and when he got a chance to call, collect of course, your numbers had been changed or disconnected," Lisa said.

Alex wanted to laugh and to cry. For so many months, he had carried around the burden of feeling responsible for Foody's death, and to know that he was alive lifted an extremely heavy burden off of his shoulders. Now that he knew Foody was among the living, Alex just wanted to kill him for not getting in touch sooner. Alex burst into peals of laughter.

"What? Damn, I'm glad he's okay. Where is he now?"

"I don't know."

"Can you trace the call? When's he coming back? Did he say what happened to the files?" Foody's resurrection was more than a glimmer of hope. He had the computer information that would prove that Alex hadn't been laundering funds.

"No, I can't trace the call, Alex, and I didn't get all of his information because the message got cut off. But I'm sure he'll call back soon. I told my secretary to accept any collect calls, and not to let him off the phone if he calls back. I even told her to book him a ticket from wherever he's at. Immediately. This is great news, right?" Lisa said, her voice positively singing.

"I can't believe it," Alex said. He was so happy he wanted to yell, "wheeee," and spin around in his chair like a gleeful child.

"I can't believe that he stowed away and they couldn't tell that they had an extra ton of cargo on board." Lisa laughed.

She and Alex laughed until they cried. It was such a relief. When Alex finally collected himself, he was able to ask an intelligent question. "He didn't say how we could get in touch with him or anything?" Alex asked, and wiped his eyes.

"No, you know Foody. I'm sure that he'll have major stories to tell when he does surface," Lisa said.

Alex glanced over at his bookcase, and his eyes focused on a picture of himself, Lisa, and Foody back in their college days. Suddenly, the world didn't seem like such a terrible place. "Damn, I'm so glad that he's okay. That's the best news I've had in months. Damn, Lisa. Thanks so much," Alex said.

"And, I have some other news for you, too," Lisa said. She went on to mention that a body had been found at Howard's house a few weeks ago.

"Why didn't you tell me? Was it Howard?" Alex asked, and his thoughts churned.

"That's why I didn't tell you. I didn't want you to get too excited. They matched the dental records, and it wasn't him. It was some guy named Wilton Royce. They estimated that his body had been there for at least two weeks before it was discovered."

Royce. The name rang no bells. But a dead body at Howard's house? It had to mean something. Alex thought about the time frame. Howard couldn't have killed him, because, according to Fortune, he was missing and presumed dead long before then.

Alex repeated the phrase that had almost become his mantra. "He must be connected to this somehow, Lisa."

"I know, Alex. Add his name to the growing list of suspects and culprits, right?"

"Right."

They continued laughing and chatting until Tiffany abruptly opened the office door, and interrupted their conversation.

"You're being downright rude, Alex. We do have guests," she said, with a glare.

Alex chuckled. "I'll call you tomorrow, Lisa," Alex said into the phone, and clicked the *off* button.

"Who was that?" Tiffany asked.

Alex looked at her with an incredulous expression. "Didn't you just hear me say, 'I'll call you tomorrow, *Lisa*'?"

"Humph. Why was it so important that you had to interrupt dinner, and run in here and shut your door?" Tiffany placed a defiant hand on her hip.

"I didn't think that you'd notice. But, anyway, I have some really good news. Foody's back."

Tiffany's face cracked. "Foody's back? And? Back from where? He's here and there, and all over the place. Why is that such a big deal?"

It came back to him that he had never told Tiffany about Foody and the role that he had played in taking down Simon's drug lab and saving both of their lives. Alex sighed when he caught the perturbed expression on Tiffany's face and thought about her asking him about the other things he hadn't told her about. Now certainly wasn't the time to bring anything else up.

"You're right. It's no big deal," Alex said. It was one of his happiest moments and he couldn't share it with his wife.

Tiffany shook her head. "You know, you get on my nerves about Lisa. I swear, whenever she calls or says something to you, you just trip out. Is that the real reason you have her staying here on our property? Is something going on between you two?"

The irony of Tiffany's words struck Alex. She had a lot of nerve, especially since she had intimated that she was capable of sleeping with another man. But to try to throw Lisa in his face? That was pure audacity. And Tiffany knew that.

So much had gone on between him and Lisa over the years, yet nothing at all intimate had ever occurred. And now, Tiffany, who had been attempting to flaunt her freedom in his face and punish him for his past indiscretions, now seemed to be a little jealous. That was something Alex had never considered. The only thing worse than a scorned woman was a jealous woman. And, above all, Lisa was the one female in Alex's life whom Tiffany had only recently been able to tolerate. If she was really jealous, Alex was now in a position he hadn't been in in months. To get some kind of response out of her. To basically pluck one of Tiffany's nerves.

"Of course not, Tiffany," Alex said, with a smirk. "Whatever would make you think that?" he winked, and brushed past his wife, leaving her with her mouth slightly agape.

SIMON HAD TAKEN quite a shine to his new assistant. He liked her style. She had recently returned from Europe, and was a graceful, curvaceous woman, and seemed to really have her act together. Yes, Simon was a bit smitten with Jessica Barnes.

Jessica had a take-charge attitude, and Simon liked that. After they had spoken that first day, she had outlined a set of plans to get Simon's business and personal life back in order. One of the first appointments Simon had Jessica schedule was a meeting with the general manager of the Grand Hyatt. If Alex was going to run for mayor, it would be the perfect place for campaign headquarters. It was centrally located and had wonderful amenities.

But Simon had ulterior motives. He figured the general manager would be so eager to get his business that he'd want to ensure that Simon had a full tour of the massive hotel. And that tour included the ballrooms, one of the guest rooms, and, at Simon's disingenuous request, the Presidential Suite.

The manager made arrangements with Edgar to have his quarters shown to an incognito Simon at 1:30 PM promptly. Simon knew that Edgar would be present, and made sure that Jessica would distract the manager, so that Simon would arrive unaccompanied.

When one of Edgar's men opened the door, Simon introduced himself, and stepped inside. The four other men drew their weapons, but Edgar, who was waiting by the balcony with a cigar in his hand, waved them down.

"Put those away, gentlemen," Edgar said. "That's no way to treat a guest. Simon, please sit down. I've been expecting you."

"That's good, Edgar. Because I think that it would be in poor taste if the hotel manager came up here, and I was either dead or dying. That would be such a shame, since I just came back from the dead and everything." Simon took a seat on the sofa, and Edgar followed suit.

"Funny, Simon. I thought you had amnesia," Edgar said, and puffed on his cigar.

Simon crossed his legs. "Oh, I do. But some things you never forget."

"I'm sure. Like how you killed Marjorie because you didn't want me to have her," Edgar said, and gnashed his teeth.

Simon squinted. "Now, that I'm a little hazy on. But, one thing I know for certain, and that I'm quite clear on, is that I don't want your damned son dating my daughter."

"*Your* daughter? Sounds like you're pretty sure of that," Edgar said, and wrinkled his forehead. "I recall a time when you weren't so sure."

"She is my daughter, just like Marjorie was my wife. You didn't get her, and you damned sure won't get Tiffany."

Edgar laughed, and blew a ring of smoke in Simon's face.

"I'm telling you, Edgar. Make this little issue go away. Or—"

"Or what? I didn't buy your wolf tickets then and I'm damned sure not buying them now." Edgar calmly rose to his feet. "Gentlemen, please show our guest to the door."

Simon stood, and coolly waved Edgar's smoke away. "You've been forewarned, Edgar. Now, this isn't the time or the place, but we'll get what's between us settled. Real soon."

"I'm looking forward to it, Simon. *Sto osservando in avanti ad esso.*"

CHAPTER 19

TIFFANY HELPED her father with his cummerbund and bow tie, and admired the way his tuxedo hung on his frame. It was almost as if she were preparing her child for his first date, and essentially, she was. Tiffany had been a little taken aback when Simon didn't ask Mrs. Bidwell to the affair. Instead, he asked Jessica to be his date, and she had graciously accepted.

Tiffany ran through her mental notes. She had given their nanny the week off between Christmas and New Year's, so she was waiting for Aunt Giselle to come and sit with the children. Tiffany was afraid that she might forget something, given how nervous she was about the event. As she thought about this evening, their first social event as a family since the accident, butterflies danced in her stomach, but Tiffany tried to stay even-keeled for her father's sake. Simon seemed calm and collected, except when he accidentally spilled black shoe polish on his gloves and insisted on washing and drying them in the basement laundry. Tiffany refused to let him do it, and she washed them herself.

It was one of the things that had made Tiffany nervous. She was a bit miffed that after she'd made a wonderful presentation, the only service Mrs. Cavanaugh had hired her for was procuring the valet-parking attendants and coat-check personnel. But it was a start, and she'd make sure that her people left a top-notch impression on Dame Cavanaugh.

Tiffany was especially tense because tonight she'd have to see Vincent while in the company of her husband. And while he'd assured her that he wasn't going to have a date, Tiffany knew that other women would be fawning over him. She didn't know how she was going to handle it.

And, then there was Alex. He had been a no-show all day, and since she had questioned him about his and Lisa's relationship, he had been distant and disinterested. And he was spending a lot of time in Lisa's apartment. The situation was really beginning to bother Tiffany, but she couldn't let him know it. But one thing was for sure. Lisa's presence on her property was coming to a screeching halt. If they wanted to engage in some little tawdry affair, they'd damn sure not do it under her roof. Tiffany would tell Alex that she wanted Lisa's ass gone by next week.

Tiffany was struggling to maintain the semblance of her marriage, but Alex had become indifferent. When she recommended that they wear similar outfits, he seemed irritated by the suggestion but reluctantly went along with it.

As she gazed at Alex's tuxedo and mask laid out on the bed, she tenderly stroked the lapel. She wondered if she was doing the right thing by staying with her husband.

SIMON LOVED IT when a plan came together. Spilling the polish had been his way of getting into the basement, to retrieve the

Cavanaugh jewel from its hiding place. Tiffany had foiled that, but then Simon, ever swift, figured that once they left for the affair, he'd act as if he'd forgotten something, like his watch or a cuff link, and double back to the Baxter house and then recover his prize. It was genius. And when he arrived at the gala of the season, he'd have everyone right where he wanted them. Ready to be skewered.

Tonight was going to be his night. For the first time in over twenty years, he'd be in the presence of all that represented good and evil in his life. Those damned Cavanaughs.

ALEX HAD SPENT THE DAY in Lisa's apartment. Lisa wasn't there, but since she'd left her car, it looked as if she were home. Alex knew that Tiffany was steaming. Because Lisa's family's company was opening an office in D.C., she had gone out with a realtor to locate either a house or a condo. But since it was New Year's Eve, Alex had expected her back home much earlier than this late hour.

Alex had milled around, until Fortune showed up. Fortune had seemed somewhat happy that Foody was alive, but less than enthusiastic when he found out that Foody would be returning to D.C. within the next month or so.

Though Fortune had been there for Alex ever since he had happened upon Simon's drug lab, they really hadn't spent a lot of time together. Or talked a great deal. But now that they had a quiet moment, it seemed like the perfect time to converse.

"What's on your mind, Alex? You seem a little down in the mouth," Fortune asked, and put his feet up on Lisa's desk.

"Female problems," Alex said, and stuck his head in Lisa's tiny refrigerator, and then cracked open a beer. "You want one?" Alex asked, and then regretted making the offer. Fortune was probably an alcoholic, and Alex didn't want to see him get drunk or enable him.

Fortune licked his lips and then wiped his mouth. "No thanks. I've, uh, kinda given that up for a good cause," Fortune said.

Alex thought about it. He hadn't seen Fortune take a drink or even smoke for weeks. Maybe even months. And he was much better kept than he had been when he'd first reentered Alex's life. His clothes were cleaner, and he even appeared to be brushing his teeth. "Word?" Alex asked. "I'm proud of you, Fortune. That's really cool." Alex slapped him five, and flopped down on Lisa's futon.

"Yeah, I'm tryin' to break some old habits. Plus, you said you got female problems. I got some, too."

Alex's left eyebrow rose. "You? Female problems? With who?"

Fortune kind of shrugged and glanced around the room.

"With Lisa?" Alex's head dipped with surprise. "Are you serious?"

"Yeah, I kind of dig her. I like her style," Fortune said. "She one of those bad-to-the-bone chicks, you know. And she can handle me."

Alex scratched his head. He had never, ever thought about those two together, but anything was possible. "Well, you should go for it, Fortune. I'm sure she'll let you know if you've got a chance."

"Oh, I'm gonna get that old girl, Alex. It's just a matter of time. I'm slowly wearin' her down with all of my charm," Fortune grinned, and revealed several gaps in his teeth.

Alex suddenly felt remiss in how he had treated Fortune. Fortune had stood with him, fought with him, and fought for him, and the least Alex could have done was look out for him. Yet, months after he had reentered Alex's life, Fortune was still scraggly and homeless, while Alex was living like the Crown Prince of Madagascar.

"I tell you what, Fortune. I want to help you. Next week, after the holiday, we're going to find you a place to live, get you to a good dentist, and hook you up with some new clothes. And get you a steady job."

"Word?"

"Word," Alex said.

"You know you don't have to do that. I'll be all right."

"I'm sure, but that's the least I can do, Fortune."

Fortune scratched his chin. "All right, that'll work. You know I don't turn down nothin' but my collar," he said. "Now, what's up with your female problems?"

Alex hunched his shoulders. "It's a long story, but let's just say that Tiffany still hasn't forgiven me. And I think that she's seeing some other guy."

Fortune scratched his neck. "You really think so? 'Cause, if you do, you know I'll go take him outta here like that," Fortune said with a pop of his fingers.

Alex sipped his beer and then shook his head. "You can't go around taking folks out, Fortune. That's how that damned Simon thought, remember? But, anyway, I'm just dealing with a whole bunch of shit right now. My marriage is crumbling, Simon is driving me crazy, and nothing seems to be going right, you know?"

Fortune reached over and shook Alex's shoulders. "You gotta get yourself together, little brother. You got too much goin' for yourself to be actin' like a sick puppy. You's a big dog now. So, if that's your woman, then go get your woman. And don't take no for no answer. From nobody. And don't let none of these big-ass bamas carry you like that and get your girl.

"And about Simon, man, forget that clown. If he's playin' a game, it's gonna come out. You know what they say, anything done in the dark come out in the light. Remember what I told you a while ago—every shut eye ain't sleep. Don't think for one minute that nigga's on the up-and-up. Don't sleep on him. But, whatever happens, you know I got your back. Simon ain't never gonna hurt you or yours no more.

"Now, if you got a date with yo' wife tonight, then get the hell up outta here. Go an' act like you know."

Alex poured the rest of his beer down his throat. "Thanks, Fortune."

"Anytime, bro. Anytime," Fortune said, and peeked out the window. "And you better hurry. I think your limo just pulled up."

AS HE RAN through his back door, Alex almost ran over Aunt Giselle, who was preparing to feed the children. He kissed his son and daughter, and ran upstairs, and then shaved, showered, and dressed in record time, while Tiffany sat quietly, with a slightly annoyed expression. She was already impeccably attired, in her black-velvet-and-satin beaded gown, and was sitting at her vanity, touching up her makeup. She was curiously quiet, and said nothing to him as he struggled with his tie. She merely gritted on him, and handed him his mask, and sashayed out of the room.

Alex watched her as she kissed the children, and said a brief good-bye to her aunt. Tiffany then wrapped her floor-length cognac-colored chinchilla fur around her shoulders, and grabbed her father's arm. They headed out the front door, and Simon escorted his lovely princess to her awaiting chariot.

SIMON POLITELY MET Jessica at her door, and she swept into the limo wearing a dark red satin gown and mink stole. After warm greetings, Jessica and Tiffany chatted about their outfits and masks, while Simon and Alex peered out of the windows. They traveled the short distance to the Cavanaugh estate and made small talk. From the street, the mansion could be seen illuminating the dark sky. Their stretch limo pulled into the circular driveway behind another limo, and they waited until their car reached the front entrance and one of the parking attendants opened the passenger door, letting the brisk December air rush in.

Tiffany and Jessica exited first, and then Simon and Alex. Just as the attendant was about to close the car door, Simon went into action. "Oh shoot. I forgot my watch," he said, and grabbed his left wrist.

Alex frowned. Something seemed fishy. "We can go back for it, Simon. That's not a problem."

Simon insisted that they go on to the festivities. "Why don't you all go in and get the place warmed up for me? I'll have the driver take me back, and I'll be back before you get in good."

"I'll ride back with you, Simon," Jessica said. "I wouldn't want to go in without my date."

Tiffany held her mask up to her face, and started walking toward the entrance. "Okay, Daddy. We'll see you in a few."

After they'd stepped away from the limo, Alex motioned for Tiffany to walk over to the front door. "I'm sorry, Tiff. I need to make a quick phone call." He watched the limo as it got stuck for a moment in the glut of cars that lined the driveway. Alex pulled his cell phone from his vest pocket and hit *speed dial,* for Lisa's number. "Lisa, I want you to get my children and Aunt Giselle out of that house. Right now. Simon's on his way back there, and I swear something's up."

THEIR LIMO DRIVER MADE IT BACK to the Baxter household in a few minutes, and Simon told Jessica to remain in the car and keep warm. He'd be back shortly.

Simon hustled into the house and quietly disarmed the alarm. He pulled his watch from his breast pocket, and went down the basement stairs, certain he'd quickly retrieve the gem, and get back to the party.

AS SIMON RUMMAGED behind the furnace, he pulled out a small black box, and smiled. He tapped the box against the concrete wall, and carefully removed a satin satchel.

"Gee, Simon, what's that?"

It was Lisa. She had arrived just as Simon dashed into the house. Alex had been right. Simon's SWAT-style actions seemed a little odd to her, so she followed him. And when she saw him crouching in the corner of the furnace room, her suspicions were confirmed. He was up to something.

"Lisa? Is that you?" Simon said. Before he turned around, he tucked the gem into his breast pocket.

"Turn around slowly, Simon," Lisa said, and when he did, he noticed that Lisa had a Glock tucked into her waistband.

"What's this all about? Why are you wearing a weapon? Especially with my grandchildren in this house. My daughter will have your head for this."

"Don't worry about your grandchildren, Simon. They're not here. I saw someone running toward this house, and I wasn't sure who it was."

"Now you know it's me, so you can go on back to your residence."

"Not so fast, Simon. What's in your pocket?"

"I don't have to answer to you. Move out of my way."

Lisa stood firm. "I'm not moving anywhere until you show me what you have. Or else."

"Or else, what? Listen, young lady, before you issue idle threats and approach people with a dangerous weapon, you may want to make sure you first have your safety off."

In the split second Lisa took her eyes off Simon and reached for her gun, he snatched it from her grasp. Simon sighed, and grabbed Lisa by the throat, and slammed her head against the concrete wall. She slid down the wall, her head slumped over to the side. Simon spoke to the unconscious Lisa. "Now, should I kill you for being so nosy, or for having such bad manners?"

"I wouldn't do either one of them if I was you, Moses," Fortune said, as he pointed a baseball bat at him. "Lisa! Lisa! Are you okay?" Lisa was unresponsive, and still slumped over.

"Moses? What are you talking about? What are you doing in here? Who are you?" Simon asked.

"Someone that knows you pretty well. I'm Fortune. Fortune

Reed. The same kid you tried to kill over fifteen years ago. Remember me now?" Simon's eyes flashed, but he said nothing. "See, I knew you was fakin' with that amnesia shit," Fortune said.

Simon pointed the gun at Fortune and tried to fire it, but he, too, had forgotten to release the safety. Fortune swung the bat, and hit Simon in the arm, and the blow sent the gun careening across the floor.

Fortune swung the bat again, but missed, and Simon caught it on the tip. He yanked it from Fortune's hands, and the two men struggled and fought as though their lives depended on the outcome. Which they did.

"You'll never live to tell about this shit, Fortune Whoever-you-are. I'm going to make sure of that."

Finally, Simon overpowered Fortune, and sent the thinner man crashing into the furnace. The blue flames from the burner cast a colorful hue on Fortune's face, as Simon brought the bat down on Fortune's wiry neck.

Satisfied that his two victims were clearly unconscious, Simon took the end of the bat and cracked the gas valve in the rear of the furnace, and fuel hissed as it escaped the hose. At the rate the vapors were filling the room, Simon knew that the house would probably explode in less than an hour. By that time, he'd be at the party, and oblivious of the tragedy that would've just occurred. Once again, he was simply brilliant.

Simon straightened his tux, and smoothed down his hair. "So long, Tweedledee and Tweedledum. I have a gala to attend."

CHAPTER 20

ALEX STRAIGHTENED his mask, and proceeded into the party with his wife. He was filled with anxiety, but steeled himself. The party was filled with movers and shakers, and he and Tiffany were greeted warmly by other guests.

The Cavanaugh's palatial home was on a grand estate, and the hostess, Sylvia Cavanaugh, was gracious and accommodating. After their coats were taken, Tiffany checked her appearance, and Alex noticed that she seemed a little anxious.

"What's the matter, Tiffany?" he asked, as he surveyed the attendees. He knew he had an agenda, but he was beginning to think that his wife had one, too.

"Nothing. I just want to make sure I look okay."

"You look perfect," Alex said, and glanced down at his watch. "You think we should wait here for Simon and Jessica? They should be back shortly, don't you think?"

Tiffany glanced around the foyer, the lights illuminating her

vibrant mask. "You can wait here if you'd like, Alex. I came to celebrate, so I'm going to go check on my personnel and mingle." She
pointed toward one of the rooms. "I'll be in there. Find me when
my father arrives."

She turned on her heel, and sauntered away. A jazz combo
played in the background, and photographers snapped pictures.

Alex tried Lisa's number again, but the call went straight to voice
mail. He was beginning to worry, when someone grabbed his elbow.

Even behind her elaborate mask, Alex recognized Winnie Sutton. She was standing next to an older gentleman, who was leaning on a cane.

"Happy New Year, Alex," she said, and embraced him. She
nodded toward the gray-haired man standing beside her, and introduced him as her husband Jake.

Alex greeted Jake, and tried to make small talk with Winnie,
who steered the conversation toward Simon.

"How's Simon doing? Is he coming tonight?" Winnie asked.
"You know, I went to visit him at the hospital, but he wasn't re-
ceiving any visitors that day."

Alex nodded. "He should be here shortly, Winnie."

"I guess that means that he's feeling better, huh?" Winnie
paused, and placed a hand on Alex's arm. "Has his memory returned yet?" Alex shook his head, and Winnie kept talking.

"Tsk, tsk. What a shame. And to think that he had so many
things on his drawing board. But I understand that you might be
interested in keeping his legacy alive. Is that correct? Are you seriously thinking about running for mayor, Alex?"

Alex had expected polite conversation and chitchat tonight, but
he'd never guessed that he'd be hit with this question before he'd
even progressed beyond the foyer.

"Well, I, uh, let's just say that I'm, uh—" Alex stammered.

At that moment, Simon walked in and interrupted the conversation.

"Good evening, everyone," he said, his voice upbeat and robust. "Did I miss anything?"

Winnie eyed Simon, and extended her hand. "Good evening, Simon."

"Hello, um," Simon snapped his fingers. "I've seen your picture in the paper. It's Sutton, right? Winnie Sutton."

Winnie nodded, and Alex could see that she was not moved.

"You'll have to forgive me, Mrs. Sutton. My memory's just not where it should be at the moment. Let me introduce you to my date. This is Ms. Jessica Barnes," Simon said.

"Charmed," Winnie said, and her eyes trailed down to Jessica's neck.

Jessica looked glamorous in her blood red gown and elegant necklace. It was a stunning piece that even captured Alex's attention. He was going to comment on it, but Simon interrupted again.

Turning toward Alex, Simon adjusted his stance. "Where's your wife, son? I'm sure she's in there rubbing elbows, like you should be doing." He winked, and turned to Winnie. "Now, if you'll excuse us, we're going to go in and mingle. Alex, are you coming?"

The three entered the room, and Simon's presence immediately caught the attention of Sylvia Cavanaugh and her family. Simon greeted some of his constituents, while Alex excused himself to go find Tiffany.

DESPITE THE THRONGS of disguised partygoers, Alex quickly spotted Tiffany from across the room. She was sipping champagne and chatting in a group. Making his way toward her, a debonair Alex worked the room, catching up with old political cronies and business associates. Tiffany noticed that her husband was coming toward her, but she had placed herself in a prime location to watch Vincent from a safe distance. He hadn't brought a date and was flirting with every unattached woman at the party. Tiffany tried to appear inconspicuous, but failed. She knew that he had seen her, but hadn't even nodded in her direction. She wanted to corner him and ask him just what the hell he was doing, but she didn't have the nerve. Eventually, she got some, and when Alex finally reached her, she sent him off to get her some hors d'oeuvres. She knew her time was short, and if she was going to talk to Vincent, she had to do it now.

Just as Tiffany was about to approach Vincent, Sylvia and her daughter-in-law Kim cut her off, and asked to be introduced to Jessica.

Tiffany reluctantly agreed, and as Sylvia twirled her around, Vincent faded from her sight. Jessica was standing by the jazz band, while Simon was off hobnobbing. Sylvia and Kim guided Tiffany to Jessica, and Tiffany quickly introduced them. Before the formalities were completed, Tiffany made a graceful departure. She was bent on giving Vincent a piece of her mind, discretion be damned.

She caught up with him in the great hall, where his eyes were riveted on some gyrating heifer in a tight red dress. She stood in front of him and tried to obstruct his view.

"Vincent, why are you doing this?" Tiffany asked, as he glanced over her shoulder at the woman in red. "Why are you treating me like this?"

"Why am I doing what? How am I treating you? I shouldn't be your concern. Aren't you here with your husband?"

"Yes, but you knew that I had a husband, Vincent. I never lied to you about that," Tiffany said.

Vincent was fixated on the crimson bombshell. "Nope, you never lied. But, you know what? You didn't have to. You know you aren't going to leave your husband. But, I'm not Joe Sausagehead. I can find better things to do with my time besides wait for you."

Tiffany couldn't believe her ears. This wasn't the patient, compassionate, understanding Vincent she had caught feelings for. "What? How can you say that to me? You act like I led you on or something childish like that."

"No, you never led me on, but you know how to play games. I'm saying, either you do me or you do him. But, it won't be me and him. I'm not having it."

Tiffany swallowed deeply, and it became extremely warm under her mask. "I can't make a decision like this right now."

Vincent took his drink and downed it. "Then, I'll make it for you. Good-bye, Tiffany," he said, and turned to walk away.

Tiffany grabbed his arm, but he pulled from her grasp. "Wait, wait, Vincent. Don't leave. I'll prove it to you. Come on. We'll find an empty guest room upstairs. Please."

CHAPTER 21

SIMON WAS having a sensational evening. He was being showered with adoration and support, and things had fallen into place even better than he had hoped. He had effectively disposed of Lisa and Fortune with minimal effort. That was an unforeseen benefit. But Simon beamed as he extensively observed his protégé, Alex, working the room like a seasoned pro. Simon was elated and proud. Alex was doing well, but Simon was bothered by the fact that Tiffany was fretting behind that damned Vincent Cavanaugh. Simon knew Alex wasn't fully aware of his wife's activities, but Simon knew the deal. That bit of information might come in handy at a later date. For now, he had all the pieces in his masterful chess game on the same board, and Simon was sure to have checkmate tonight.

When Simon returned with a drink for Jessica, she appeared a little flustered. When he questioned her about it, she took the glass of sherry and then touched the ruby pendant. "Let's just say that this jewel of yours is garnering all types of attention. Sylvia Cavanaugh came over and practically removed it from around my neck."

Simon smirked, but tried to be sensitive. "There, there, Jessica. I'm sure that Madame Cavanaugh wasn't only admiring your jewels, but your whole outfit. And the sensational way you look in it."

Jessica smiled and sipped her cordial. "I guess. But I felt a little outnumbered. But that's another story."

"For another time, I suppose?" Simon asked, and stroked her chin.

For now, it was just a matter of time before the Cavanaughs played their hand. Simon had known that when they spotted the jewel, it was going to be on. But Simon was prepared, as he always was. That gem was the cornerstone of that family, and now he was going to use it to ensure that they self-destructed because of it.

Simon's assessment was truly on point. Within moments of returning to Jessica's side, the Cavanaughs requested that he, and the gem, join them in the library.

IT WAS THE MOMENT Simon had waited years for. He'd had possession of the real stone all of those years, and they never knew it. When they led him into the library filled with huge men in dark suits, Simon was ready. Harrison, Edgar, and their sons were all present, and anxious to draw Simon's blood. When Harrison questioned Simon about the jewel, Simon played his trump card.

"Edgar gave it to me. He thought he could buy my wife with it," Simon said, and the room went up in a fury.

Of course, Edgy denied it. And when Harry's son Joey examined it, Harry smashed a heavy lead-crystal decanter down on it, and it shattered all over the conference table that they were seated around.

Simon's blood pressure threatened to blow off the top of his head, but he calmed down quickly. Although he had been taken by that damned Jules the jeweler, his mind instantly clicked. There was no better defense than a good offense, and if the Cavanaughs had thought he had their jewel, then that meant that they now knew they didn't have the real one either. Whoever had the jewel had done Simon a favor, and though his revenge had not gone off as he had planned, Simon still felt avenged. The fact that he knew that the Cavanaughs didn't have any clue as to where their precious heirloom was was satisfying enough for him. This was turning out better than Simon could ever have imagined.

"Well, Simon. My brother gave you a fine piece of glass for your wife's honor. I guess he didn't think too highly of your dear Marjorie," Harry said, and glared at Simon.

Simon shrugged. "I still think that I got the better end of the deal, Harry."

Harry sniffed, and motioned for Simon to go. "Consider yourself dismissed, Simon. I have no further use for you."

Simon gloated, but left. His work was done. Harry and Edgy were back at odds, and certain to cancel out each other. And Simon was walking away unscathed. He was always a winner. And always would be.

THEY KISSED, PASSIONATELY licking each other's lips and sucking tongues. Tiffany was so turned on that she was having difficulty breathing. When she felt Vincent's swelling arousal, she rubbed her taut body against his.

She and Vincent had found a small guest room upstairs, and wasted no time groping each other. Vincent pushed Tiffany down on the double bed, and began unzipping her gown. Her shoulders were almost exposed when there was a loud bang on the door.

"Who's in there?" a man asked. His voice was thick, with a heavy New York accent.

Tiffany nearly jumped out of her skin. She hopped off the bed, pulled her dress back over her shoulders and started straightening her hair. "My husband could've sent someone to look for me," she whispered. "Please, don't say anything."

Vincent leaned back on the bed and watched Tiffany panic. "Fuck him. I'm not scared of him," he said, with an amused expression. "Who are you?" Vincent yelled toward the door, and the blood drained from her face as she headed for the closet.

"Vincent? Is that you?" The man asked. "Your father needs to see you. Right now."

Two of the massive goons from downstairs burst into the room, and grabbed Vincent, while Tiffany cowered by the closet door.

"What the hell is this all about?" Vincent yelled. "Who are you? Get your goddamned hands off of me!"

"You'll see. Just come on," the other hulking figure said.

As he was being led out of the room, he glanced back over his shoulder at Tiffany. "Don't worry, sweetie. I'll be back in a couple of minutes," Vincent said, and puckered his lips at her.

CERTAIN THAT THEY WERE GONE, a twitchy Tiffany collected herself, and headed back to the party. That had been a close call, and she had no idea why she had done something so stupid. It was careless and reckless, and inexcusable. Maybe that was how Alex felt. Foolish and irresponsible. Now, she felt even worse. Thank God Alex hadn't come looking for her. She had to get back to him and cover her tracks before some other near-tragic event occurred.

IT WAS ALMOST MIDNIGHT when Tiffany sidled up to Alex and hugged him as if she was actually glad to see him.

"Hello, darling. I was wondering where you were," Alex said. He caught the next waiter and grabbed two glasses of champagne. "They're getting ready to do the countdown."

Tiffany grabbed the glass and took a long sip. "Oh, I was around. You know, checking on my employees and catching up with old friends and what not." She glanced around. "Where are Father and Jessica?"

"Here we are," Simon said. With Jessica draped on his arm, he was looking quite content. "Just in time to bring in the New Year with my loved ones." Simon and Jessica lifted their glasses as the countdown began.

"Five—Four—Three—Two—One! Happy New Year!" The crowd roared, while horns and noisemakers blew and gold-metallic balloons and streamers were released from the ceiling.

As the band played "Auld Lang Syne," Alex reached to kiss his wife, and instead of giving him a peck, she actually kissed him. For a moment, the world was shut out, and Tiffany looked at him with watery eyes, and they just held each other. She buried her face in his chest and clung to him as though she hadn't seen him in years.

"Isn't that sweet," Jessica said, touching her now bare neck.

Simon nodded. "I'll say. That's the right way to start the New Year."

SHORTLY AFTER THE MIDNIGHT festivities concluded, Lisa and Fortune crashed the party and hunted Alex down. The attendants at the door had refused to let them in, but they sneaked in anyway, and found Alex, who had gotten separated from Tiffany, Simon, and Jessica.

They cornered their startled friend and told him that Simon had tried to kill them. Or, at least that's what they thought.

"When? What happened?" Alex asked. Simon had been buzzing around all evening, being his congenial self. He certainly hadn't seemed like someone who had attempted murder earlier that evening. But, then again, they were talking about Simon. How else would he be acting besides unaffected? "Really? Are you sure?"

Lisa and Fortune glanced at each other. "Yeah, uh, we're sure," Lisa said. "I've got a lump on the back of my head that says so."

"I know a lot has gone down, but this doesn't fit. Why would he try to kill you? For what purpose?"

"I'm not sure," Lisa said. "All I know is that I came across Simon snooping around your basement, and when I woke up, Fortune was carrying me out of there. Gas fumes were everywhere."

"What? Where are the children? Aunt Giselle? Did you get them out? Are they okay?" Alex asked, and turned, as if ready to bolt out the door.

"They're fine. But, no thanks to Simon," Fortune said.

"I sent them to her house when you asked me to, thank goodness," Lisa said.

"Yeah, well, I know he tried to kill me, too," Fortune said. "But, he just knocked my ass out, an' expected the gas to either smother us or blow us up. An', I know he's been fakin' all of this time."

Alex rubbed his face. "Really? Did he say anything to incriminate himself?"

"No, uh, not really," Fortune said. "But it's a feeling I got."

Alex exhaled, and balled his fists up by his side. "We've had that feeling for a while now, but it's still not proof of anything. Damn. All of this happened when he went back to my house? I knew he was up to something. But what was he doing there?"

"He got something out of your basement. What, I don't know. But it must've been pretty important," Lisa said.

"What could it have been? I thought you went over my house with a fine-toothed comb."

"I did. But I guess I just missed something."

"Or maybe he planted it there after he moved in," Fortune said.

This was yet another mysterious piece of the puzzle, and thinking about it made Alex's head hurt. They still had nothing more concrete than they'd had before. Simon, with his wily, Teflon-coated self, had done his dirt, and slipped away unsullied. Alex was so incensed and absorbed in their conversation that he didn't notice that the music's volume had been brought down, and that Sylvia Cavanaugh was speaking.

"I'm so tired of this shit," Alex said, his voice wavering with anger. "Simon always does just enough to get what he wants, but never enough to get caught. Damn! I just want to go find him and beat the truth out of his ass."

"Well, there he is, tiger. Let's go get him," Fortune said, and pointed to the podium on which Sylvia stood. With Tiffany and Jessica on either side, Simon stood to the right of Sylvia, his white teeth beaming through his mask. The crowd exploded with applause as she announced that they had raised almost one hundred thousand dollars for their charity, but Alex noticed very little of this. He focused his eyes on Simon, and didn't move.

After the applause died down, Alex watched as Simon made his way to the podium and then grabbed the microphone. "Very nice, Sylvia. Very well done," Simon said, and raised his mask. "Now, I hope that you'll allow me to beg your indulgence for a moment and digress. I'd like to thank all of you who have supported me over the years, although I'm kind of memory challenged these days." The crowd responded courteously, and Simon continued.

"Although I'm unable to adequately continue my tenure in public office, nothing brings me greater joy than to announce that my son-in-law, Alexander Baxter, is going to run for mayor of our fair city. Alex! Come on up here, son!"

A bewildered Alex exchanged glances with Lisa and Fortune, and stood still. He was shocked that Simon had put him on the spot like this, and Alex realized that his options were few. In a split second, he made a decision that Simon would've been proud of. He was going to play this role to the hilt. If it took everything that he had, he'd beat Simon at his own game.

Armed with a renewed determination, Alex slowly made his way to the mic. The band played a very upbeat tune, and the entire audience seemed to be in concert with Simon's announcement. Alex smiled, and placed his hand over the mic. "I know what happened at the house, Simon. Lisa and Fortune told me that you tried to kill them."

"Lisa and who? I don't know what you're talking about, Alex. I did no such thing. Frankly, when someone accosts you, and she's armed with a gun, and then someone else comes after you with a weapon, it's normally called self-defense."

"Why didn't you tell me about it?" Alex asked through gnashed teeth. "You've been in here acting like nothing's been going on, while all of this occurred."

"I didn't bother you because I didn't want you to worry. I called the police, just to be on the safe side. And face it, if there was any problem with a gas leak, it probably came when that boy was swinging that bat at me. He probably hit a pipe or something."

"Oh, really, Simon? I didn't mention anything about any gas."

Simon sneered and then shrugged. "Oh, um, that's what the police told me later, son. But, someone from the gas company fixed that." Simon smirked, and then narrowed his eyes at Alex. Simon waved, and smiled at the crowd. "Smile for the cameras, son. And for your wife over there," Simon said, and turned Alex in Tiffany's direction. She was actually smiling. "And if you want her back, you'll play ball. Can't you see? She wants to be the mayor's wife."

Simon swatted Alex on the back. "Face it, Alex. It's a done deal. Now that you're officially a candidate, your whole life has become a matter of public record. And I'd hate for any skeletons to come flying out of your closet. Like for instance, any financial impropri-eties. Hmmm, very interesting. Now, if you just play the game, and act like you know, we'll get along fine. But, if you choose not to, well, then my little memory might just come back, and I might find myself remembering those little things like getting stabbed with a knife." Simon smirked and again whacked Alex on the back, like a rowdy politician.

"Welcome to the wonderful world of politics, son. But I've got your back. Always remember that."

CHAPTER 22

ALEX AWOKE the next morning with a splitting headache and belching up day-old liquor through hot pipes. All he could think about was getting water into the Sahara Desert that was his mouth. Hungover from an overdose of heady accolades and excessive drink, Alex cracked his eyes open, and blinked, trying to figure out where he was. Seeing the light passing through venetian blinds, he realized that he had passed out on the sofa in his home office, still fully dressed in his tuxedo and shoes.

He touched his face, and felt the leathery couch pattern pressed on his skin. He wiped the corners of his eyes and yawned. Struggling to sit up, Alex cringed at the sound of bells ringing in his head. They sounded eerily like the noisemakers from last night's ringing in of 1993. He dropped his head and cupped his ears.

Simon had hinted that he was faking amnesia, in his slick, contrived way, but he had not outright admitted it. Alex had been completely thrown off guard by Simon's public announcement that Alex was going to run for mayor. Whatever behind-the-scenes moves Simon had planned, the consequences were now going to be played out in a very public arena.

It would be just as Simon had said. Now that Alex was officially running for office, his life was going to be under a microscope. And that's probably just how Simon wanted it.

Making his way over to his mini-fridge, Alex guzzled down two plastic bottles of spring water he got from it, before slumping behind his desk. He picked up a pen and a piece of paper, and wrote Simon's name, and drew a huge circle around it. Then, he arranged every person and event that had occurred in his life since he had known Simon and tried to connect them using "what-if" scenarios.

What if Simon had contacted Howard after the accident, and Howard had helped him convalesce? It would make sense. Since Howard was playing both ends against the middle, he would've helped Simon. And, if the Cavanaughs found out, that would've sealed Howard's fate. It was beginning to click.

The other body at Howard's house? Probably someone who was helping Howard take care of Simon. And that person wound up dead because Simon was finished with him and his services. Alex jotted down some dates. They seemed to coincide with the time frame of Simon's reappearance.

Alex scratched his head. The timing of Simon's reappearance might reveal something, too. He thought back. There were the deaths of those drug dealers. But they were peons compared to Simon. But perhaps their deaths, as Fortune had said, signaled that the Cavanaughs were ready to take over the city's drug market. That would have been reason enough for the egomaniacal Simon to return.

How, Alex thought, did he himself play in all of this? By reappearing, Simon had made a very dangerous move, especially knowing that Alex knew who he really was. Simon's bravado was supported by something. He knew that Alex wasn't in a position to expose him. Why? Because he had no proof. And what proof Alex had, only implicated Alex.

He chuckled and shook his head. "That's why Simon came back when he did," he said. "And he probably sent those pictures as a diversion."

How could he not have seen it before? Perhaps he should have gotten drunk sooner. It had brought a level of clarity to his mind that he'd never had stone sober.

THE HOUSE WAS UNUSUALLY QUIET as Alex stuck his head out of his office. He climbed the stairs, careful not to make any noise. The door to Simon's bedroom was cracked open, and Alex peeked in to find it vacant. He continued down the hall to his and Tiffany's bedroom, and he nudged the door open, to find Tiffany buried beneath the covers, snoring loudly.

He grabbed a pair of jeans, a copper-colored rugby turtleneck, and some underwear, and headed for the bathroom down the hall. He quickly showered, and was on his way over to Lisa's when the aroma of brewing coffee wafted from the kitchen. His nose led him in that direction.

Wearing one of his long-sleeved oxford shirts, and with her hair sticking out in various directions, Tiffany was leaning against the counter, studying the hot stream pouring into the carafe.

Alex thought about how good she looked, even with smudgy, day-old makeup on. The sight of her shapely legs still made him weak. "Good morning, Tiff," Alex said, and she instantly brought a finger to her lips.

"Shhhh," she said through slitted eyes. "Not so loud, okay?"

"I guess you tied one on, too, huh?"

Tiffany grabbed two mugs from the cabinet, and filled them up to the rim. "I think I tied two on," she said, and handed Alex one

of the cups. She took a massive gulp from her cup, and tipped toward the doorway, drops of coffee spilling on the floor. "I hope
you want yours black this morning."

"Gee, thanks," he said, and wished she had left a little room in
the cup for some cream and sugar. "Um, do you have any plans for
the day?"

Tiffany rubbed her eyes and yawned. "I'm going to get the
children, later on. I was supposed to do brunch with Lily and
some of our friends, but I think I'll pass. Right now, the only thing
I want to do is chew on some BCs, chase that with some Alka-
Seltzer, and sip this coffee. And go back to bed." She blinked and
then squinted at Alex. "I take it you're going out? Well, don't forget that you're supposed to be meeting with Daddy this afternoon
to discuss your strategy. I think he said four o'clock, but you know
how he is about promptness." She placed a gentle hand on his
shoulder. "Congratulations, Alex. I think you really deserve it."

ALEX POURED HIS COFFEE into a travel mug, and threw on a black
skullcap and Triple F.A.T. goose down jacket. The sky was clear
and it was bitingly cold, and the few steps to Lisa's studio seemed
like a mile-long stretch.

Alex knocked on the door, and after a few moments, a groggy
Lisa finally called out to him.

"Wait a minute," she said, and Alex rubbed his hands against
the insulated cup.

Lisa finally answered, clasping her robe closed. Her hair was
standing all over her head, and she looked as if she was barely
awake. Alex pushed his way through the door and removed his hat.
"Damn, girl. Don't you know it's freezing out there?" He nearly
stumbled over a pair of black brogans, and he cut his eye at Lisa.

"Oh, I'm sorry. Did I interrupt something?" Alex overheard
the sound of running water in the bathroom, and his eyes flashed.

"Shut up, Alex. It's not what you think," Lisa said as she shut the door.

Alex pointed at her gaping robe. "I think I just interrupted your groove, sis."

It had been so long since Alex had had sex that he'd forgotten that was a natural activity. "Don't let me CB any more than I have. Give me a call when your company leaves."

"Company? I ain't no company," Fortune said as he emerged from the bathroom. His lean chest was bare, and he was wearing a pair of Lisa's too short, too baggy, sweatpants.

Had the world gone mad? Alex looked at each of them, and then burst into laughter. "You've got to be kidding," he said, and nearly snorted.

"Shut up, Alex," Lisa said. "And don't be so loud. Nothing happened last night. We came in here and started doing tequila shots with Corona chasers. We just had too much to drink."

"Way too much," Fortune chimed in, and pulled a Hilliard Institute sweatshirt over his head. "I hadn't had a taste in a minute, so you know I was tore up from the floor up."

Alex shuddered. "You two must think I'm stupid or something. You mean to tell me you just drank yourselves into a stupor? Yeah, right."

"After the stunt you pulled last night, I'm surprised we both didn't get more than drunk," Lisa said, and she whacked Alex in the stomach and then dashed into the bathroom. "I can't believe that you're actually going to run for mayor. That blows my mind," she said, and shut the door.

"She blows my mind," Fortune whispered. "I think I'm really gonna need that crib you promised me."

Alex looked at Fortune and shook his head. "I'll make sure we get to it this week, I promise." He tilted his head toward the bathroom door. "I've got it under control, Lisa," he said in her direction. He looked at Fortune. "I hope you two have whatever's going on here under control, too."

THINGS SETTLED DOWN after Alex regained his composure and a fully dressed Lisa appeared from the bathroom. He was then able to share his revelations with his friends, who were in concert with his theories.

"That's pretty good, Alex," Lisa said. "I was thinking along the same lines myself."

"I haven't figured everything out yet, but I think I'm going in the right direction. I want him to think that I'm going along with his program, so that he'll get cocky and maybe slip up. The more static I give him, the more he's going to squeeze me," Alex said, and sipped his now cold coffee.

"Now, if I can get him real confident again, he's going to focus all of his energy and attention on this election. That's his forte. And trust me, he's chomping at the bit. He's even got a campaign meeting scheduled for me this afternoon. He's intent on me becoming mayor. And my goal is to get something on him that's going to prevent that from ever occurring."

"Sounds like a plan, Alex," Fortune said. "But, you know what you're dealing with. You've gotta build a better mousetrap to catch Simon. Shoot, forget a mousetrap, you gotta get a rat trap for his ass. He'll gnaw his way through any other contraption."

"You have such a colorful way with words, Fortune," Lisa said, with her face twisted with sarcasm. "You're under the gun now, Alex. With that election scheduled for April, you only have a few months to pull this off. And look how long it's taken us to get here."

"I know. But, I'm banking on Foody being back by then, and he'll be able to clear me of those online transactions."

Lisa nodded, and Alex continued. "Okay, so that gets me off the hook. But, it won't necessarily implicate Simon. That's what I have to focus on now. Finding something illegal that he's done that he can't wiggle out of. Something in his past. Something like—"

"Like what? When he had his old lady killed?" Fortune asked. "There's no one around that knows he ordered that hit. Those dudes are long gone, and we all know that I can't testify to anything."

When Fortune had been a child, he'd participated in a scam that led to Simon's wife Marjorie's death. He ran out in front of her car, and when she swerved to avoid hitting him, she hit a parked car. Some hoods, working under Simon's direction, beat her to death, and made her injuries look like the result of the accident.

"I know," Alex said. "I thought about that. We can't prove that just like we can't prove that he ordered the hit on you that killed my brother."

"All that points back to Blinky, now," Fortune said.

"What about Winnie's husband? Alex, Fortune told me that Simon was behind her husband's getting beaten and robbed. All because Simon wanted her out of the way so that he could get the vote on his precious stadium pushed through," Lisa said.

"That's right, but again, that'll go right back to Blinky," Fortune said. "Simon never got his hands dirty like that."

"Damn!" Alex exclaimed. "It seems like every path we take, Simon's already blocked it off." He stood up, and walked toward the window, and stared at his home. "Simon's good, but he's not perfect. He's slipped up somewhere, somehow, and I have to figure it out."

"Tick-tock, my brother," Fortune said, and nodded toward the wall clock. "Don't talk about it, be about it."

CHAPTER 23

LATER THAT AFTERNOON, Alex could barely focus as Simon steamrolled through his campaign plans. They were gathered in Alex's office, and with Jessica scribing, Simon detailed how he was going to make Alex a winner as his unofficial campaign manager.

"Identify the competition and eliminate them. That'll be my job. Any formidable opponent has already made his intentions known, and so far, we only have Smalls and that self-serving Councilman Monty Montgomery. Diffusing their campaigns will be as simple as that," Simon said, and snapped his fingers.

"We'll start working on your advertising campaign, and get you some public appearances scheduled. I'll get you the best PR firm in the area. Whichever that is," Simon said, and motioned for Jessica to underscore that thought. He was pacing, while Jessica was perched on the edge of the sofa, and Alex was seated behind his desk, with his chin in his hand.

Simon droned on, and Alex's thoughts drifted to Tiffany. She was gone by the time he'd returned home, and she hadn't returned yet. It was past five, and Alex wondered where she was.

Then, he thought about Lisa and Fortune getting busy. A familiar ache crept down his loins, and he realized why he was so envious. It had been months since he and his wife had made love. And when she'd made her insidious remark about sleeping with someone else, it had made sense. She probably was out there now screwing some other guy.

He made it through the meeting, but not without Simon noticing his distraction. When he questioned Alex about it, Alex tried to gloss over it, but Simon honed right in.

"Hmph. You seem like a man who's got a lot on his mind, Alex. You should be floating on a cloud, yet you seem kind of dejected." Simon glanced at the clock, and it was after six. "Your professional life is about to soar—could it be a personal matter that has you a little troubled?"

Alex twisted his jaw and pokered his face. "Not at all, Simon. Not at all."

Simon reached into his breast pocket and pulled out a pipe. It wasn't his old fraternity pipe, but a nice ivory one that Alex hadn't seen him with. In fact, it was the first time since Simon had reappeared that Alex saw him attempt to smoke. "For some reason, I've been craving a puff," Simon said, as he practically read Alex's mind. "But, anyway, I'm glad to hear that your family life is okay. And, I told you that Tiffany would be elated if you ran for office." Simon prepared his pipe by stuffing in a bit of tobacco, and lighting it. "And, that's a good thing. You have a lovely wife, and she was getting an awful lot of attention last night from a lot of gents. But, especially from that Vincent Cavanaugh. She says that he reminds her of that fellow she used to see in college. I think she said his name was Sid." Simon scratched his face and puffed, a sly smile crossing his lips. "Yes sir, the last thing you want to happen is for some amorous young man to pick up on her dissatisfaction, fill her head with a bunch of nonsense, and ultimately mar your image. Believe that."

Vincent Cavanaugh? Alex didn't even know who that was. But to know that he reminded Tiffany of Sidney, the beast that had tried to rape her, caused his thoughts to jumble, while his rage simmered. Simon's glibness had unearthed a caveman element in Alex. He was furious at the thought of another man touching his wife. Though he had initially dismissed Tiffany's comment about seeing another man, now it kind of stood to reason. He could barely wait to confront her about it, but he played it cool.

"That's the least of my concerns, Simon. When I'm named mayor, my wife will be right by my side. You can believe *that*."

BY THE TIME Tiffany and the children arrived home, it was well after seven. Alex was alone, but still seething, as he mindlessly stared at the television screen.

Simon and Jessica had decided to go to dinner, and Alex spent his moments mulling over Simon's innuendo. With his jaws tight, he helped put the children to bed, but could hardly contain himself until they were tucked in before he began questioning her about where she'd been.

"Don't even go there, Alex. You don't have a right to ask me about my comings and goings. I thought we had established that already." She pushed past him, and walked into the hallway.

"I have every right. You're my wife, damnit."

"So?"

"I want to know who the hell Vincent Cavanaugh is."

"Who?" Tiffany asked. Her tone was innocent, but the color had drained from her face.

"You heard me. Vincent Cavanaugh. I understand you were getting pretty chummy with him last night."

Tiffany raised an eyebrow. "Oh, Vincent? I don't know what

you're talking about. Now, if you don't mind, I'd like to go get some rest."

"Not so fast," Alex said, and grabbed her arm. "Don't try to play me stupid. You've been coming and going as you please, keeping all kinds of inappropriate hours. And now that our lives are really going to be under public scrutiny, I'd appreciate knowing if you're out there catting around. I want to know if you're sleeping with this guy, because you're damned sure not sleeping with me."

Tiffany pulled away, and eyed Alex with a defiant look. "And I'm not going to. You blew that, Alex. And, and if you want to know the truth—"

"Yeah, I want to know the truth, Tiffany."

"It's none of your damned business."

"You are my business."

"Fine. If you really want to know, I have been sleeping with Vincent. And it's been incredible."

Alex's face dropped, and he punched the wall, dangerously close to where Tiffany was standing. Tiffany shrieked as the impact from his knuckles left an imprint and shook the wall. He grabbed her by her wrists and shook her. "You're lying. I don't believe you."

Tiffany's eyes flashed, and she jerked her head back. "I don't care what you believe. Vincent and I have been having each other for weeks now. Everywhere and in every way possible."

Alex's face crumbled and he dropped her hands. "You make me ill," he said, and turned away.

TIFFANY WATCHED HER HUSBAND as he walked into the guest room and slammed the door. Even as the words had fallen from her lips, she couldn't believe what she was saying.

The lies took wings and flew. She wanted to hurt him, she really did, and now that she had, she wished that she hadn't. The look in his eyes had said it all. She had hurt him more deeply than she had planned.

She didn't rest too well that night. After a steaming hot Jacuzzi bath, her muscles were relaxed, but her mind was restless. Though she tried not to listen for him, Alex was eerily silent behind his closed door. When Anya cried, she heard him go to their daughter, and stay with her until her cries ceased. Suddenly, she felt worse about what she had said. She thought about going to him, to tell him it was all a lie, but then she thought better. He had caused her enough pain, and perhaps a night of imagining her having wild sex with another man would do him some good. She decided to tell him in the morning, and finally drifted off to sleep.

To Tiffany's surprise, Alex was out and gone by the time she awoke. While she waited for the nanny to arrive, Tiffany needed a sympathetic ear, and telephoned her aunt. Giselle instantly knew that something was amiss with her niece.

After a little prodding, Tiffany finally gathered enough nerve to tell her the truth. "I told Alex that I had been with another man."

The phone went dead for a moment. "What do you mean, Tiffany? How could you do something so inappropriate? You're not supposed to cheat on your husband."

Tiffany wanted to cry, but didn't. "I wanted to hurt him, that's all. But I didn't mean to destroy him."

Giselle exhaled, and the phone rustled in Tiffany's ear. "I don't believe this, Tiffany. Whom have you been cavorting with?"

Tiffany bit her lip. "I told him I was seeing Vincent Cavanaugh."

Giselle was silent. Tiffany had fully expected her aunt to be shocked, but even she wasn't prepared for her aunt's escalating tone. "Is that Edgar's son? Is it?"

Tiffany couldn't stop the tears from filling her eyes. "Yes."

"Oh, my God. Tiffany, no! Tell me you did not sleep with your half brother!"

Tiffany almost dropped the phone. "My half brother? What are you saying, Aunt Giselle?" Tiffany repeated herself twice more, before Giselle responded.

"I'm coming to get you, right now," Aunt Giselle said, while a muted Tiffany just held the phone. "I'll be there in twenty minutes, and if your nanny isn't there by then, we'll bring the children with us."

As Giselle promised, she was there in seventeen minutes, arriving at the exact moment the nanny did. A pale Giselle whisked the shocked Tiffany into the back of her waiting limousine, and she slid the privacy glass up as the town car drove through Rock Creek Park, heading downtown, toward the Tidal Basin.

Giselle removed her huge black designer sunglasses, and then hugged her niece, gently patting her shoulder. "Tiffany, I love you, so very much, and I owe you an apology. A major apology. An extreme disservice has been done to you, and unfortunately, I have been a party to it." Giselle proceeded to tell Tiffany about her mother's liaison with Edgar Cavanaugh, and her subsequent plans to divorce Simon. It was almost unheard of in the 1960s, and the family had tried to keep it under wraps.

Tiffany felt as though the sides of the car were crushing in around her. So, her parents' marriage wasn't the fairy tale she had thought. Her mother had been having an affair. Had Marjorie lived, she would have divorced Simon. What other of her lifelong thoughts or memories could be destroyed?

Tiffany went to the well of hysteria, but came back empty. She couldn't even force herself to cry. She was numb. Wounded. Deflated. As they passed the Kennedy Center, Tiffany glanced at the landmark and felt lost. She realized that from this moment on she would never see anything the same again.

She swallowed deeply, the breath cutting into her lungs like broken glass. She pulled away from her aunt, and slid next to the door, where she stared at her mother's sister.

"You mean to tell me that Edgar Cavanaugh may be my father? That Simon Blake really is not? How could you keep something like that from me?"

Giselle reached for her niece, who shrank from her touch. "I know, dearest, and I guess that I never thought that this conversation would ever be necessary. The fact is, I really don't know if Edgar is your father. Your mother was my best friend, but she didn't share a lot of specifics with me. All I know is that she and Edgar were in love. You see, they were seriously involved before Marjorie went away to school, and their love was rekindled years later when Marjorie returned home. They were friends for a while, but, Marjorie became disillusioned with her marriage, and ultimately, she and Edgar had an intimate relationship while your parents were married.

"But then, Marjorie succumbed in the accident, and I was devastated. My main priority was to care for you. Shortly after your mother's death, Edgar left the area. What were the chances of you ever meeting him or his son? But, I should have told you, when you became old enough to know. It's my mistake, and I'm so sorry. But, I thought that I was doing the right thing. I thought that was what Marjorie would've wanted."

"I don't think so, Aunt Giselle. From what you've told me about my mother, she would've never wanted anything like that. She wasn't like you. She was determined to do what she wanted to do. She wasn't afraid of what people thought, nor did she care. She would have never lied to protect anyone. Never. You lied to protect yourself from any embarrassment."

Tiffany closed her eyes, and tried not to scream. "And you continued the lie. When I was looking at the pictures and asked you who Edgar was, you said you didn't recall."

Aunt Giselle tried to get a word in edgewise, but Tiffany didn't let up. "You are unbelievable, Aunt Giselle. You're so hung up on image and pedigree that you couldn't be honest with me. Yet you claim to love me so much. Ha! Do you know what you've done by keeping your little secrets and trying to protect my mother's image? You could have ruined my life.

"It wasn't only Vincent. I grew up with the Cavanaughs, and I could've become involved with any of them. Dating your first cousins isn't acceptable anymore, either, in proper society, you know. I can't believe that you knew. And that my father knew, too."

"Simon knew?"

"Yes, I told him I was seeing Vincent," Tiffany said, her voice trembling. "And he said nothing. Absolutely nothing. Why would he do that to me? Do you know that I almost slept with him?"

Giselle's eyebrows arched. "You mean you didn't?"

"No, I didn't. But I feel sick to my stomach even thinking about it."

Giselle heaved a sigh of relief. "Oh, thank God, thank God."

"You should be thanking Him, Aunt Giselle. Because I would literally lose my mind if something had happened with Vincent. And it would've been your fault."

Giselle held her hands to her lips, in a praying manner. "I know."

"And I want to know who my father is. I think that I have a right to know."

"Tiffany," Aunt Giselle said, and touched her niece's hand. "Does it matter? Simon has loved and been there for you all of your life. What good will come from your dredging up a lot of old hurt and discomfort?"

TIFFANY DIDN'T DIGNIFY Giselle's question with an answer. She just insisted that Giselle return her to her home and then do what she did best. Keep her mouth closed.

She had almost committed adultery and incest in one fell swoop. What more was she going to be expected to take?

She was ashamed, hurt, and angry. Angry at the man she called her father. The rest of the day passed with Tiffany's mind in a fog. She feigned being ill and locked herself in her room. Alex didn't even bother to check on her. Tiffany heard him go into his room, and then he left shortly afterward. When her father tapped on her door, she pretended to be asleep. The phone rang often, with Aunt Giselle, Lily, and some of her other girlfriends calling, but Tiffany had the nanny take messages. She was grateful that Vincent hadn't called her on her cellular phone. She had no human contact, other than spending some time with her children. Her sweet, innocent babies. They were the ones who gave her motivation to go on, because she was otherwise totally and completely stymied. And she had no one that she could talk to. Tiffany knew she had to do something, but what?

She thought about her mother. What would she do? Tiffany couldn't imagine her taking to her bed. Faking an illness. She'd do something to create her destiny, and not have destiny create her. By the end of the first day of her self-imposed exile, Tiffany roused herself from bed, and decided to take charge of her life.

The next morning, she took a long, hot bath, and made appointments for a facial, a manicure, and to get her hair styled. And, she made some serious decisions about her life. She decided that if her marriage was going to be over, it wasn't going to be because of some lie. She'd tell Alex the truth, and although he probably wouldn't believe her, her conscience would be clear. That's one thing Tiffany knew her mother did do. She stood on her convictions and her misdeeds and dealt with them. It was tragic that her life ended before she was able to see what it would've been like if she and Edgar had gotten together.

And Tiffany would find out who her father was. If not for her own sake, then for her children's. She bore no shame, and wouldn't now. If Marjorie had lived, she would've held her head high. Just as Tiffany was going to do.

And lastly, she was going to finish the memorial to her mother.

She richly deserved one, and now Tiffany felt more reason than ever to honor her mother's memory. For the woman she was, not the woman everyone purported her to be. Her decision to walk away from her marriage indicated that she had as much strength as she had beauty. And though Tiffany didn't know who her father was, she knew who her mother was. She was definitely Marjorie's child. Now she just had to act like it.

CHAPTER 24

SIMON DRUMMED HIS FINGERS on the desktop, and fiddled with a large, unmarked manila envelop. It was a package from one of his closest cohorts, an ex–special agent named Finley. Simon smiled, and leaned back in his chair, placing his elbows on the chair arms. He was at his former residence, sitting in the drawing room in the mayor's mansion.

As he surveyed the room, the sealed moving boxes and barren walls disturbed him. He didn't care if they had thought he had drowned. They should not have packed up his belongings as though he were a vagrant. He'd have to make sure that someone paid for that little transgression.

Simon Blake had built this city with his blood and sweat. He had taken command of D.C. two terms after the Feds had basically appointed a puppet, and were jerking his strings. They knew not to pull that crap with him. He was Simon Blake, after all. Educated, articulate, polished, and with a magnetic personality.

It had all worked in his favor, and he was able to carry out his double duties while doing an exceptional job as mayor. And even though this little hiccup called Alex Baxter had come along, he was still going to make it work to his advantage.

Getting Alex into office would be relatively simple. Smalls really posed no great threat. He had a slight gambling problem, and his father used to run numbers back in the day. Monty might be a little more challenging. Simon didn't know of any vulnerabilities of his, except that his ego was too large. He had relied heavily on his association with the Black Panthers to create some sort of militant image that impressed some of his constituents. Simon had contracted Finley to dig up some dirt on Smalls and Montgomery. Finley was extremely reliable, and usually pretty thorough.

When Simon opened the package, he was pleased with the contents. Both Smalls and his wife had a thing for Atlantic City, and it seemed that they had some pretty big markers out at the Sands. And with some unseemly 'Lang City types. This was just what Simon needed to dispense of Phillip Smalls.

What was unearthed from Monty Montgomery's background was a little less incriminating. It appeared that he had forgotten about a minor gun charge from the early seventies. But, that might play into his tough-guy image. Instead, Simon figured, if he could get someone to implicate Monty in a crime, the speculation about it would be damaging enough. In politics, who really cared if anything was true? It was all about public opinion.

Simon cracked his knuckles and sneered. Things were truly falling into place. He'd sit on this newly acquired information until it became necessary to use it. After all, timing was everything. And it had to be perfect, especially since he was dealing with such a condensed time frame. Everyone and everything had to work together, like the gears in a crankshaft. He had to keep Alex right where he was. Guessing. Dropping that Vincent Cavanaugh tidbit on him had been genius. It was enough to keep him off-balance and worried about his little home life. Simon knew Alex's mettle, and his Achilles' heel. And that would be Tiffany.

DESPITE DEALING WITH THE DEMONS of his marriage, Alex kept his promise to Fortune, and the next day, he leased a house at Twelfth Street and Maryland Avenue, Northeast. It was a small two-family dwelling on the expanding area of Capitol Hill, in a neighborhood that was undergoing significant gentrification. The two-story upstairs had been renovated, but the basement was only a third completed. Alex had an option to buy it, and as soon as he got his finances together, he was going to make a gift of it to Fortune.

After checking out the place, the two men headed over to District Heights, where Alex made a down payment on a late-model Honda Accord. Fortune was ecstatic, even after he was told that he'd have to get his driver's license before he could be insured. Car insurance was another thing added to the growing list of things Alex had promised to get, but he was going to keep his promises. Especially to an extremely grateful Fortune.

By the end of the day, Alex was exhausted, and begged off any other excursions. The utilities were scheduled to be turned on the following day, and then Alex would take Fortune shopping. He'd have to make appointments for the dentist and doctor, but Fortune understood.

"That's no problem, Alex. Not at all. We'll get to it," Fortune said, as they were driving back from the auto dealer.

"I'm glad you understand. I'm beat, and I've got a lot on my mind. I need to see what tasks Simon has lined up for me, but we'll get you squared away. I promise."

"I believe you. I just can't thank you enough for helping me to get my life back together," Fortune said. "I really owe you."

"You don't owe me anything. I owe you my life."

Fortune reached over and cranked up the stereo, to the tune of "Nuttin' But a G Thang," by Dr. Dre.

FROM BEHIND HER CLOSED BEDROOM DOOR, Tiffany overhead Alex rush in and head immediately for the shower. That was kind of odd, she thought, so she went into his bedroom. His down jacket was thrown across the bed, and when she moved it, two stapled sets of papers fell out of the pocket.

She picked up the documents, and read them, her eyes disbelieving the words. It was a house lease and sales papers for a 1990 Accord. Her fingers shook. Was he really planning to move out on her? And to that part of Northeast, of all places?

It didn't make any sense to her. Not unless—Tiffany dropped the documents and clasped her hands. Not unless he had set some heifer up in a love nest and the car was hers. She committed the address to memory. "Oh, hell no," Tiffany said, and she placed the papers back in his jacket and rearranged it on the bed. She'd find out what was going on. If it was the last thing that she did.

AND, IT WAS THE FIRST THING that she did the next morning. With her cousin Lily driving, Tiffany rode over to the address on Twelfth Street. After a few minutes of last-minute strategizing and Lily's pep talk, Tiffany was ready to confront the unknown. She convinced Lily to stay in the car, with the doors locked and the engine running.

Armed with pepper spray and outfitted in rugged wear, Tiffany brazenly walked up to the door. It was chilly, but her adrenaline was keeping her warm. She wasn't sure what she was going to do, but she was determined to do something.

It took her a moment, but she finally knocked. The door swung open, and a tall, thin man stood there, with a shocked expression on his face. He was holding a drill, which he absently dropped by his side.

"Is the woman of the house here?" Tiffany asked, and the man just stared, his mouth gaping. She slipped the pepper spray into the pocket of her shearling coat.

"Huh?"

"What's the matter with you?" Tiffany said, and looked over his shoulder. She repeated her original question.

"I, uh—Don't know, I mean, there's no lady living here," he finally said, barely able to look at her.

"What? Then who are you?"

"I'm, I'm, uh." He raised his hand and shrugged his shoulders. "I'm, uh."

"Who are you? I want to know who lives here? Are you working for Alexander Baxter?"

The man smiled with a nervous twitch. "No, I don't work fo' him. I live here. I'm Fortune."

The name struck a chord in Tiffany. "Fortune?"

"Yeah, that's me."

"Where have I heard your name before?" Tiffany tilted her head. "And you look kind of familiar, too."

"'Cause I'm an old friend of Alex and his brother, Ivan." Fortune peered at Tiffany, and then invited her in. "Why don't you tell your friend out there you might be here for a few minutes?"

Tiffany stepped back and shook her head. "I don't know about that. I don't know you like that."

Fortune extended his hand. "Come on in. We're like family."

TIFFANY CONVINCED LILY to run down to Union Station and have some coffee, while she talked to Fortune. She didn't know why she trusted this stranger so much, but there was something affable about him. She didn't fear him.

Fortune told Tiffany about his and Alex's relationship, and she was flabbergasted. There was so much about Alex's childhood and life that she apparently didn't know, and so much he had kept from her.

Seated on a rickety milk crate, Tiffany just stared at Fortune. "How come he didn't tell me about you now?"

Fortune shrugged. "I'm thinkin' that the timing just hasn't been cool. We have a very complicated relationship, you know? He always blamed me for Ivan's death, so it wasn't like we was in contact all of those years. But, I, uh, always tried to look out fo' him. Especially now."

"Why now?"

"Because, he really needs it. Yo' husband is a good man, Tiffany. He's helped me out so much, and he's that kinda dude. And I, well, we share a lot. I kinda keep his feet on the ground, and he kinda helps me get my life together."

It was almost too much for Tiffany to digest. Here was someone so integral to her husband's life that he gave him a place to live, and a car, yet never even mentioned Fortune to her.

"I'm sorry about the way I approached you," Tiffany said. "I had no right, but I'm just glad that you weren't—"

"What? Some chick?" Fortune laughed. "You're somethin' else, girl. Why in the hell would you think that, fine as you are?"

Tiffany had to smile. "Thank you. But so, so much has happened between Alex and me. And I thought that either he was planning to move out, or had moved some woman in here that he was seeing."

"Get real, girl. That's the last thing on that brother's mind. He loves you to death. He always has. Whatever he did do, I can tell you, it didn't mean nothin' to him. You've always had his heart. Ever since y'all was back in school."

"He told you about that?" Tiffany's eyes lit up.

"Of course. I'm tellin' you. If there's one thing I know, is that he loves you. And them kids, too. Everything he's done has been because of y'all."

Tiffany's heart melted. How could she have been so blind? How could she have tried to hurt her husband so badly? She grabbed Fortune and hugged him, and thanked him for filling in so many blanks.

"You're welcome," he said, and hugged her back. "I'm tellin' you, you two is meant to be together. Y'all have been through so much shit, I mean stuff, that you just need to be together for the rest of your lives. You just gotta learn how to shut out all of this noise an' listen to each other, you know? I mean really listen to each other. From the heart."

Tiffany kissed Fortune's cheek, and then wiped his jaw. "I'm so glad that I finally met you," she said. "And, you're right. You are just like family. If there's ever anything I can do for you, I will. Okay?"

It was Fortune's turn for his eyes to light up. "Well, there is something you can do, if you wouldn't mind."

"What's that?"

"Alex is real busy, an' I really didn't want to bother him. An' I know you really know 'bout clothes and stuff. So, I was wondering if you wouldn't mind takin' me shoppin'? I mean, I have my own money an' what not."

Tiffany smiled and grabbed Fortune's hands. "That's the least I can do. I'd love to take you shopping. We'll have a ball."

"Cool."

"Now, there's one thing you can do for me, Fortune. Please don't tell Alex about this. I want to tell him myself."

SHE LIT THE CANDLE, the twelfth one she had placed around the family room. The fire was blazing, and Tiffany had spread a checkered picnic blanket in the center of the floor and on it arranged serving dishes containing a sumptuous feast of cracked crab claws, hot potato salad, and fire-roasted asparagus. She had two bottles of Moët chilling beside it in a glass bucket, with two crystal flutes.

Tiffany wrung her hands. She was more nervous than she had been the first time she and Alex had made love. It was almost nine o'clock, and she had paged him a half hour ago, asking that he come home.

The children were fast asleep, and now that Simon was so enthralled with Alex's campaign, he was spending more time at the mayor's mansion and with Jessica. Tiffany called him to tell him that she and Alex needed some privacy tonight, and she was pleased to know that he wasn't going to interrupt them later.

With only the light from the candles and the fire illuminating the room, Tiffany caught a glimpse of herself in the reflection from the fireplace doors, and smiled. She felt good about her appearance. The bronze spandex catsuit with the zippered front suggested that she was ready and willing, but not desperate.

She grabbed the stereo's remote and turned on the CD player. She had programmed a number of songs, mostly Alex's favorites, to enhance the mood. When R. Kelly's "Honey Love" came on, Tiffany swayed with the music.

When she saw his headlights turn into the driveway, Tiffany lowered the volume, and adjusted her stance. She wanted to appear casual, but welcoming.

Alex came through the kitchen door and called her name.

"I'm in here," she said, and she heard him taking off his coat.

"What's all this about, Tiffany?" Alex asked, and stood in the doorway.

"It's about you and me," she said, and motioned for him to join her on the floor.

"What do you want? I think you said all you had to say the other day, right?"

Tiffany stood and reached for her husband, who withdrew from her grasp. Alex took a seat on the edge of the sofa, and Tiffany nestled in between his legs. He tried to close them, but she pried his knees open.

"I want to apologize, Alex. I was wrong for saying what I said.

It wasn't true." She looked deeply in his eyes, but they were cold and empty.

Alex sucked his teeth. "Oh, so now it isn't true. What makes you think that I'd ever believe a word you have to say? Especially about something as detrimental as what you said?"

Tiffany hung her head, but then looked up at her husband. Her long eyelashes were moist from the tears that threatened to fall from her lids. "Because it is true, Alex. I was hurt, and I wanted to hurt you. So, I lied about the one thing that I knew would hurt you. And I'm sorry."

"I don't know, Tiffany."

"I know you don't. And I don't know what I can say to make you feel or believe otherwise. All I can tell you is how I feel, and what the truth is."

"The truth, huh?"

"The truth. And the truth is that I would have committed suicide if I had slept with Vincent. Honestly."

Alex's brow furrowed. "What do you mean?"

Tiffany took her hand and caressed her husband's cheek. "I'm so ashamed, Alex. But I didn't sleep with him. I didn't. In fact—I just found out that Vincent may be my brother."

Alex grabbed Tiffany's chin. "What?"

She tried to hang her head, but Alex lifted her chin. "I just found out that my mother and Vincent's father Edgar were having an affair. And, well, I, I just might be Edgar's child."

Tears filled her eyes. "I need to know who my father is. Do you know how that makes me feel?"

Alex inhaled deeply and scratched his head. How could that be? How could Simon know that Tiffany was seeing her half brother? It couldn't be true. Simon was a heartless, cruel son of a bitch, but this was just sick. More than ever, he wanted to protect his wife.

He took his wife in his arms, and held her while Tiffany

sobbed. "I'm so sorry. We were both hurt. And I was wrong for shutting you out and acting the way that I did when those pictures showed up. But, I'm not perfect. I reacted, and just kept reacting. I never listened to you like I should've."

Alex stroked the back of her hair and tried to find comforting words. But his words were thick, mired in the swelling anger he had for Simon. "We have to forgive each other, honey. We were both wrong, Tiffany. I was wrong for never telling you about that night with Stacey, and you were wrong for not listening to me. But I guess that's what happens when you hurt. I'm sorry, too."

Tiffany sniffed, and buried her face in his chest. "I'm sorry, baby. I really am. I just want things to be right between us."

"I want things to be right between us, too. But we have to trust each other," Alex said. "And there may come a time when I really need for you to trust me. Me and only me. Do you think you can do that?"

Tiffany raised her head. "I'll try. If you will."

"That's all we can do for right now," Alex said, and he swept his wife into his arms. Putting all thoughts of Simon aside, Alex concentrated on his wife, and she on him. And that night, for the first time in months, Mr. and Mrs. Alexander Baxter communicated and shared. They talked and listened to each other. About their family, their lives, their plans, goals, and dreams. They laughed and cried. And then they made love. Just like the first time.

CHAPTER 25

FINALLY, there was a positive energy in the air. Alex and Tiffany were again of one accord, and she had finally met Fortune and had welcomed him into their family. Lisa continued to investigate Simon, although she was progressing slowly, since Alex's schedule was so taken up with the election. They now had to steal moments to sync up, but Lisa made sure that she knew where he was at any given moment. She had chosen a property and was waiting for the closing, but had already moved her office into part of it. Alex knew that Tiffany would be glad when Lisa moved out of their house.

Lisa had tracked Alex down and insisted that he swing past her new office before he went to a luncheon that day. Foody had called again, and this time, Lisa had actually held a conversation with him.

He was in Singapore, and Lisa had immediately tried to make arrangements for him to catch the first plane out, but because

Foody didn't have the appropriate identification to get through customs, it was going to take a couple of days to get his documents and overnight them to the U.S. embassy.

The good news was that Foody said that he had sent the files to his AOL account. The bad news was that it had now lapsed. Alex and Lisa would have to wait until he returned to the States so he could re-establish his account.

"Well, then wire him enough money so that he can buy a laptop there. He can start working before he even gets back. Time is of the essence." Alex paused, and then snapped his fingers. "Why don't you send somebody over there with a laptop and with Foody's documents? That way, we'll have all the bases covered, and have someone in-country, in case he gets jammed up."

"That's a great idea, but—" Lisa rubbed her fingertips together.

"Just put it on my tab," Alex said. "I'll make sure it gets paid."

FOODY'S REAPPEARANCE REJUVENATED ALEX. Every lead they had pursued had been a dead end in their quest to remove the tightening noose from Alex's neck. Foody's info had always been their ace in the hole. Now it was up to Alex to take that noose and place it firmly around Simon's neck.

A FEW EVENINGS LATER, after a full day of prepping for debates, shaking hands, and kissing babies, an exhausted Alex came home and went straight to his children's room. He was playing with them and their squeaky toys when Tiffany burst in, holding an overstuffed folder.

"Darling, look," she said, as she sat down on the floor beside him. She opened the folder in front of Alex, and then scooped up Anya, kissing her cheeks.

"What's this?" Alex asked, and Tiffany reached over and brushed his lips.

"I've found a sculptor to do my mother's bust," she said. "His name is Clive, and the Corcoran referred him."

"That's great, Tiff," he said, with his son gurgling on his shoulder.

"I'm pleased," she said, her voice filled with pride. "And, I met with him, and he's going to be able to get started immediately. I've decided to use this picture." She removed a beautiful photo of her mother from the folder. "I told him that he had to include this, too." Tiffany pulled another paper from the stack and showed it to Alex. It was an enlarged copy of a handwritten note.

"What's this?" Alex asked, and focused in on the photocopy.

"It's my mother's signature. I want that to be part of the sculpture."

Alex glimpsed at the document, and his mind immediately flashed back to the signature he had seen on Tiffany's mother's will. They were not the same.

"That's a pretty distinctive signature, isn't it?" Alex said, with a casual tone.

"Yes, it is, isn't it? It was one of the things my mother was most proud of."

Alex continued staring at the paper. He smiled, and as Tiffany continued talking about the memorial, he became more excited. He might have found the answer to his problems.

THE NEXT DAY, Alex made sure that he caught up with Lisa. "You have to get these documents analyzed by a handwriting expert," Alex said, as he tossed copies of Marjorie's will and the handwritten note on top of Lisa's desk.

"I've been up almost all night, Alex," a bleary-eyed Lisa said. "Foody's still being detained while they confirm his identity, and I've been working on that." She yawned and stretched. "Now, what's this you've just thrown at me?"

After Alex explained what the documents were, Lisa's tired face filled with doubt. "You know this is a reach, right Alex? I don't want you to get your hopes up too high on this," she said.

"This is it, Lisa. Look at them. They're similar, but not the same. See, everything's falling into place. Foody's on his way here, and once we get this analyzed, we can charge Simon with forgery. That's a federal offense."

"I understand your enthusiasm, but, I'm just saying—let's not get too excited."

"Okay, okay," Alex said. "But, I'm telling you, it's not her signature."

Lisa rolled her eyes and then picked up the telephone. She made a few calls, and then one of her men knocked on her door. Before she handed him the copies, she made another set for safekeeping.

"Samuels says that he can get these analyzed before the week's over, best case. Worst case, it might take two weeks." Lisa said. "Then you'll have your answer."

Two weeks. Alex could live with that. He wanted to get Simon well before the election so that it wouldn't have to go to the eleventh hour. He punched his fist in his hand. "See? That's what I'm talkin' about. Progress."

There was another knock on the door, and when Lisa opened it, more progress walked in. It was Fortune, quite spiffy and polished, looking good in a pair of crisp jeans, a thick black leather jacket, and a bright red turtleneck. Even Lisa's face registered that she was impressed.

"What's up, lady?" Fortune said, with a grin. His teeth were bright, and he filled the office with the scent of cologne. He slapped Alex five. "What's up, my brother?"

"Looking good," Alex said.

"Yeah, your girl really hooked me up, huh?" Fortune took his jacket off and then struck a model's pose. "Things are really lookin' up for a brother. I got my license, my wheels, and even a little j-o-b," Fortune said, and eyed Lisa.

"Yeah, I figured I could use Fortune to help out with some investigative work," Lisa said, looking at the ceiling.

"Well, that's good," Alex said. "And we've got good news, too." Alex ran down the day's events.

"Word is bond," Fortune said, with his eyes focused on Lisa. "Sounds like you might finally get that old bastard."

"Yeah," Alex continued. "Now, I just need to—" He stopped short when he noticed that Lisa and Fortune were staring at each other. "Do you two need a moment?"

"What?" Lisa said. "No, I was just, well, I was listening."

"Yeah, right," Alex said.

Just then, the phone rang. Lisa answered, and then hit the speakerphone button.

"Yo! what's up!" It was Foody.

"Foody! What's happening, man? You had us worried to death," Alex said. "Is everything okay?" Foody's voice sounded like music to Alex's ears.

"Ain't no need to worry, Alex. You know me, I got it all under control," Foody said. "But, I ain't gonna lie. I was a little worried when Lisa's guy showed up at the embassy. I thought I was about to get arrested or something."

The trio laughed as Foody continued. "So, anyway, our flight leaves in the morning, which means I'll be getting in the next day, at around six in the morning. At JFK, okay? And, I've got the laptop, and I'm going to hook this bad boy up right now, and get your files. By the time we land, I should have something for you. As soon as you tell me what it is you need."

Lisa quickly chimed in. "We need for you to confirm exactly which computer requested those overseas transactions. And how it was done. Right now, it looks like they were coming from Alex's, but—"

"But they were probably made from a PC that was networked into Alex's. I got it now. I can get that. Not a problem," he said.

"Yo, thanks, Foody. I knew you'd come through for me," Alex said.

"Don't worry about it, bro. I'm traveling business class, and until then, I'll be eatin' and drinkin' like a king, on your dime. So I'm cool."

Alex laughed. "Well, eat up, Foody. That's the least I can do because I do owe you big-time," Alex said.

"Square biz," Foody said, with a laugh. "Square *bid*-ness."

HE WAS UNABLE TO SUPPRESS HIS GRIN, and looking at Lisa and Fortune only made Alex want to smile harder. But, they'd have to celebrate later when Foody arrived. Right now, Alex had to put in some face time with Simon, which would serve a dual purpose. Keeping Simon appeased, and allowing Alex to keep an eye on him.

"Well, I guess I better fly," Alex said, and then picked up his jacket. "Simon has me on a short leash. Almost every moment of my time is accounted for. And if it's not, then he's paging me." Lisa and Fortune barely noticed as Alex took a few steps toward the door, and then reached back to retrieve the copies of Marjorie's note and will from the end table where he had placed them. He accidentally brushed them onto the floor, and Fortune picked them up.

Fortune peered down at the will, and looked at each page. When he reached the last page, he shook his head. "I don't know about old girl's signature bein' real, but you better check out this notary. 'Cause if this is the 'Julius Canty' I've heard of, you might have Simon by the balls."

"Julius who?" Alex asked, and then it clicked. Julius was Simon's former client, the drug dealer whom Simon had eliminated so that he could take over his business. "Fortune, you might have something there. First, we need to determine if that really is Julius Canty, because if it is, and he was a convicted felon at the time, then he couldn't have notarized that document. When was it signed?"

"January sixteenth, 1970," Lisa said.

"I was just thinkin' that if Julius had anything to do with it, it had to be shady," Fortune said.

"Shady? Try felonious. Even if Marjorie's signature isn't a forgery, we'll have Simon on fraud," Alex said, with a sneer that rivaled his former mentor's. "Then it's bye-bye Simon."

CHAPTER 26

STANDING IN the living room of Tiffany and Alex's house, Simon tapped the face of his watch. It was a little past three, and Alex should have been there and ready by now. They were scheduled to meet with the Rotary Club at three-thirty and then do a photo-op at the Boys and Girls Club. How dare he be late?

Simon cracked his knuckles. Everything was coming together. Jessica was a whiz at the administrative tasks, and he felt comfortable with her assistance. Alex had fallen back into line and was doing a fine job in the mayoral race. Simon closely monitored the polls, and according to yesterday's *Washington Post,* Alex was leading the pack with a forty-five percent rating. His closest competitor was Councilman Montgomery, whom Simon didn't perceive as a threat—yet. If he got closer to Alex in the polls, Simon was prepared to make public certain damning information.

Simon peered out the window. January was slowly coming to

an end, and the promise of spring was in the air. He predicted that by April, his world would once again be in perfect order. Alex owed him for destroying his business, and yes, payback was a bitch. But, revenge was even sweeter. Finley had confirmed that Edgar and company had made an unceremonious departure from the city, and that the Cavanaugh dynasty was now in chaos. Simon laughed when he recalled the events at the holiday party, where Edgar's fate was finally sealed. Simon was simply gleeful at the news of the Cavanaughs' squabbles. It meant that they wouldn't be making any strides in taking over Simon's coveted markets, and it would require minimal effort from Simon to make his business flourish again. Especially when Alex took office.

The house was quiet. The children were upstairs with the nanny, and Tiffany was out, busily working on her mother's memorial. "Some memorial," Simon thought. "Hmph. Commemorating a tramp." He had been livid about Marjorie's immortalizing, until he realized that Tiffany had planned to do the same for him, too, when she thought that he was dead. He'd have to make sure that he had a statue, one day. A big one. And he planned on being around to see it, too.

It was three-fifteen when Alex came rushing through the back door, and Simon plastered on a smile and called his name.

"Simon? I'm sorry I'm running late," Alex said. "I got caught up with some potential voters and didn't want to be rude." He was lying, but it didn't matter. He knew how to play the game.

Simon eyed him up and down. "You need to change," he said. Alex was wearing a brown suede car coat, shirt, and tie. "This jacket's fine for when we go to the Boys and Girls Club, but you need a conservative suit for the Rotaries. You're young, and they're not too keen on that, so you need to make sure you always look like a leader when you meet with them."

"I understand," Alex said. "I'll just need a few minutes to change."

Simon helped Alex take his jacket off and slapped him on the shoulder. "You've got five minutes. We can't be late."

Alex didn't protest and ran up the stairs. Simon shook his head, and then realized that he was still holding Alex's jacket. He grunted, then tossed the jacket onto the sofa, and some folded papers fell out. He picked them up and his face dropped. What the hell was Alex doing with a copy of Marjorie's will?

"Maybe Alex isn't as in line as I thought," Simon said out loud, and looked up the stairs. "I guess I'll just have to see to it that he does get there, and his ass stays there. Once and for all."

TIFFANY'S DAY WAS FULL ALSO. She had spent the morning with her personal shopper at Neiman Marcus, picking out outfits for a college alumni dinner she and Alex were scheduled to attend, and afterward, she had finalized the details of her mother's sculpture with Clive. Her next appointment was with her doctor. She wanted to discuss blood types and paternity.

After a high level overview from her doctor, she found out that her mother's blood type was A-positive, while Tiffany's was O-negative. Armed with her newfound knowledge, she needed to know Simon's blood type. That would be simple enough, she thought. She decided that she'd get a copy of Simon's hospital records, under the ruse that his primary physician needed them. Or, if that didn't work, she'd suggest that Alex give blood at the Red Cross. She dialed Jessica on her mobile phone and arranged it.

Tricking Jessica into scheduling that event was quite easy. Now all Tiffany had to do was be present and cajole her father into donating. That would be a guaranteed way to get his blood type without raising suspicion. With the plan set into motion, Tiffany felt much better. Perhaps she really was Simon's daughter. She had learned how to wheel and deal with the best of them.

With Simon clocking his every move, Alex completed his candidate duties at the Rotary Club. They settled into the back of their Lincoln, and during the ride back from the club, Simon congratulated Alex for a job well done.

"Yes, the old boys at the Rotary Club are quite impressed," Simon said. "You have a strong platform, and you're presenting yourself very well. I must say that you're doing a good job."

"Thanks, Simon. But, this schedule is killing me. I need a little more time for myself."

Simon removed a pipe from his breast pocket and lit it. "This is the road you're traveling on now, son. After the election, you can be a little more selective with it. But for now, you have to get out here and beat the streets."

Forget the streets. Alex wanted to beat the hell out of Simon. "I hear you, Simon. But, I still have to have a life. I want a little more input with regard to my schedule. It's already Wednesday, and I haven't taken care of one personal item yet."

Simon puffed on his pipe and nodded. "Point well taken, Alex. I'll have Jessica put together your schedule on a weekly basis, and we'll update it daily." Simon opened up a Day-Timer, and pointed to a typed page with Alex's schedule. "Your tomorrow is pretty tight. You have a meeting with your PR firm in the morning, and then you're supposed to go around to some of the city agencies in the afternoon. But Friday was supposed to be clear, with the exception of a Hilliard Alumni fund-raiser in the evening. Well, one more thing was just added. Jessica called and said that your lovely wife thought that it would be a good idea if you gave blood, so, at eleven on Friday, you'll be at the Red Cross with your sleeve rolled up."

Friday morning? That was when Foody was scheduled to arrive, and Alex was planning to be there.

"Tell Jessica to move that to next week. I have a conflict," Alex said.

"Conflict? What kind of conflict?"

Alex hedged, but then decided to tell the truth. Simon didn't know that Foody was involved, so he was safe. "My college roommate is coming into town. And I planned to spend the day with him."

Simon puffed and pursed his lips. "Gee, I thought you would want to keep your wife happy. Oh, well, I'll see to it that she moves it."

"You do that, Simon."

SHE WAS RESTING IN HIS ARMS, sitting in a steamy bubble bath, when Alex broke the news. He felt Tiffany's body tense up, when he told her that he'd rearranged the visit to the Red Cross.

"Why'd you do that? I think you need to do it as soon as possible."

"You don't think next week is soon enough? I know they might have a shortage, but my pint isn't going to stop the gap."

Tiffany sighed. "I was going to donate, too, Alex. And I was going to get Dad to also."

Alex kissed the back of her head. "I'm sure he will, baby. Even next week."

"But, you don't understand. I was going to find out what his blood type was. To see if he could be my father. You know I told you that I wanted to find out who my father was."

"Oh," Alex said. He knew that blood type could only determine who couldn't be the father. But from Alex's perspective, maybe Tiffany would be satisfied to find out if Simon could be her father. So he decided to encourage it. "That's great. Why didn't you tell me that's what you wanted to do?"

"Because, I know you have a lot on your plate, and I figured it was something I could do. But, if I have to wait until then, well, then I will. But what do you have to do Friday?"

Alex told her about Foody, and she was happy to know that he was coming into town. But then her body tensed up again.

"Where's he going to stay?"

Alex chuckled, and squeezed the loofah onto Tiffany's back. He could hear in Tiffany's voice that she was ready for Lisa to go and probably glad that Simon wasn't there as often. But she wasn't ready to have another houseguest. "I hadn't thought about it, baby. But I'll make sure that he's got a place to lay his head, even if it's not here."

Tiffany folded her arms and nestled into Alex's chest. "We'll, see, huh. A few days might not be so bad, and you know that I love Foody, but with everything that's going on, I'll be glad when we have our house back to ourselves. Which reminds me. Won't it be something if you're elected, and we move into the mayor's mansion? It'll be so odd living there again."

Alex hadn't even thought about that. Probably because he had no intention of ever becoming mayor. But he agreed, and stroked his wife's shoulders as she continued on about the official residence. He'd never realized how important his being elected was to his wife.

IT WAS FRIDAY MORNING before Alex knew it. When Fortune opened Lisa's office door, Alex was shocked to see his old friend Foody sitting at the head of the conference table eating out of a Styrofoam container.

"Alex!!" Foody yelled, and ran to him and gave him a big bear hug. Foody had lost weight, and grown a mustache and beard. He wasn't tiny, but most of his former flab was a lot tauter.

"What's up, Foody? Damn, let me look at you. We're going to have to get you a new nickname," Alex said.

Foody grabbed his stomach and jiggled it. "Naw, I'll always be the Foodster, man."

"I'll say," Lisa said. "He's been eating me out of house and home since he got back."

"There's nothin' like salmon cakes and grits from the Georgia Mile, you know what I'm sayin'?"

"What'd you lose, about fifty pounds?" Alex asked.

"Fifty pounds? You kiddin' me, right?" Fortune said, and

pointed to Foody's backside. "I think I found it. It's right behind him."

"That's all right, Slim. You could use about fifty to keep the wind from blowing you over," Foody said with a laugh.

"All right, you two," Alex said with a grin. It was so good to finally have everyone together. "So, what's up? Foody, what'd you find out?"

Lisa motioned for Alex to join them at the table, and Foody plopped down and ran through the details in between mouthfuls. "It's like this, Alex. I tracked down all of those transactions, and whoever did it had some kind of program installed that mimicked your computer. I was able to prove that the transactions didn't originate from the location where your PC was. But the location where the actual transactions were made is phantom."

"What do you mean?"

"I'm sayin' that although we can prove that you didn't key in the requests, we'll never be able to prove who did. They go back to the location of the warehouse, which we all know isn't linked to you. So, at least that gets you off the hook."

"In some ways. It means that if it's ever made public, I would still have the shadow of wrongdoing hanging over my head. The public doesn't want to hear about the specifics of an IP address or some other bullshit. It'll still seem like I was involved some kind of way."

"True dat," Foody said.

"Lisa, we need to make that money disappear. Dissolve those trust funds with my kids' names on them, and send that money to Zurich. Pay off whomever you need to pay off, but I want it to appear that it was never there. If Simon goes looking for it, I want to make sure he can't find it. And he's going to want it, especially if he plans on starting his business back up. I might be able to use it as leverage to get him off my back. He might want that money bad enough to exchange it for my freedom."

"I got it," Lisa said. "But I'll make sure that we keep enough out to cover the cost of this investigation, okay?"

"Okay," Alex said. "So what else is up?"

Lisa told him that the jury was still out on the handwriting analysis. The two samples had been sent to two other experts, who were still working on their results.

Alex scratched his head. "So, we've got nothing on the signature. What about Julius's notary status?"

"Another question mark, Alex," Fortune said. "The only thing we know right now is that Julius didn't have a conviction until the mid-seventies. But, I'm still checkin'."

"What, you work here now?" Foody asked, and Fortune gritted on him. "Well, damn, I want a job then, too."

Alex felt stymied. A few days ago things were looking up and now everything was in a state of flux. "I don't know what else we can do now."

"Don't throw in the towel, Alex. All we gotta do is think. We can come up with something," Foody said, and finished his food.

"You comin' in here late, Foody," Fortune said. "We've thought about everything, an' we ain't got shit."

"I don't know if we need to keep adding things to the mix, Alex. We probably have the answers, we just have to wait for them," Lisa said.

"No, Lisa. That's not good enough. I have no intention of waiting until the last minute before I check Simon. I'm not going to let him make me win this election, and then have to step down. No way. We've got to come up with something now."

THEY RETRACED THEIR STEPS. They retold Simon's past, highlighting and detailing it on the whiteboard on the wall. They explored everything, twice again, and still came up with the same thing. Nothing.

Then it hit Alex. The truth resided in a will, but not Marjorie's. It had to be in Julius's.

"Fortune. You said that Simon had Julius eliminated so that he could take over his estate, right?"

"I told you that a long time ago."

"Yeah, I know, but now it's all coming together. I believe that Marjorie's will is fake, but I also think that it's going to be hard to prove. And Simon probably knew that the Newtons would dissect any legal documents that pertained to Marjorie. But, I bet he wasn't so careful with Julius's."

"What do you mean?" Foody asked.

"I mean that we need to find Julius's will. And if we can find that, we should compare his signatures. And, I bet it'll be a forgery. Lisa?"

"I'm on it," Lisa said.

CHAPTER 27

A LEX CONTINUED going through the motions, but Tiffany became increasingly anxious about determining Simon's blood type. She had confirmed that her mother was definitely A-positive, and by the time they reached the Red Cross that next Friday morning, she was nearly shaking.

Alex smiled, rolled up his sleeves, and willingly gave blood, while Tiffany coerced Simon.

"Me? I'm an old man. Nobody needs my blood."

"Sure, I—I mean, we do." She nudged him in the arm. "And plus it'll make a great picture."

Simon rubbed his hands together, and began taking off his suit coat. "Well, I guess you have a point there, missy."

Tiffany nearly clicked her heels when Simon sat down at the desk and filled out his forms. When the aide asked if he knew what his blood type was, Simon responded with a powerful voice. "Of course I know. It's red." And the room fell out.

"No, I'm just kidding. It's O."

"O what, Father?"

"O-negative," the aide responded.

Tiffany's heart dropped, and she bent down and kissed her father's cheek. She fluttered over to Alex's cot, where he was lying down, sipping juice, and eating cookies. "Alex, baby," she whispered. "Daddy's O-negative like me. I must be his daughter."

Alex sipped his drink, and forced a smile. He'd been hoping that Simon would have some rare blood type that would eliminate the possibility of him being her father and give creedance to the fact that he had motive to kill Marjorie since she had cheated on him and had another man's baby. Instead, what Tiffany had found out really didn't prove anything. But he decided not to tell her. Perhaps it was better if she did think that Simon was her father. The fact was O-negative blood was pretty common. And the only way she would know definitively if Simon was her father would be to find out if Edgar's blood type ruled him out. And, the only way she was going to get that information was from a Cavanaugh. And it wasn't like she could just broach the subject over tea and crumpets one afternoon. So Alex let it ride, and hoped that she wouldn't delve further into it, at least not until much later.

"Tiff, darling. That's great. At least that will put your mind at ease."

"At ease? Darling, you just don't understand. I feel like a ten-ton weight has been lifted from my shoulders. This is the best Valentine's gift I could ever receive."

EASING TIFFANY'S MIND was a good decision for Alex. To have her running around frantic and upset would have only created more stress. Now she could focus on her interests, while Alex grappled with their dubious reality.

Even with Lisa, Fortune, and Foody looking for Julius's will, it still hadn't turned up. It had not been recorded in the city archives, and it was a footrace to find it. They were even scouring through the storage vaults, looking through the old boxes from Simon's former practice. It was a tedious, time-consuming process, and time was running out. Alex pushed his team to their limits.

After a pleasant but quiet Valentine's Day, the election was right around the corner. Tension was in their midst, and it seemed that everyone was scrambling, except for Simon. He was cool and controlled, and continued his routine of monitoring the polls and pushing Alex toward victory.

The Thursday before the election, Alex's lead slipped slightly, and he was elated. He and Simon were sitting in the campaign office, watching the local news, when they broadcast the latest polls. Monty Montgomery was gaining, with thirty-two percent, and Alex had slipped to forty-two percent.

Alex wanted to leap from his seat, but played it cool. "Oh, well, Simon. It looks like old Monty's pouring it on. I guess I couldn't lose to a better man, huh?"

"Lose? That's not in our vocabulary, son. Polls are like women. They're fickle. You just stay tuned," Simon said, and leaned back in his chair.

"Stay tuned to what?" Alex asked, but Simon just smirked. He searched Simon's blank face, and then went back to reviewing his schedule for the next two days. The election was next Tuesday, and every minute of Alex's time till then was mapped out. The plan was to move headquarters into the Grand Hyatt on Sunday, where they'd reside until after the election.

Lisa called Alex on his cell phone. "Can you talk?" she asked.

Alex glanced over at Simon, who was within earshot. "Sure, what's up, Foody?"

"I've got some news for you. Can you swing past here or can we meet somewhere?"

"I'm not sure. My schedule's pretty tight today. And I probably won't be home until after six."

"Okay, well, Marjorie's analysis came back today. It's inconclusive."

"Really?" Alex asked, but kept his voice light. He forced a laugh. "Unbelievable."

"I know. And we did confirm that Julius was a notary at the time. He wasn't incarcerated then."

"Get out of here," Alex said, again with a forced laugh.

"The good news is that we extended the search to include Virginia and Pennsylvania, and guess what? We found out that Julius's will was recorded in Lynchburg. Foody and Fortune are going to ride down there tomorrow and pick up a copy. Then we can compare the signatures."

Alex folded his arms, but never took his eyes off Simon. "Okay, that's cool. But, don't you think it's too cold to grill tonight?"

"Huh? What are you saying? You want me to meet you at your house this evening? All of us? Oh, okay, I got you. We'll have dinner at your house tonight. Are you going to clear this with Tiffany?"

"I'll talk to Tiffany. You just do your thing, man."

Before Alex could turn off the phone, Simon was beckoning him back to the television. "Take a gander at this," Simon said, and pointed at the "late-breaking news" bulletin that was flashing across the screen.

The local news was still on, and the newscaster announced that they were about to broadcast live from Councilman Montgomery's campaign headquarters.

"This just in," the reporter said as she stood outside Monty's office. "It has just been reported that Councilman Montgomery was arrested in 1972 on a gun charge. This information was previously undisclosed, and we understand that the councilman is going to address these claims. Also in is a report that a convicted felon by the name of Lionel Walker has implicated Councilman Montgomery in an armed robbery that occurred in 1972."

The reporter continued, and Simon gloated. Alex held his chin and shook his head as he watched Monty proclaim that the allegations were false, and that he was cooperating with the investigation. Alex had to admit, Simon was awfully good. That's why he'd been so cool about the dip in the polls.

"Oh, well, Alex. I guess old Monty's got his own concerns to worry about now, huh? And, I don't think that being elected mayor is going to be one."

Alex forced a weak smile. "Poor guy," he said. *Poor me,* he thought.

ALEX COULD HEAR THE CLOCK ticking in his head. Lisa coordinated the barbecue, and Tiffany was even warm to the idea of Alex having a final hurrah with his best friends prior to D.C.'s Super Tuesday. Alex also invited his father, Mrs. Owens, and Aunt Giselle, in case he needed someone to distract Tiffany, so that he and his friends could conduct their business.

Tiffany loved playing hostess. Foody cooked up a feast of smoked ribs and grilled fish, then while Tiffany, Aunt Giselle, and Mrs. Owens put the final touches on the rest of dinner, Alex and company retreated to the basement rec room, where they could play spades and finalize their plans.

Alex, Foody, Lisa, and Fortune sat around a card table, while Gerald stood behind the bar.

"First off, everyone, let me tell you all how much I appreciate what you've done for me. I know that I couldn't have done it without you. But, you know this is probably the last time we'll all get together before the election, right?" Alex asked, and shuffled the cards. "From here on out, I'll probably be out of reach. Saturday, we'll be checking into the Hyatt, and my every move will be captured by the media or Simon. Plus, I've got a tight schedule to maintain. So if you need me, send a text message to my pager."

Foody reached behind the bar and grabbed an icy Corona.

"Cool. We've got the trip worked out for tomorrow. Me and Fortune are heading down to Lynchburg first thing in the morning to get Julius's will."

Alex nodded and dealt the cards. "You've got to get that to the handwriting expert immediately. We don't have a moment to spare. I have to have the results back by Monday."

"That's pretty important stuff, Alex. I think I should ride with these fellows, just in case," Gerald said, and sipped on his beer.

Both Fortune and Foody turned toward Gerald and gave him an incredulous look. "We don't need no chaperone, Mr. Baxter," Fortune said, and picked up his cards.

"I'm not going as one. I'm going because it's in the best interest of my son," Gerald said.

"I think that's a good idea, Mr. B.," Lisa said. "There's safety in numbers."

"I'm cool with that," Foody said.

"Now, while they're gone, I need for you to make sure that you have security in place, Lisa. The next three days are going to be serious. If Simon gets wind that anything out of ordinary is going on, he's going to try something. So, watch him. And, I'd like for you to do one more thing. I know that Simon poisoned Tiffany that night of the fundraiser. When my father took her to the hospital, I told him to make sure they checked her system. There should be a tox screen in her records. Would you try to get a copy of it? I think it might be more good info to have just in case I need evidence that Simon tried to kill her."

"I'll get right on it. And, Alex," Lisa said, and reached into her purse. "I think you need to hang on to this." She handed him Ivan's old penlight/switchblade knife.

"It's like your mojo, bro," Fortune said. "Your good luck piece."

Alex flicked the switch and watched the blade spring out. "Thanks, Lisa. But, I hope I won't have to use it this time."

"Keep it as a 'just in case' type a thing," Foody said.

"Okay," Alex said, and then retracted the blade and placed it in his pant's pocket. "Until I have proof positive in my hands, we have to be as normal as possible. We can't let on anything."

Lisa picked up her cards and fanned them out. She cut her eyes over at Alex. "What if Julius's will is real?"

Alex laid his hand down, and glanced toward the stairs. "I have a couple of long shots. I really didn't mention this to you all, but Tiffany started questioning whether Simon is really her father."

Everyone except Fortune looked surprised. "I know, I know. It's a long story, and I'll tell you another time. But, based on Simon's blood type, he could be, but then we don't know what the other man's type is."

"And, what's that gonna prove?" Fortune asked.

"Nothing, really. But maybe you could blackmail him," Lisa said. "I'm sure the great Simon doesn't want the world to know that he was cuckolded and Tiffany's not his child."

Alex tapped his cards on the table. "It's a stretch. Plus, I don't think we have enough time for that, Lisa. If Julius's will doesn't do it, then I'll have to bluff. I have Marjorie's will, and once Lisa gets Tiffany's tox screen, I'll have to make my move with that. I can threaten to expose his wife's murder and Tiffany's attempted murder. And, it'll have to work."

There was a loud clatter, and the sound of breaking glass. Tiffany was standing at the base of the steps and had dropped a pitcher of lemonade.

"What do you mean, once Lisa gets my 'tox screen'? And what murder are you talking about, Alex? I want to know what the hell's going on in here. Right now!"

CHAPTER 28

T HERE WAS no sugarcoating, no fast-talking, and no glossing it over. The day of reckoning had come, and Tiffany was not about to let it go without complete disclosure.

Alex leaped to his feet, and, stepping through the broken glass, tried to get her to go upstairs, but Tiffany was defiant. "I'm not going anywhere, Alex. Nowhere. I'm sick of this. You better tell me what you and your band of merry men and women are talking about. Right now."

Everyone hung their heads as Alex stuttered. "Tiff, Tiffany, it's not what you think."

"Oh, that you're down here discussing my business with your friends? That's exactly what I think and exactly what it sounded like."

"There are a lot of things you don't know."

"What am I, a child? I'm not playing with you, Alex. So help me God, I will not be handled with kid gloves anymore. You told me that you'd never lie to me or keep anything from me, and I walk in on the tail end of some more secrets. I thought we were going to communicate with each other. So, tell me the truth."

"You need to tell your wife the truth, son," Gerald said, and rubbed the back of his neck.

Alex grabbed his wife's arm, and led her to the sofa. "I don't know where to start."

"Start at the get-go," Fortune said, and then he stood to go clean up the beverage spill.

Alex paused and rubbed his hands together. "Tiffany, remember I told you that there might come a time when you needed to trust me and only me? Well, now's the time. I have my doubts about Simon being your father. Namely, because he tried to kill you the night of the boating accident. He poisoned you, and the tox screen from the hospital would show that. I never told you about it, but he tried to kill me that night, too." Alex reached in his pocket and pulled out the knife. "This was my brother's knife. The same one I used when I stabbed Sid back at Hilliard. And if I hadn't had this, he would've killed me. I had to stab him to protect myself."

In between Tiffany's words of disbelief, Alex elaborated on that night's events. He glossed over the fact that he knew that Simon was a major drug dealer, but attributed their confrontation to his discovery that Simon had been involved in some dubious business dealings. He told Tiffany about the questionable nature of Marjorie's death, her will, the resurfacing of the pictures, their house being bugged, and the funneled money he had put in Alex's name. He brought her up to the present.

"He bugged our house? Our home? He put money in your name to make it look like you had done something illegal?"

"Yes, baby. He stooped that low. That's why I didn't want to move back into the house after the accident. And why I've been acting so strangely. I was concerned that he'd use those offshore accounts to blackmail me." Alex sighed. "I hate to tell you, but I even doubt that he has amnesia," he said as Tiffany's eyes glazed over. "It's too damned convenient."

Tiffany fell back on the sofa. "Well, how—why did you keep this from me for so long?" she asked, and her voice cracked.

"Because he was trying to protect you," Lisa said.

Tiffany dropped her head in her hands. "I just don't understand how my father could do something like this. He was the mayor of the city. How could he be so corrupt?"

"Because he is, Tiffany."

Tiffany closed her eyes and mumbled. "Oh, no. Aunt Giselle had told me that my parents' marriage had been in trouble, and that there was some doubt about who my father really was. It makes sense now. That's why he snapped that day. When I mentioned that I wanted to do a memorial for my mother, my father became very belligerent, but then he tried to play it off. But it bothered him because he was still angry with her for wanting to divorce him. I can't believe this, Alex. I just can't."

Alex lifted her chin. "I know you can't; that's why I never told you. Hell, I don't even believe all of it. But, even now, despite everything that's happened, Simon wants me to become mayor so he can get back into his dirty dealings, with me covering for him. I don't want to do it. But I haven't been able to get any evidence against him, so I have to go along with it."

Tiffany closed her eyes and when she opened them, she looked into each of their faces. "So, this is why you all are here. You've been helping Alex."

Everyone mumbled and nodded, while Fortune swept up the broken glass. "We had to help Alex, Tiffany," he said. "His life was as fucked up as this pitcher here. An' in almost as many little pieces."

Alex patted Tiffany's hand. "They're my family, Tiff. I mean our family. They're the only ones I could trust."

Tiffany shook her head. "And yet you didn't trust me enough to let me help you, too."

Alex grabbed her shoulders and moved his face close to hers. "It's not that I didn't trust you, Tiff. You had your own stuff you were dealing with. And I didn't want to get you involved and be hurt any more than you had to."

"Nothing's more important than you and our children, Alex. Can't you see that? I've learned so much about my life over the past few months that I'm not sure about anything other than you and our family." She inhaled deeply, her chest heaving. "You carried around all of this trying to protect me, but we're in this together. I want to know what I can do to help you now."

"That's what I'm talkin' about," Fortune said, and flung the broom down, and bobbed his head.

IT WAS GOOD that Tiffany knew, and it mitigated some of his fears, but added new ones. Alex was concerned that her emotions would get the best of her and somehow arouse Simon's suspicions.

They went over the plan countless times, with each action and reaction checked and rechecked. Handoffs and timing were critical. There could not be a misstep or a lapse. Especially since most of this was going to be played out in a very public forum.

By the time they'd hammered out every detail, it was well past one in the morning. Everyone ventured back to their respective homes, for at first light, the plan would be set in motion.

Alex barely slept that night. When the sun rose, he knew that his folks were headed to Virginia, and these were the final hours. He prayed for strength and protection, and kissed his wife's forehead. He had a job to do, and he was going to do it. And he was more than ready for it.

Alex went about his day, making his appearances, with Simon always on the periphery. Tiffany stayed close to him, too, holding his pager and cell phone. She took every opportunity to tell him how much she loved him, and her strength complemented his. Alex was able to play it cool, joking and laughing, and appearing upbeat and confident. With Monty scrambling to defend himself against those trumped-up allegations, Alex's approval rating had soared to over fifty-five percent. He was a shoo-in.

Around noon, while they were having lunch at Ben's Chili Bowl, Tiffany whispered in his ear that the "deed was done." Lisa had left the cryptic message that meant the will had been picked up and was on its way to be analyzed. Phase one of the plan was complete.

Alex sighed with relief, and inhaled his half-smoke. Smiling for the cameras, shaking hands and answering mundane questions was becoming second nature for him, but with Simon sitting on his shoulder, Alex felt phony and deceitful. He couldn't wait for this to be over.

By evening, Lisa had paged again, with news that she had gotten Tiffany's hospital records. Tiffany's blood level showed an elevated level of phenobarbital, a barbiturate. It could have killed her, had Alex not induced vomiting or had she not gotten to the hospital when she did.

TIFFANY AND ALEX relocated their family to the Hyatt, and the last-minute campaigning intensified. They had a block of rooms on the fifteenth floor, where everyone had set up camp. Simon, Jessica, Gerald, Lisa, and some of Alex's staff had suites and rooms on that floor. Fortune and some of Lisa's agents kept a close eye on the smug Simon and Alex and his family, while Lisa and Foody electronically monitored them.

With a flurry of appearances scheduled, Alex could barely maintain his train of thought, much less maintain his face. But, he was staging a masterful performance, even with that clock loudly ticking in his head.

Saturday and Sunday passed without incident, and on Monday, judgment day had arrived. There was still no word from the handwriting expert, and the grains of sand were almost out of the hourglass. He muddled through a last-minute debate with his opponents, and by Monday evening, he was on the brink of winning the biggest race of his life, and losing the most critical element in his life. His integrity.

It was after eight o'clock that night when the analysis was finally completed. Lisa paged Alex immediately and informed him that it was ninety-eight percent conclusive that Julius's signature on his will was forged. And the icing on the cake was that it had been notarized by an M. Newton. "Marjorie Newton" had notarized the will, a full seven years after her death. How could Simon have become so cocky that he'd committed such a damning error?

Alex picked Tiffany up and spun her around in his arms. "Baby, we're free!" he yelled.

"Shhhh. You'll wake the babies." Tiffany struggled until her feet reached the ground. "What happened? Was the signature on Julius's will forged?"

"You know it," he said and gave her a big, sloppy kiss. "I knew I'd get him. Julius's will was signed in 1977, and guess who 'notarized' it? Your mother."

"You're kidding, right? Why would he do that?" Tiffany asked. "Why would he use her name like that?"

"Why does Simon do half the things he does? He's cruel. It was probably another way to disrespect her memory. And, he's greedy, and he never thought that anyone would think to go and look up Julius's will way down there in Lynchburg. Think about it. Look how long it took us to figure it out."

"So, this is all over now? You're really not going to be mayor?" Tiffany asked, and her eyes registered slight disappointment.

Alex leaned over and kissed her forehead. "Don't be sad about this. Maybe one day I will run, and maybe one day I'll win. But, I want to do it because I want to do it, not because someone thinks that I should."

"But you'd make a good mayor, Alex."

"Thanks, baby. But I don't deserve to be mayor. Simon has pulled so many strings and leveled so many lives that I don't want to be a part of that. I want to stand on my own merit. Nothing else."

Tiffany rubbed his cheek. "If that's how you feel, then you need to do what you think is right. I'll stand behind you."

"Thanks, Tiff. Now, I'm going to go have a little chat with your father. And put an end to this game."

JUST AS ALEX WAS about to leave his suite, Lisa phoned. "Your boy just gave us the slip," she said. "Simon's MIA."

"What do you mean, Lisa? I thought you all were watching him. Where'd he go?"

"I have no idea. But, we're looking for him."

"That's not good enough. I need to know where he is. You know I can't bow out of the race until I confront him."

"Do you think he might've gotten word of what we were doing?"

"I don't know," Alex said.

"What's going on?" Tiffany asked.

Alex told her about the latest turn of events, and Tiffany's face went blank. "I'm thinking that someone at the records office in Lynchburg contacted him," he said finally.

"You're probably right. You know Dad has friends everywhere, and he probably had someone there that knew to contact him if anyone ever came looking for that will."

Lisa overheard what Tiffany had said and agreed. "I guess we screwed this one up, didn't we?"

"Damn!" Alex yelled. "I could kick myself. Why didn't I think that he'd have some twenty-year safety net in place?"

"I'm going to pour myself a drink," Tiffany said, and walked over to the fully stocked bar. "Do you want one?"

Alex nodded, and began to pace.

"Why would he disappear?" Tiffany asked, and handed Alex a cognac.

"He has to be up to something," Alex said.

"Maybe he just wants to be a ghost until after the election," Lisa said. "Maybe he figures that you wouldn't have the nerve to resign then."

Alex sipped his drink. "He doesn't know the nerve I've got. Lisa, we have to find him. Even if I have to get out there myself and look, we have to find Simon. Right now."

CHAPTER 29

LISA DISPATCHED a full team of agents to search for Simon, but to no avail. Tuesday morning came, and the polls opened. A sleep-deprived Alex reluctantly made his rounds, with Tiffany in tow. Fortune insisted on shadowing them, and was sticking to Alex like velcro.

Everywhere Alex went, he and Fortune searched the faces in the crowd for Simon. Though Alex was met with rousing support, he was becoming unnerved. He didn't know what Simon had up his sleeve. And then he found out. Lisa called. Simon was showing up at various polling places, encouraging voters to come out. The moment Lisa's men arrived, he vanished. Only to show up forty-five minutes later at another location.

It was Alex's worst nightmare. Simon was taunting him in a game of cat and mouse, and it continued throughout the entire morning. When they were on their way to another appearance, he called Lisa.

"Why can't you find him, Lisa? Why is Simon running all over town, yet we can't seem to get him?"

"Because he don't want to be gotten, Alex," Fortune said. "No disrespect, Tiffany, but your old man is a shysty, slick-ass son of a bitch, and he's gamin' Alex. He's tryin' to unnerve you."

"Fortune's right," Lisa said. "You've left messages for him, I've had Jessica page him, but he's ignoring everyone. He's playing you out in front of the media, and there's nothing you can do about it. We can't even get a make on the car he's driving. I swear, I think he's changing them, too."

Tiffany was changing the channels on the limo's television, and shook her head. "Look at Channel Seven. Dad's over in Southeast at one of the polling places on Minnesota Avenue."

"Did you hear that, Lisa?" Alex said, and then glanced at the TV. "Turn up the volume, Tiff."

Simon was regaling for the cameras, smiling and chatting it up with the voters. He was promoting Alex to the max, with every other word about making Alexander Baxter the mayor.

"And I'm not just saying that because he's my son-in-law," Simon quipped. "I'm telling everyone to come on out and vote for Alex because he's the best man for the job."

"Get somebody on him, Lisa. If he's in Southeast, there's no telling where he's going next."

"Mayor Blake," the reporter said. "We're surprised that you're not with Alex right now. Is this some kind of new strategy?"

Simon pulled out his pipe and started puffing. "Not at all, not at all. Alex and his lovely wife are making their rounds, and I'm out here doing what I do best. Standing with my people." Simon stared into the camera. "I'm doing what I do best."

Alex took that directly to heart. "Lisa, don't bother. There's no way you're going to find him. He's not going to face me until the bitter end. And when he wants to see me, he'll make it known."

"He's not goin' to see you unless he sees me, Alex," Fortune said.

"And I'm still going to keep trying. We've come too far to blow it now," Lisa said.

Alex hung up the phone, and Tiffany grabbed his hand. "She's right, you know. You have come too far to give up now. Maybe it's meant for you to win this election, baby."

Alex turned and stared out the darkened window, unwilling to accept the hand fate was dealing him. "Where are we due now?"

THE GAME CONTINUED for the rest of the day, until Alex was scheduled to return to the Hyatt and watch the tallying of the votes and reports from each ward with his staff. It was almost seven, and the polls were scheduled to close at eight. Simon was still a no-show, and Alex was teeming with rage. It was the one trick he hadn't seen coming. And, it was simply brilliant.

They dropped Fortune off at the corner of Eleventh and G Streets, so that he could enter the hotel without being seen. Alex and Tiffany made their grand entrance on the carpeted valet area, and amidst the flashing bulbs and bright lights of the television cameras, they made a perfect picture.

Lisa and a few of her men escorted them through the crowd, and Alex noticed that Fortune was waiting near the elevators.

"Alex, my feet are killing me," Tiffany said. "I need to go change these pumps before we go into the ballroom." She adjusted his tie. "I think you should change your shirt, too. It looks a little unkempt."

Alex motioned for one of Lisa's men to accompany Tiffany upstairs. "I need to talk to Lisa for a moment, and then I'll be up." He kissed her on the cheek. "I love you."

"I love you, too," Tiffany said, and then headed toward the elevator.

"There's still no sign of him, Alex," Lisa said, before Alex even asked the question.

"Where's Foody?"

"With your family in the ballroom. There's a nice buffet in there, so I don't even know why you asked that question," Lisa said.

"If he's gonna make his move, it's got to be soon," Fortune said, and glanced around. "You got your folks covering all the entrances and exits, right?"

"They're even working the service elevators," Lisa said.

Alex hunched his tired shoulders. "I'm done. I'm going to go up and change, and I'll be back in a few."

"I'll go with you, man," Fortune said.

"And I'll be out here in the lobby," Lisa said.

ALEX AND FORTUNE headed into the service elevator, where one of Lisa's agents was waiting. The elevator doors closed, and the agent pressed fifteen. Alex started to speak, but Fortune nudged him, and then glanced at the guard. Before Alex could utter a word, the agent spun around, and pointed a .45 at Alex, and then at Fortune. "Your presence is requested on the roof."

When they reached the roof, Alex and Fortune reluctantly stepped out of the elevator, and the guard stuck Fortune with a stun gun. He went down like a lead balloon.

"Why'd you do that?" Alex asked, and bent down to help Fortune, but the guard pressed the barrel of the gun against his temple.

"Keep moving."

In the air was a familiar scent. Alex could see Simon's silhouette against the backdrop of the city. Simon was puffing on his pipe. The city lights sparkled, and the sounds of moving traffic barely reached them. For a split second, Alex wanted to rush him and knock him over the railing, even if that meant they both would plummet to their deaths.

"Simon. You've been a hard man to catch up with today."

Simon kept puffing and spoke without turning around. "Alexander Baxter. You've been quite an active young man yourself. And to think that I thought that you'd be busy campaigning, and you're out playing I-Spy."

"So, you know, huh?" Alex asked.

Simon spun around. "Don't you know that I know everything? Look around you. I made this city. Haven't you learned that yet? A rat can't piss on Florida Avenue and I not know about it. How many times am I going to have to teach you that lesson?"

"Oh, so you admit your memory finally returned. Just in time. Now perhaps you can explain some of your actions," Alex said.

"Explain what? I don't explain anything to you. You work for me, remember?"

Alex rubbed his hands. The night March air had a clinging chill to it. "I used to. Not anymore. If you don't play your cards right, the only work you'll be doing is pressing out license plates."

Simon smirked and smoked. "Very funny. Seems like we had this conversation before, and we know how that ended up. You'll never win, Alex. You can't win. You'll never beat me."

"Never say never, Simon. You might live to eat those words."

"If I do eat them, it won't be from any meal you're serving," Simon said, and folded his arms across his chest. "You know, you disappoint me, Alex. You're so bright, yet you can't follow instructions. You just can't leave well enough alone, can you?"

"I'll never listen to you again, Simon. And I mean that. You have done everything in your power to control and destroy my life, and it's over. This twisted little game of yours is over."

"I'll say when it's over. And it's not yet," Simon said. "Not until you give me my money back. . . . That's right. I went looking for my money, and it was gone. And I want it back."

Alex laughed. "You've got to be kidding. I don't know what you're talking about. What money? Was that another part of your sick little game? Come on, I'll play with you, because you proba- bly went looking for it to try to make it seem like I had some finan- cial improprieties going on. But guess what? I beat you to it. I beat you, Simon, you sick son of a bitch."

Simon raised his eyebrows. "Well, we sure are confident these days, aren't we? But confidence is only part of what you need if you want to play with the big boys. And if you think for one minute I'm going to let you walk away with my ends, you don't have half the brains I thought you did."

"So, what do you want, Simon? You want your money back? Your money and then you'll get out of our lives forever? Yeah, right. You must think I'm stupid."

Simon blew ringlets of smoke into the air and yawned. "You know, Alex, you bore me. I can't believe that this is the best you were able to come up with. I can always make more money. But you'll never live to spend a dime of it. You or your wife."

"My wife? Or do you mean your daughter?"

"What?"

Alex glanced over his shoulder to see if Fortune had awakened, but he only saw the guard standing in the shadows. "You heard me. How does it feel to know that you tried to kill your own child? Tiffany is your daughter, in case you didn't know it." Alex hoped that he could maintain a poker face.

Simon drew his pipe from his lips. "What are you talking about? Tiffany isn't my child."

"She is. You proved it the other day when you had your blood taken. You have the same blood type. Based on his blood type, Edgar Cavanaugh couldn't possibly be her father," Alex lied.

Simon pursed his lips. "I don't believe you. And anyway, it doesn't matter."

"Oh, but it will. Because I can prove that you tried to kill your own daughter. And as you say, an allegation may actually be worse than the truth."

"My, my, my. You have been a busy little bee, haven't you?" Simon's eye twitched. "I'd be proud of you, if I wasn't furious at your deception."

"Deception? You're the king of deception. And manipulation. I don't want you to be proud of me, because anything you're proud of is clearly wrong.

"And speaking of deception, I'm not sure how you plan on beating a forgery rap. Make that two forgery raps. We both know that you faked your wife's and Julius's wills." Alex could feel the air being sucked out of Simon's lungs.

"Humph, you have really done your homework, Alex. You've undone more in six months than most men have tried in my lifetime. You have really thought this thing through. Like, the money trail."

"It no longer exists," Alex said, and he felt confidence swelling in his chest. "You have nothing to hang over my head. I'm no longer dancing to your tune."

Simon shrugged. "Well, I guess you got me. The teacher has been beaten by the student."

"You mean the slave has finally revolted against his master. Now, it's time for you to dance to my tune. I'm going to withdraw from this election, and then you're going to disappear. This time, for good. And if I ever hear or see anything unsavory about you, I swear that I'll have you locked up so fast that you won't know what hit you."

Simon clapped his hands, and the sound echoed across the roof. "Bravo, Alex," he said, and then motioned for his guard to leave. By this time Fortune was waking up, and clutching his head.

"Alex! Are you all right?" Fortune asked.

"I'm fine, Fortune. Just fine," Alex said, and smirked at Simon.

Simon tamped his pipe against the concrete wall, and blew out the tobacco particles. He walked toward Alex and extended his hand, but Alex refused to shake it. "Well, Alex, I guess I have to agree to your terms. But, before we go down and you make your concessions, I had arranged for you to meet one of your constituents. I told her that you'd love to meet her and her family."

The elevator door opened, and a young woman, a teenage girl, and a little boy walked onto the roof. "Alex, I think you know this young lady. Her name is Stacey. But, I don't think that you've met her daughter, Mya, before."

Stacey stood beside her daughter, a pretty young lady who looked as if she was in the midst of adjusting to braces, bras, and a budding body. "Hi, Alex," Stacey said, and she smiled a weak smile. "Mayor Blake said that you wanted to see us. I was real surprised."

Alex's face dropped as Simon walked over and grabbed Stacey and Mya by the shoulders. Then he bent down and picked up the little boy. "And this, is—What's your name, little man?"

"I-van," the little boy said.

"That's right, Ivan. You should really meet this little guy, Alex. Seems like he's someone you need to know. Like your son."

Alex caught Fortune's eyes and wanted the roof to swallow him up whole.

"Alex, man. You didn't," Fortune said. "Stacey, is that you?"

"Fortune?" Stacey said, and peered over her shoulder.

When Stacey walked over to Fortune, Simon sidled up to Alex, still holding Ivan, who was playing with Simon's tie.

"Now, do you plan on including this in your concession speech, or should we drop by the fifteenth floor to get Tiffany's input on it? Huh?" Simon cooed at Ivan, and then squinted his eyes at Alex. "Now, who's beat whom? If this doesn't teach you not to fuck with me, nothing will. Always remember that, you stupid little punk. I own your ass, lock and key. Always remember that."

CHAPTER 30

ALEX HAD COME too far and endured too much to be beaten by Simon now, but time was against him. He had Simon on the forgery, but that wasn't enough to trump Simon's Stacey play. Simon had outwitted him once again, but he wasn't going to give up. He shoved his right hand in his pants pocket and felt Ivan's knife. It took all of his might not to take that knife and, this time, make sure Simon died. But that wasn't the solution.

While Fortune and Stacey talked, Alex again laid his cards on the table.

"I don't care, Simon. I'll tell Tiffany about this myself. I'm not going to let you destroy everyone, just so you can get what you want. I swear I'm going to make sure you go down this time."

Simon shrugged. "We'll see, Alex. I don't believe for one second that you'll throw everything away just because you want me to go away. You're too smart for that. Why should you care about a few wills? Trust me, by the time I'm done with the spin, no one else is going to care about it. And remember, I have been diagnosed with amnesia. The charges will never stick."

Simon clutched Alex's shoulder and turned him around. "Now, why don't you go have your little conversation with your wife. Or should I bring Stacey and family down to meet your lovely wife and children. You'll have one big happy family." Simon's expression turned thoughtful. "I don't think so. You know what, we'll skip the introductions for now, and I'll go on downstairs with your illegitimate child as the ballots are counted, and get ready for your acceptance speech. I hope you're prepared."

Alex jerked away from Simon's grasp. "I'll be prepared. You just get prepared to exchange your jewelry for a set of steel bracelets," Alex said, and stood nose to nose with his former mentor.

Stacey appeared confused as Simon reached for her hand. "Come on, Stacey," Simon said, pushing Alex aside. "We have a celebration to attend."

Fortune approached Alex, his face filled with disappointment. "Man, Stacey told me what happened. But how could you do it? With Stacey of all people. That was Ivan's girl," Fortune said. "I understand what she said, but, I swear, I just don't get it. You know I got yo' back 'bout a lotta stuff, but this? I don't know. Somehow I feel like you disrespected my boy."

"Fortune, I can't change what happened. I'm not asking you to back me on this one, but I don't feel like I disrespected Ivan. If anything, I tried to care for the woman that he loved. Because that's what she needed."

"Yeah, but you the one that's gotta kid with her."

"I don't know that for sure."

"You know you did her without coverin' up, don't you?" Fortune waved his hands and turned away. "But that's beside the point right now. Simon's got yo' ass again, doesn't he?"

"No doubt. And now, I have to either go on and play his game, or go talk to my wife. Either way, I'm screwed."

Fortune shook his head. "Give your girl a little more credit. Y'all done been through hell and it ain't over yet. You don't have a choice but to go talk to her. 'Cause if you don't, you're letting Simon get at you with no resistance. An' I know you ain't tryin' to go out like that."

Alex held out his hand for Fortune to slap. "Not at all, Fortune. Not at all."

ALEX FELT LIKE A DEAD MAN walking as he and Fortune exited the elevator on the fifteenth floor and silently made their way down to the suite where Tiffany waited. The night's events had spiraled away so quickly from what he had planned, and though he had tried to anticipate Simon's every action and reaction, he had no backup plan for this scenario.

As he reached his suite, Fortune grabbed his shoulder. "You want me to come in?"

"No, I don't think so," Alex nodded. "This is one conversation that my wife and I have to have alone."

Fortune nodded. "I'll go down and keep an eye on Simon and Stacey." He gave Alex some dap. "Be strong, my brother. Be strong."

WHEN ALEX ENTERED the suite, Tiffany was in the living room, wearing a navy blue worsted wool suit, holding two pairs of black shoes. "Alex, I'm glad you're here. Have you decided if you're going through with this? Either way, I'm going to be by your side, but I want to look my best. I can't decide which pair of shoes to wear. I don't want to appear matronly, but I'm not sure. I was going to ask Aunt Giselle, but she's in the back with the children."

Alex smiled at his wife and pointed at the pair in her right hand. "Tiffany, I need to talk to you."

Tiffany set the discarded pair on the floor and slipped her feet into the black pumps Alex had suggested. "About what? What took you so long?"

Alex guided her to the sofa, and he sat down beside her and inhaled deeply. He took her hands and kissed them. "It's your father. He finally showed up."

Tiffany twitched. "What happened? What did he say when you told him about the wills? Was he angry?"

"He didn't react like I thought he would. I thought he'd concede defeat, but he didn't. He pulled something else out of his sleeve."

"What?"

"Stacey."

"Stacey? Who's that?"

Alex rubbed her hand. "The girl from the pictures. My brother's ex-girlfriend. Stacey. Evidently, Simon was the one that sent the pictures, and he made it his mission to find her and bring her here tonight."

"Why would he do that?"

"Because—Stacey has a child. And he might be mine."

Tiffany snatched her hand from Alex's grasp, and shouted, "What? You've got to be kidding."

"Tiffany, please keep your voice down. Isn't Aunt Giselle back there?"

"I don't care."

"Tiffany, I didn't know. Stacey never told me anything. She never contacted me."

"Alex. How could you let something like this happen?" Tiffany stood and glared at him. "How could you?"

"I didn't. Simon did."

"Simon didn't create that child. You did."

Alex tried to face his wife, but she turned away. He reached for her, and she smacked his face. "I can't believe you, Alex. We have been through so damned much, and just when I think that I've taken all that I can, you come up with something else."

Alex rubbed his jaw and wondered if he'd have a handprint on the side of his face. "Tiffany, I'm not excusing the fact that I slept with Stacey and her child might be mine, but Simon pulled these strings. Can't you see that Simon is behind all of this? He's been faking his amnesia, probably since day one. Somehow he must have figured out that I was on to him, and he brought her into this. From day one, he's manipulated and hurt everyone who's ever come in contact with him."

"What do you mean?"

"I know that he is personally responsible for the deaths of two of the most important people in our lives. Hell, my brother was killed because of him, and he killed your mother because she was going to divorce him."

Tiffany gasped. *"What?"*

Alex told Tiffany about Fortune's firsthand account of Ivan's and her mother's deaths, leaving out no details.

Tiffany started shaking. "My father never talked about my mother. Or visited her grave. And I thought it was because he was hurt by her death, but maybe he never loved her. Everything I've thought I knew about him has turned out to be a lie. I don't know what is true anymore."

Alex reached for his wife, and this time she didn't withdraw. "I had hoped that I'd never have to tell you the extent of your father's wrongdoings, but he's given me no choice. He doesn't care about anyone other than himself. Not even his grandchildren. He put illegal funds in an offshore account in Alex's and Anya's names."

Tiffany grabbed Alex by the collar. "No, Alex. No he didn't. He didn't use our children."

"Yes, he did Tiffany. We're just pawns to him. And he'll destroy us if we allow the issue of Stacey's son to ruin us."

Tiffany released Alex's collar and looked at him. "Alex, you're asking me to deal with so much. I—"

"I know I'm asking for an awful lot, Tiff. But consider the circumstances. Now that you know, I'm willing to go through with being mayor, but we've got to resolve this Stacey situation. And we can't do it tonight. Can we work it through together?"

"I don't know if I can."

"You love me, don't you?"

"Of course I do, Alex. I just can't take any more surprises."

"I promise not to bring anything else to bear on you, Tiffany. I promise. But I need you to get through this."

Tiffany looked into her husband's eyes and then raised hers to the ceiling. "I do love you, Alex. And I'll try to be here with you. But, it's not going to be easy."

Alex reached for his wife's hands. "I know. But it has never been easy. But, now you know everything. And with you and this," Alex said, and withdrew Ivan's knife from his pocket, "I know I'll make it through tonight."

"Alex, what are you going to do with that? You aren't going to—"

"No, Tiff. I want you to keep it for me. Hopefully, it'll bring us some luck. We're going to need it."

WHILE ALEX CHANGED into the blue pinstripe suit Tiffany had laid out for him, Tiffany took Alex's lucky charm and slid it inside her handbag. The couple looked at each other, their eyes reflecting their resolve to take on Simon and whatever else awaited them in the ballroom.

"Aunt Giselle?" Tiffany called out, as they were just about ready to leave. "Are you coming?"

Aunt Giselle walked out into the living area looking a little shaken. "My, don't you two look wonderful. Just the picture of an enterprising young power couple." She reached over and gave them both a hug and a kiss. "I just called Mrs. Owens, dear, and as soon as she comes over to stay with the children, I'll be down. Good luck, Alex," she said, and gave them a final once-over.

"Tiffany, dear. Are you sure you need your handbag? It may get in the way with all the activity going on."

Tiffany paused and then gave her aunt her purse. "Would you mind bringing it down when you come? Thanks, Auntie," Tiffany said, and she reached for Alex's hand. "I guess we're ready, huh?"

"We're more than ready, baby," Alex said.

THE BALLROOM WAS FILLED with TV monitors, reporters and cameramen, well-wishers and rabble-rousers. By the time Alex and Tiffany made their grand entrance, the polls had closed, and the results were streaming in. By all accounts, Alex was going to win the election by a landslide.

They were immediately swarmed. Camera lights flashed and reporters shoved microphones in his face, but Alex, with Tiffany holding his arm, downplayed his pending victory.

"It's not over until it's over," Alex said, and forced a smile. "I have some very strong opponents, and there's no telling what the final results will be. I'd like to reserve comment until that time."

"Mr. Blake, more than half of the polling places have reported their results, and it's almost inevitable that you will be declared the winner. Won't you give the public a little something?" a young woman reporter asked.

Alex smiled and kissed his wife's forehead. "Yes, you can tell them that I'm a very thankful and blessed man. No matter what the outcome."

They maneuvered through the crowd, and Alex surveyed the room, hoping to locate Simon. He noticed that Aunt Giselle and his father had arrived. As she had promised, she was carrying Tiffany's bag as they were guided through the crowd by one of Lisa's security guards. Alex then spotted Lisa, Fortune, and Foody standing in a far corner, and Stacey and family seated at a table near the rear. Alex was so swamped with the paparazzi that he couldn't break free to get to his friends. But he knew that Fortune had already clued Lisa and Foody in, and that they were all keeping a watchful eye on the events.

Simon managed to reach Alex and Tiffany, and leaned over and gave Tiffany a kiss on the cheek. "Hello, darling," he said, and Tiffany bristled.

"Father," she said coldly.

Simon smirked and guided them over to an area near the podium where a large screen TV was set up. "I trust this means that you're going through with your obligation, Alex," he whispered. "I was wondering if I'd have to make a proper introduction between Tiffany and your bastard child. But, perhaps another time."

"It's only a matter of moments, now," Simon announced to the room. "But it looks like our guy is going to be the next mayor of our fair city."

The room exploded with thunderous applause, and almost on cue, reporters rushed Alex, as the newscasters made the announcement. "With over eighty-nine percent of the polls reporting in, we are pleased to announce that Alex Baxter has been elected the new mayor of Washington, D.C."

Alex's heart sank. His moment of reckoning was here. Tiffany hugged him amid an explosion of flashbulbs and camera lights, as red, white, and blue balloons and confetti were released from the ceiling.

Alex's father and Aunt Giselle joined Tiffany and Alex next to the stage. The roar from the crowd was overwhelming, and it was difficult to hear.

"Congratulations, son," Gerald said, and hugged Alex so tightly, that he could barely breathe. "You're going to make a fine mayor."

"Yes, you will, Alex," Aunt Giselle agreed, and had barely uttered her comments before Simon commandeered the podium. He seized the microphone, and gestured for Alex and family to join him on the stage.

"May I have your attention please." Simon's request was met with a few catcalls and wolf whistles as the crowd continued to cheer. He motioned for the crowd to quiet.

Simon was beaming. He was in his element. Once again the city was his stage and all of its citizens his fans. As the television cameras zoomed in on his face, his image appeared on all of the television screens in the ballroom.

"I am so very proud to stand before you today. What I am about to do is to introduce to you not only a very special member of my family—"

Before Simon could complete his sentence, Aunt Giselle had quietly sidled next to him, and was reaching for the microphone. "Simon, I hope you don't mind if I say a few words before your speech," she said, with a slight smile.

A look of confusion briefly crossed Simon's face, but he quickly smiled as the camera lights flashed. "Giselle?" He glanced around and adjusted his shirt collar. "Why, this is quite unexpected. Well, sure. After all, you are family." Simon handed her the mic, but held on to it momentarily. "I trust that you'll be brief. This is live television, you know." Simon smiled and winked for the camera, and the audience applauded.

He stepped aside as Alex and Tiffany glanced at each other, then shrugged and focused on Aunt Giselle.

The audience quieted down as Aunt Giselle slowly cleared her throat. "I think that it is most appropriate that before our new mayor is introduced, we recognize the person most responsible for making this all possible. Simon Blake."

Simon stepped closer to Giselle and waved, and the audience roared again. Giselle cleared her throat and continued. "I have known this man for over thirty years, and I can truly say that he has a way of making things happen.

"When my sister, Marjorie, first started dating you, I accepted you into my family because she truly loved you. Or at least she loved the man she thought you were. And when she realized you weren't that man, you decided she no longer deserved to live."

The audience gasped and fell silent. Simon's smile froze upon his face. Giselle continued. "I didn't know that you were a murderous scoundrel, but for years, I wondered about you and what really lay behind that smug façade of yours. You never even grieved after my sister died. But, I thrust myself into the love and care of my niece, my sister's child, and tried to shield her from the ills of your world. And I thought that I had, until I learned that you had tried to kill her, too. Apparently, she has also done something to have fallen out of favor with you.

"When will it end, Simon? With Tiffany's children? I think not, for I understand that you've already preyed upon their innocence for your own selfish gain. I shudder to think what you will do to them once they outlive their usefulness."

Simon reached for the mic, but Giselle snatched it away. "Giselle, please," Simon pleaded. "I think you've said enough. Security? This woman is deranged. I don't think that she's taken her medication today."

Giselle kept talking. "I couldn't live with myself if I allowed your reign of harm to continue. You have hurt the people I love for so long that it's second nature for you. It's who you are. It's what you do. But you won't cast your web over another generation of my family. You are a disease that sickens me and threatens to spread to others. And now, I'm going to do the city and the world a favor."

Giselle reached into Tiffany's bag, pulling out Alex's knife. The audience gasped as the blade projected. Simon reached for the knife, but Giselle quickly plunged it into Simon's heart.

Simon clutched his chest and fell backward.

"Oh, God!" Tiffany screamed as she and Alex rushed to Simon's side.

"Jesus!" Simon gasped, blood pooling under his hand. "Somebody do something."

Security circled the stage, and the crowd rose to its feet as Gerald held Giselle's arm as she stood riveted in the same place.

"Somebody call an ambulance!" a face in the crowd yelled, as the reporters scrambled to move in closer.

"Cut the cameras!"

"Keep rolling!"

In the middle of the melee Alex knelt down beside Simon, and stared at his wound. Tiffany held his head in her lap and wiped his forehead.

Simon coughed, and blood trickled from his lips. "Well, Alex. I didn't see this coming."

Alex opened up Simon's jacket and watched as the blood poured from his chest. "Me neither."

"Shh, Father. Don't try to talk," Tiffany said.

Wheezing, Simon struggled to breathe. "Somehow I feel cheated. I would've never thought that old bag had it in her."

"Being hurt makes you do crazy things, Simon. And I guess you finally hurt the wrong one," Alex said.

Simon coughed again, and spit up bloody mucus. "I would've felt better had you beat me. But, at least you didn't."

"*I* might not have beat you, but you lost. Therefore, I've won. We all have." Alex said as Simon's eyes closed for the final time.

A team of medics arrived and immediately started administering CPR. "He's crashing!" one medic shouted, and then called for a defibrillator. They lifted Simon onto a gurney, while still trying to revive him.

Tiffany followed the medics, while the police led away an unresponsive Giselle.

Lisa instructed her men to keep the reporters at bay, and then she, Fortune, and Foody surrounded Alex. They stared at him, but Alex's face remained blank.

Fortune finally broke the silence. "Did he say anything?"

Alex rubbed his face. "He didn't see it coming."

"Unbelievable," Lisa said. "I would never believe this if I hadn't seen it myself." Foody nodded in agreement.

Alex grunted. "It is unbelievable. Imagine how Simon must've felt. He looked at everyone and everything as a challenge. He always had to think five moves ahead of you. He always had to manipulate you into doing what he wanted you to do. He always had to outwit you. He had to beat you. He had to destroy you. And he ended up losing to the one person he wasn't even playing against. She beat him and he never even had her in the game." Alex sighed and rubbed his hands. "I'm sure that Simon's more bothered by who killed him than the fact that he got killed. How ironic is that?"

"It's called what goes around, comes around," Fortune said.

"It's karma."

"Kar-what?"

"Nevermind, Fortune. I'm too tired to even talk about it any more."

Fortune grabbed Alex's shoulder. "Alex, you should be beat. You know what I said a long time ago, yo' life's been like that game of Simon Says. Hmph. But now, Simon ain't got nuttin' to say, except for—"

"Game's over," Alex said.

EVERY SHUT EYE

A Reader's Guide

COLLEN DIXON

READING GROUP
QUESTIONS AND TOPICS FOR DISCUSSION

The questions and discussion topics that follow are intended to enhance your group's reading of Collen Dixon's *Every Shut Eye*. We hope they will provide new insights and ways of looking at this suspense-filled novel.

1. When Alex and Tiffany's marriage begins to unravel, Tiffany wonders if she and Alex got married too young. Should Alex and Tiffany have waited until they were older to get married? Are younger people able to understand the lifelong commitment that successful marriages require? Should people attain a certain age before they get married?

To print out copies of this or other Strivers Row Reading Group Guides, visit us at www.atrandom.com/rgg

2. As soon as Fortune meets Lisa he knows that he is interested in her. As the months go by, Fortune cleans up his act with the hope that Lisa will become attracted to him. Is it fair that Fortune changed his entire lifestyle while Lisa changed nothing about herself? Are there times when one member of a couple must step up and make significant life changes to please his or her partner? Would you consider changing something about yourself to be with someone who had not expressed interest in you?

3. Although Simon was mayor of one of this country's most prominent cities, he was not content with his job—he developed an alter ego and became a criminal kingpin. Why would someone in Simon's position take up such a dangerous and illegal second line of work? Does Simon have any chance of being remembered for all the good work he did as mayor, or is his reputation irreparably tarnished by his illegal actions? Do you think that Simon would have ever given up his corrupt activities?

4. Despite his own wishes to the contrary, Alex is elected mayor of Washington. Do you think that he will accept the position? If he does accept the position, will he make a good mayor? Will Alex's time as mayor be marred by the fact that Simon played an important role in his campaign? If Alex turns down the job, do you think that he will one day decide to run for mayor on his own terms?

5. When Tiffany finds out that Alex lied when he said Tiffany was the only woman he had slept with, she contemplates committing adultery with Vincent. Would Tiffany's adultery have been worse than Alex's premarital betrayal? Should Alex have come clean with Tiffany earlier, or was he right to attempt to spare his wife's feelings? If Tiffany had committed adultery, would Alex have been able to forgive her?

6. Alex's friend Foody nearly dies in his attempt to remove files from Moses' warehouse. Do you think that Alex is appropriately

grateful to Foody for his loyalty and the ordeal he went through? Can Alex do anything that would properly repay Foody for his work? If the situation demanded it, would most friends be as loyal as Foody is to Alex?

7. When Tiffany finds out that Simon might not be her father, she feels compelled to discover the truth. If Simon were not Tiffany's father, do you think that Tiffany would have cut him out of her life? If Simon were her father, would Tiffany have been more likely to forgive him for his betrayals? Is it possible for a child to simply stop caring about the person they believed was their father for almost thirty years? If you were in Tiffany's position, would you have wanted to know who your biological father was?

8. Simon doesn't particularly value any of his aides. After Howard nurses him back to health, Simon never pursues his apparent murder by the Cavanaughs. And, shortly after Royce signs on to be his assistant, Simon murders him. Why doesn't Simon express greater gratitude for Howard's help? Could Simon ever take on a partner for his illegal activities? Is Simon a cold-blooded killer, a calculating businessman, or both? Are people as greedy as Simon is capable of having fulfilling relationships with friends or family?